STEP INTO A WORLD OF GENTLE PEOPLE, PROPER BEHAVIOR . . . AND THE CLEVEREST OF MURDERS

- a rejected novelist seeks revenge
- love and money inspire the foulest of deeds
- an overly eager sleuth stumbles over one too many corpses
- an Agatha Christie tour of London provides plenty of mystery . . . and a touch of murder!
- and discover the answer to the question: "Why are English villages so lethal?"

Other Malice Domestic Titles from
Avon Books

MALICE DOMESTIC 7
MALICE DOMESTIC 8

Joan Hess

PRESENTS

MALICE DOMESTIC 9

AVON
TWILIGHT

AVON BOOKS, INC.
An Imprint of HarperCollins*Publishers*
10 East 53rd Street
New York, New York 10022-5299

Contents

CONTENTS

Joan Hess, Agatha Award winner for Best Short Story, is the author of the long-running mystery series with bookstore proprietor and sleuth Claire Malloy and her teenage daughter Caron (who Only Speaks in Initial Capitals); and the novels featuring chief of police Arly Hanks in the eccentric town of Maggody, Arkansas, which include Murder@Maggody.com.

Introduction:
The Four H's:
Hearth, Health, Home,
and Homicide

Joan Hess

Q: Hey, you! Editor of this anthology—okay, maybe just the broad what writes the introduction—where do you get your ideas?

A: Please lower your voice. The children are napping and Nanny is in the cupboard, brewing something exotic for tea. She's been quarreling with the vicar for quite some time, but they still go walking together on the moors and she inquired about borrowing a thermos. The parlormaid's been experiencing some sort of intestinal distress lately, mostly in the mornings, but that's expected when one feeds exclusively on day-old crumpets. She's a dear young thing, ever so comely and innocent. I understand the vicar has been offering guidance in the parsonage.

As for my ideas, I order them from Peoria.

Q: So Malice Domestic means the nanny's gonna kill the vicar and the butler's gonna freak out and collapse in the trifle. What the hell's a trifle, anyways?
A: A trifle is a layered dessert consisting of pudding and ladyfingers.

Q: I think I'm about to throw up.
A: Ladyfingers are cookies, you dolt. If the subgenre of so-called Malice Domestic novels and stories was limited to nannies, butlers, and vicars, none of the wonderful authors who burst onto the scene in the mid-1980s, such as Nancy Pickard, Margaret Maron, Jill Churchill, Dorothy Cannell, M.D. Lake, Charlotte MacLeod, Carolyn Hart, Lia Matera—

Q: They never had no nannies.
A: Your attitude is beginning to annoy me. I will admit many of them might have profited with a more structured upbringing in the nursery. However, they and many other delightful purveyors of venom most subtle have learned that the infamous "mean streets" are the alleys behind the MGM studios. Crimes of the heart, of the soul, of the writhing confusion created by everyday greed and lust, may strike the classroom mother or the aerobics instructor, the scout leader or the basketball coach, the retiree with the lovely flower beds, the ninth-grade English teacher just down the hill. Malice Domestic doesn't necessarily take place in the parlor; it takes place wherever real people live.

The stories in this anthology are about real people: no drug dealers, no secret agents, no gangbangers, no serial killers, no stalkers. Here you'll find a commonality that's more frightening. Lock your door, fix a cup of tea, and curl up on the sofa. Leaves rustle in the wind, you know. Dogs bark and cats yowl. Headlights flash as cars race by much too quickly. A mourning dove calls out for its mate. A whippoorwill haunts the night.

Listen, instead, for the curling of a lip, the intake of a breath, the padding of slippers as someone comes up behind you, holding not an assault weapon but merely a pillow to slip behind your back. Perhaps. But not to worry. You're home, where all is safe and snug.

Q: You got that address in Peoria?
A: No.

*In this classic case of a restless military man, Agatha
Christie's alter ego, mystery novelist Ariadne Oliver, makes
a memorable appearance with sleuth Parker Pyne. In Mrs.
Oliver, the reader can see Mrs. Christie's gentle lampoon-
ing of her chosen profession.*

The Case of the
Discontented Soldier

Agatha Christie

Major Wilbraham hesitated outside the door of Mr.
Parker Pyne's office to read, not for the first time, the advertisement from the morning paper which had brought him
there. It was simple enough:

> ARE YOU HAPPY? IF NOT, CONSULT
> MR. PARKER PYNE, 17 Richmond Street.

The major took a deep breath and abruptly plunged
through the swing door leading to the outer office. A plain
young woman looked up from her typewriter and glanced
at him inquiringly.

"Mr. Parker Pyne?" said Major Wilbraham, blushing.

"Come this way, please."

He followed her into an inner office—into the presence of the bland Mr. Parker Pyne.

"Good morning," said Mr. Pyne. "Sit down, won't you? And now tell me what I can do for you."

"My name is Wilbraham—" began the other.

"Major? Colonel?" said Mr. Pyne.

"Major."

"Ah! And recently returned from abroad? India? East Africa?"

"East Africa."

"A fine country, I believe. Well, so you are home again—and you don't like it. Is that the trouble?"

"You're absolutely right. Though how you knew—"

Mr. Parker Pyne waved an impressive hand. "It is my business to know. You see, for thirty-five years of my life I have been engaged in the compiling of statistics in a government office. Now I have retired and it has occurred to me to use the experience I have gained in a novel fashion. It is all so simple. Unhappiness can be classified under five main heads—no more, I assure you. Once you know the cause of a malady, the remedy should not be impossible.

"I stand in the place of the doctor. The doctor first diagnoses the patient's disorder, then he recommends a course of treatment. There are cases where no treatment can be of any avail. If that is so, I say quite frankly that I can do nothing about it. But if I undertake a case, the cure is practically guaranteed.

"I can assure you, Major Wilbraham, that ninety-six percent of retired empire builders—as I call them—are unhappy. They exchange an active life, a life full of responsibility, a life of possible danger, for—what? Straitened means, a dismal climate, and a general feeling of being a fish out of water."

"All you've said is true," said the major. "It's the boredom I object to. The boredom and the endless tittle-tattle about petty village matters. But what can I do about it? I've got a little money besides my pension. I've a nice cottage near Cobham. I can't afford to hunt or shoot or fish. I'm not married. My neighbors are all pleasant folk, but they've no ideas beyond this island."

"The long and short of the matter is that you find life tame," said Mr. Parker Pyne.

"Damned tame."

"You would like excitement, possibly danger?" asked Mr. Pyne.

The soldier shrugged. "There's no such thing in this tin-pot country."

"I beg your pardon," said Mr. Pyne seriously. "There you are wrong. There is plenty of danger, plenty of excitement, here in London if you know where to go for it. You have seen only the surface of our English life, calm, pleasant. But there is another side. If you wish it, I can show you that other side."

Major Wilbraham regarded him thoughtfully. There was something reassuring about Mr. Pyne. He was large, not to say fat; he had a bald head of noble proportions, strong glasses, and little twinkling eyes. And he had an aura—an aura of dependability.

"I should warn you, however," continued Mr. Pyne, "that there is an element of risk."

The soldier's eye brightened. "That's all right," he said. Then, abruptly, "And—your fees?"

"My fee," said Mr. Pyne, "is fifty pounds, payable in advance. If in a month's time you are still in the same state of boredom, I will refund your money."

Wilbraham considered. "Fair enough," he said at last. "I agree. I'll give you a check now."

The transaction was completed. Mr. Parker Pyne pressed a buzzer on his desk.

"It is now one o'clock," he said. "I am going to ask you to take a young lady out to lunch." The door opened. "Ah, Madeleine, my dear, let me introduce Major Wilbraham, who is going to take you out to lunch."

Wilbraham blinked slightly, which was hardly to be won-dered at.

The girl who entered the room was dark, languorous, with wonderful eyes and long black lashes, a perfect com-plexion, and a voluptuous scarlet mouth. Her exquisite clothes set off the swaying grace of her figure. From head to foot she was perfect.

"Er—delighted," said Major Wilbraham.

"Miss de Sara," said Mr. Parker Pyne.

"How very kind of you," murmured Madeleine de Sara.

"I have your address here," announced Mr. Parker Pyne. "Tomorrow morning you will receive my further instructions."

Major Wilbraham and the lovely Madeleine departed.

It was three o'clock when Madeleine returned.

Mr. Parker Pyne looked up. "Well?" he demanded.

Madeleine shook her head. "Scared of me," she said. "Thinks I'm a vamp."

"I thought as much," said Mr. Parker Pyne. "You carried out my instructions?"

"Yes. We discussed the occupants of the other tables freely. The type he likes is fair-haired, blue-eyed, slightly anaemic, not too tall."

"That should be easy," said Mr. Pyne. "Get me Schedule B and let me see what we have in stock at present." He ran his finger down a list, finally stopping at a name. "Freda Clegg. Yes, I think Freda Clegg will do excellently. I had better see Mrs. Oliver about it."

The next day Major Wilbraham received a note, which read:

On Monday morning next at eleven o'clock go to Eaglemont, Friars Lane, Hampstead, and ask for Mr. Jones. You will represent yourself as coming from the Guava Shipping Company.

Obediently on the following Monday (which happened to be Bank Holiday), Major Wilbraham set out for Eaglemont, Friars Lane. He set out, I say, but he never got there. For before he got there, something happened.

All the world and his wife seemed to be on their way to Hampstead. Major Wilbraham got entangled in crowds, suffocated in the tube, and found it hard to discover the whereabouts of Friars Lane.

Friars Lane was a cul-de-sac, a neglected road full of ruts, with houses on either side standing back from the road. They were largish houses which had seen better days and had been allowed to fall into disrepair.

Wilbraham walked along peering at the half-erased names on the gateposts, when suddenly he heard something that made him stiffen to attention. It was a kind of gurgling, half-choked cry.

It came again and this time it was faintly recognizable as the word "Help!" It came from inside the wall of the house he was passing.

Without a moment's hesitation, Major Wilbraham pushed open the rickety gate and sprinted noiselessly up the weed-covered drive. There in the shrubbery was a girl struggling in the grasp of two enormous Negroes. She was putting up a brave fight, twisting and turning and kicking. One Negro held his hand over her mouth in spite of her furious efforts to get her head free.

Intent on their struggle with the girl, neither of the blacks had noticed Wilbraham's approach. The first they knew of it was when a violent punch on the jaw sent the man who was covering the girl's mouth reeling backwards. Taken by surprise, the other man relinquished his hold of the girl and turned. Wilbraham was ready for him. Once again his fist shot out, and the Negro reeled backwards and fell. Wilbraham turned on the other man, who was closing in behind him.

But the two men had had enough. The second one rolled over, sat up; then, rising, he made a dash for the gate. His companion followed suit. Wilbraham started after them, but changed his mind and turned towards the girl, who was leaning against a tree, panting.

"Oh, thank you!" she gasped. "It was terrible."

Major Wilbraham saw for the first time who it was he had rescued so opportunely. She was a girl of about twenty-one or -two, fair-haired and blue-eyed, pretty in a rather colorless way.

"If you hadn't come!" she gasped.

"There, there," said Wilbraham soothingly. "It's all right now. I think, though, that we'd better get away from here. It's possible those fellows might come back."

A faint smile came to the girl's lips. "I don't think they will—not after the way you hit them. Oh, it was splendid of you!"

Major Wilbraham blushed under the warmth of her glance of admiration. "Nothin' at all," he said indistinctly. "All in day's work. Lady being annoyed. Look here, if you take my arm, can you walk? It's been a nasty shock, I know."

"I'm all right now," said the girl. However, she took the proffered arm. She was still rather shaky. She glanced behind her at the house as they emerged through the gate. "I can't understand it," she murmured. "That's clearly an empty house."

"It's empty, right enough," agreed the major looking up at the shuttered windows and general air of decay.

"And yet it *is* Whitefriars." She pointed to a half-obliterated name on the gate. "And Whitefriars was the place I was to go."

"Don't worry about anything now," said Wilbraham. "In a minute or two we'll be able to get a taxi. Then we'll drive somewhere and have a cup of coffee."

At the end of the lane they came out into a more frequented street, and by good fortune a taxi had just set down a fare at one of the houses. Wilbraham hailed it, gave an address to the driver and they got in.

"Don't try to talk," he admonished his companion. "Just lie back. You've had a nasty experience."

She smiled at him gratefully.

"By the way—er—my name is Wilbraham."

"Mine is Clegg—Freda Clegg."

Ten minutes later, Freda was sipping hot coffee and looking gratefully across a small table at her rescuer.

"It seems like a dream," she said. "A bad dream." She shuddered. "And only a short while ago I was wishing for something to happen—anything! Oh, I don't like adventures."

"Tell me how it happened."

"Well, to tell you properly I shall have to talk a lot about myself, I'm afraid."

"An excellent subject," said Wilbraham, with a bow.

"I am an orphan. My father—he was a sea captain—died when I was eight. My mother died three years ago. I work in the City. I am with the Vacuum Gas Company—a clerk. One evening last week I found a gentleman waiting to see me when I returned to my lodgings. He was a lawyer, a Mr. Reid from Melbourne.

"He was very polite and asked me several questions about my family. He explained that he had known my father many years ago. In fact, he had transacted some legal business for him. Then he told me the object of his visit. 'Miss Clegg,' he said, 'I have reason to suppose that you might benefit as the result of a financial transaction entered into by your father several years before he died.' I was very much surprised, of course.

" 'It is unlikely that you would ever have heard anything of the matter,' he explained. 'John Clegg never took the affair seriously, I fancy. However, it has materialized unexpectedly, but I am afraid any claim you might put in would depend on your ownership of certain papers. These papers would be part of your father's estate, and of course it is possible that they have been destroyed as worthless. Have you kept any of your father's papers?'

"I explained that my mother had kept various things of my father's in an old sea chest. I had looked through it cursorily but had discovered nothing of interest.

" 'You would hardly be likely to recognize the importance of these documents, perhaps,' he said, smiling.

"Well, I went to the chest, took out the few papers it contained and brought them to him. He looked at them, but said it was impossible to say offhand what might or might not be connected with the matter in question. He would take them away with him and would communicate with me if anything turned up.

"By the last post on Saturday I received a letter from him in which he suggested that I come to his house to discuss the matter. He gave me the address: Whitefriars,

Friars Lane, Hampstead. I was to be there at a quarter to eleven this morning.

"I was a little late finding the place. I hurried through the gate and up towards the house, when suddenly those two dreadful men sprang at me from the bushes. I hadn't time to cry out. One man put his hand over my mouth. I wrenched my head free and screamed for help. Luckily you heard me. If it hadn't been for you—" She stopped. Her looks were more eloquent than further words.

"Very glad I happened to be on the spot. By Gad, I'd like to get hold of those two brutes. You'd never seen them before, I suppose?"

She shook her head. "What do you think it means?"

"Difficult to say. But one thing seems pretty sure. There's something someone wants among your father's papers. This man Reid told you a cock-and-bull story so as to get the opportunity of looking through them. Evidently what he wanted wasn't there."

"Oh!" said Freda. "I wonder. When I got home on Saturday I thought my things had been tampered with. To tell you the truth, I suspected my landlady of having pried about in my room out of curiosity. But now—"

"Depend upon it, that's it. Someone gained admission to your room and searched it, without finding what he was after. He suspected that you knew the value of this paper, whatever it was, and that you carried it about on your person. So he planned this ambush. If you had had it with you, it would have been taken from you. If not, you would have been held prisoner while he tried to make you tell where it was hidden."

"But what can it possibly *be*?" cried Freda.

"I don't know. But it must be something pretty good for him to go to this length."

"It doesn't seem possible."

"Oh, I don't know. Your father was a sailor. He went to out-of-the-way places. He might have come across something the value of which he never knew."

"Do you really think so?" A pink flush of excitement showed in the girl's pale cheeks.

"I do indeed. The question is, what shall we do next?

You don't want to go to the police, I suppose?"

"Oh, no, please."

"I'm glad you say that. I don't see what good the police could do, and it would only mean unpleasantness for you. Now I suggest that you allow me to give you lunch somewhere and that I then accompany you back to your lodgings, so as to be sure you reach them safely. And then, we might have a look for the paper. Because, you know, it must be somewhere."

"Father may have destroyed it himself."

"He may, of course, but the other side evidently doesn't think so, and that looks hopeful for us."

"What do you think it can be? Hidden treasure?"

"By Jove, it might be!" exclaimed Major Wilbraham, all the boy in him rising joyfully to the suggestion. "But now, Miss Clegg, lunch!"

They had a pleasant meal together. Wilbraham told Freda all about his life in East Africa. He described elephant hunts, and the girl was thrilled. When they had finished, he insisted on taking her home in a taxi.

Her lodgings were near Notting Hill Gate. On arriving there, Freda had a brief conversation with her landlady. She returned to Wilbraham and took him up to the second floor, where she had a tiny bedroom and sitting room.

"It's exactly as we thought," she said. "A man came on Saturday morning to see about laying a new electric cable; he told her there was a fault in the wiring in my room. He was there some time."

"Show me this chest of your father's," said Wilbraham.

Freda showed him a brass-bound box. "You see," she said, raising the lid, "It's empty."

The soldier nodded thoughtfully. "And there are no papers anywhere else?"

"I'm sure there aren't. Mother kept everything in here."

Wilbraham examined the inside of the chest. Suddenly he uttered an exclamation. "Here's a slit in the lining." Carefully he inserted his hand, feeling about. A slight crackle rewarded him. "Something's slipped down behind."

In another minute he had drawn out his find. A piece of dirty paper folded several times. He smoothed it out on the table; Freda was looking over his shoulder. She uttered an exclamation of disappointment.

"It's just a lot of queer marks."

"Why, the thing's in Swahili. *Swahili*, of all things!" cried Major Wilbraham. "East African native dialect, you know."

"How extraordinary!" said Freda. "Can you read it, then?"

"Rather. But what an amazing thing." He took the paper to the window.

"Is it anything?" asked Freda tremulously. Wilbraham read the thing through twice, and then came back to the girl. "Well," he said with a chuckle, "here's your hidden treasure, all right."

"Hidden treasure? Not *really*? You mean Spanish gold— a sunken galleon—that sort of thing?"

"Not quite so romantic as that, perhaps. But it comes to the same thing. This paper gives the hiding place of a cache of ivory."

"Ivory?" said the girl, astonished.

"Yes. Elephants, you know. There's a law about the number you're allowed to shoot. Some hunter got away with breaking that law on a grand scale. They were on his trail and he cached the stuff. There's a thundering lot of it—and this gives fairly clear directions how to find it. Look here, we'll have to go after this, you and I."

"You mean there's really a lot of money in it?"

"Quite a nice little fortune for you."

"But how did that paper come to be among my father's things?"

Wilbraham shrugged. "Maybe the Johnny was dying or something. He may have written the thing down in Swahili for protection and given it to your father, who possibly had befriended him in some way. Your father, not being able to read it, attached no importance to it. That's only a guess on my part, but I dare say it's not far wrong."

Freda gave a sigh. "How frightfully exciting!"

"The thing is—what to do with the precious document," said Wilbraham. "I don't like leaving it here. They might come and have another look. I suppose you wouldn't entrust it to me?"

"Of course I would. But—mightn't it be dangerous for you?" she faltered.

"I'm a tough nut," said Wilbraham grimly. "You needn't worry about me." He folded up the paper and put it in his pocketbook. "May I come to see you tomorrow evening?" he asked. "I'll have worked out a plan by then, and I'll look up the places on my map. What time do you get back from the City?"

"I get back about half past six."

"Capital. We'll have a powwow, and then perhaps you'll let me take you out to dinner. We ought to celebrate. So long, then. Tomorrow at half past six."

Major Wilbraham arrived punctually on the following day. He rang the bell and inquired for Miss Clegg. A maid-servant had answered the door.

"Miss Clegg? She's out."

"Oh!" Wilbraham did not like to suggest that he come in and wait. "I'll call back presently," he said.

He hung about in the street outside, expecting every minute to see Freda tripping towards him. The minutes passed. Quarter to seven. Seven. Quarter past seven. Still no Freda. A feeling of uneasiness swept over him. He went back to the house and rang the bell again.

"Look here," he said, "I had an appointment with Miss Clegg at half past six. Are you sure she isn't in or hasn't—er—left any message?"

"Are you Major Wilbraham?" asked the servant.

"Yes."

"Then there's a note for you. It come by hand."

Wilbraham took it from her and tore it open. It ran as follows:

Dear Major Wilbraham:

Something rather strange has happened. I won't write more now, but will you meet me at Whitefriars? Go there as soon as you get this.

Yours sincerely,
Freda Clegg

Wilbraham drew his brows together as he thought rapidly. His hand drew a letter absent-mindedly from his pocket. It was to his tailor. "I wonder," he said to the maid-servant, "if you could let me have a stamp."

"I expect Mrs. Parkins could oblige you."

She returned in a moment with the stamp. It was paid for with a shilling. In another minute Wilbraham was walking towards the tube station, dropping the envelope in a box as he passed.

Freda's letter had made him most uneasy. What could have taken the girl, alone, to the scene of yesterday's sinister encounter?

He shook his head. Of all the foolish things to do! Had Reid reappeared? Had he somehow or other prevailed upon the girl to trust him? What had taken her to Hampstead?

He looked at his watch. Nearly half past seven. She would have counted on his starting at half past six. An hour late. Too much. If only she had had the sense to give him some hint.

The letter puzzled him. Somehow, its independent tone was not characteristic of Freda Clegg.

It was ten minutes to eight when he reached Friars Lane. It was getting dark. He looked sharply about him; there was no one in sight. Gently he pushed the rickety gate so that it swung noiselessly on its hinges. The drive was deserted. The house was dark. He went up the path cautiously, keeping a lookout from side to side. He did not intend to be caught by surprise.

Suddenly he stopped. Just for a minute a chink of light had shone through one of the shutters. The house was not empty. There was someone inside.

Softly Wilbraham slipped into the bushes and worked his way round to the back of the house. At last he found what he was looking for. One of the windows on the ground floor was unfastened. It was the window of a kind of scullery. He raised the sash, flashed a torch (he had bought it at a shop on the way over) around the deserted interior, and climbed in.

Carefully he opened the scullery door. There was no sound. He flashed the torch once more. A kitchen—empty. Outside the kitchen were half a dozen steps and a door evidently leading to the front part of the house.

He pushed open the door and listened. Nothing. He slipped through. He was now in the front hall. Still there was no sound. There was a door to the right and a door to the left. He chose the right-hand door, listened for a time, then turned the handle. It gave. Inch by inch he opened the door and stepped inside.

Again he flashed the torch. The room was unfurnished and bare.

Just at that moment he heard a sound behind him, whirled round—too late. Something came down on his head and he pitched forward into unconsciousness . . .

How much time elapsed before he regained consciousness Wilbraham had no idea. He returned painfully to life, his head aching. He tried to move and found it impossible. He was bound with ropes.

His wits came back to him suddenly. He remembered now. He had been hit on the head.

A faint light from a gas jet high up on the wall showed him that he was in a small cellar. He looked around and his heart gave a leap. A few feet away lay Freda, bound like himself. Her eyes were closed, but even as he watched her anxiously, she sighed and they opened. Her bewildered gaze fell on him and joyous recognition leaped into them.

"You, too!" she said. "What has happened?"

"I've let you down badly," said Wilbraham. "Tumbled headlong into the trap. Tell me, did you send me a note asking me to meet you here?"

The girl's eyes opened in astonishment. "*I?* But you sent *me* one."

"Oh, I sent you one, did I?"

"Yes. I got it at the office. It asked me to meet you here instead of at home."

"Same method for both of us," he groaned, and he explained the situation.

"I see," said Freda. "Then the idea was—"

"To get the paper. We must have been followed yesterday. That's how they got on to me."

"And—have they got it?" asked Freda.

"Unfortunately, I can't feel and see," said the soldier, regarding his bound hands ruefully.

And then they both started. For a voice spoke, a voice that seemed to come from the empty air.

"Yes, thank you," it said. "I've got it, all right. No mistake about that."

The unseen voice made them both shiver. "Mr. Reid," murmured Freda.

"Mr. Reid is one of my names, my dear young lady," said the voice. "But only one of them. I have a great many. Now, I am sorry to say that you two have interfered with my plans—a thing I never allow. Your discovery of this house is a serious matter. You have not told the police about it yet, but you might do so in the future.

"I very much fear that I cannot trust you in the matter. You might promise—but promises are seldom kept. And you see, this house is very useful to me. It is, you might say, my clearing house. The house from which there is no return. From here you pass on—elsewhere. You, I am sorry to say, are so passing on. Regrettable—but necessary."

The voice paused for a brief second, then resumed. "No bloodshed. I abhor bloodshed. My method is much simpler. And really not too painful, so I understand. Well, I must be getting along. Good evening to you both."

"Look here!" It was Wilbraham who spoke. "Do what you like to me, but this young lady has done nothing—nothing. It can't hurt you to let her go."

But there was no answer.

At that moment there came a cry from Freda. "The water—the water!"

Wilbraham twisted himself painfully and followed the direction of her eyes. From a hole up near the ceiling a steady trickle of water was pouring in.

Freda gave a hysterical cry. "They're going to drown us!"

The perspiration broke out on Wilbraham's brow.

"We're not done yet," he said. "We'll shout for help. Surely somebody will hear. Now, both together."

They yelled and shouted at the top of their voices. Not till they were hoarse did they stop.

"No use, I'm afraid," said Wilbraham sadly. "We're too far underground and I expect the doors are muffled. After all, if we could be heard, I've no doubt that brute would have gagged us."

"Oh!" cried Freda. "And it's all my fault. I got you into this."

"Don't worry about that, little girl. It's you I'm thinking about. I've been in tight corners before now and got out of them. Don't you lose heart. I'll get you out of this. We've plenty of time. At the rate that water's flowing in, it will be hours before the worst happens."

"How wonderful you are!" said Freda. "I've never met anybody like you—except in books."

"Nonsense—just common sense. Now, I've got to loosen these infernal ropes."

At the end of a quarter of an hour, by dint of straining and twisting, Wilbraham had the satisfaction of feeling that his bonds were appreciably loosened. He managed to bend his head down and his wrists up till he was able to attack the knots with his teeth.

Once his hands were free, the rest was only a matter of time. Cramped, stiff, but free, he bent over the girl. A minute later she also was free.

So far the water was only up to their ankles.

"And now," said the soldier, "to get out of here."

The door of the cellar was up a few stairs. Major Wilbraham examined it. "No difficulty here," he said. "Flimsy stuff. It will soon give at the hinges." He set his shoulders to it and heaved.

There was the cracking of wood—a crash, and the door burst from its hinges.

Outside was a flight of stairs. At the top was another door—a very different affair—of solid wood, barred with iron.

"A bit more difficult, this," said Wilbraham. "Hello, here's a piece of luck. It's unlocked."

He pushed it open, peered round it, then beckoned the girl to come on. They emerged into a passage behind the kitchen. In another moment they were standing under the stars in Friars Lane.

"Oh!" Freda gave a little sob. "Oh, how dreadful it's been!"

"My poor darling." He caught her in his arms. "You've been so wonderfully brave. Freda—darling angel—could you ever—I mean, would you—I love you, Freda. Will you marry me?"

After a suitable interval, highly satisfactory to both parties, Major Wilbraham said with a chuckle, "And what's more, we've still got the secret of the ivory cache."

"But they took it from you!"

The major chuckled again. "That's just what they didn't do! You see, I wrote out a spoof copy, and before joining you here tonight, I put the real thing in a letter I was sending to my tailor and posted it. They've got the spoof copy—and I wish them joy of it! Do you know what we'll do, sweetheart? We'll go to East Africa for our honeymoon and hunt out the cache."

Mr. Parker Pyne left his office and climbed two flights of stairs. Here in a room at the top of the house sat Mrs. Oliver, the sensational novelist, now a member of Mr. Pyne's staff.

Mr. Parker Pyne tapped at the door and entered. Mrs. Oliver sat at a table on which were a typewriter, several notebooks, a general confusion of loose manuscripts, and a large bag of apples.

"A very good story, Mrs. Oliver," said Mr. Parker Pyne genially.

"It went off well?" said Mrs. Oliver. "I'm glad."

"That water-in-the-cellar business," said Mr. Parker Pyne. "You don't think, on a future occasion, that something more original—perhaps?" He made the suggestion with proper diffidence.

Mrs. Oliver shook her head and took an apple from the bag. "I think not, Mr. Pyne. You see, people are used to reading about such things. Water rising in a cellar, poison gas, et cetera. Knowing about it beforehand gives it an extra thrill when it happens to oneself. The public is conservative, Mr. Pyne; it likes the old well-worn gadgets."

"Well, you should know," admitted Mr. Parker Pyne, mindful of the authoress' forty-six successful works of fiction, all best-sellers in England and America, and freely translated into French, German, Italian, Hungarian, Finnish, Japanese, and Abyssinian. "How about expenses?"

Mrs. Oliver drew a paper towards her. "Very moderate, on the whole. The two Negroes, Percy and Jerry, wanted very little. Young Lorrimer, the actor, was willing to enact the part of Mr. Reid for five guineas. The cellar speech was a phonograph record, of course."

"Whitefriars has been extremely useful to me," said Mr. Pyne. "I bought it for a song and it has already been the scene of eleven exciting dramas."

"Oh, I forgot," said Mrs. Oliver. "Johnny's wages. Five shillings."

"Johnny?"

"Yes. The boy who poured the water from the watering cans through the hole in the wall."

"Ah, yes. By the way, Mrs. Oliver, how did you happen to know Swahili?"

"I didn't."

"I see. The British Museum, perhaps?"

"No. Delfridge's Information Bureau."

"How marvelous are the resources of modern commerce!" he murmured.

"The only thing that worries me," said Mrs. Oliver, "is that those two young people won't find any cache when they get there."

"One cannot have everything in this world," said Mr. Parker Pyne. "They will have had a honeymoon."

Mrs. Wilbraham was sitting in a deck chair. Her husband was writing a letter.

"What's the date, Freda?"

"The sixteenth."

"The sixteenth. By Jove!"

"What is it, dear?"

"Nothing. I just remembered a chap named Jones."

However happily married, there are some things one never tells.

"Dash it all," thought Major Wilbraham, "I ought to have called at that place and got my money back." And then, being a fair-minded man, he looked at the other side of the question. "After all, it was I who broke the bargain. I suppose if I'd gone to see Jones something would have happened. And anyway, as it turns out, if I hadn't been going to see Jones, I should never have heard Freda cry for help, and we might never have met. So, indirectly, perhaps they have a right to that fifty pounds!"

Mrs. Wilbraham was also following out a train of thought. "What a silly little fool I was to believe in that advertisement and pay those people three guineas. Of course, they never did anything for it and nothing ever happened. If I'd only known what was coming—first Mr. Reid, and then the queer, romantic way that Charlie came into my life. And to think that *but for pure chance* I might never have met him!"

She turned and smiled adoringly at her husband.

Yorkshireman Robert Barnard provides a caustic tale of malice in a nursing home. Barnard, winner of an Agatha Award for Best Short Story and an eight-time Edgar nominee, is the author of numerous mysteries including The Corpse at the Haworth Tandoori, *and an appreciation of Agatha Christie,* A Talent to Deceive.

Nothing to Lose

Robert Barnard

When Emily Mortmain finally consented to go into an old people's home, her relatives predicted a spate of suicides by the other residents before her first week was over. If other possible outcomes of the move occurred to them, they did not speak of them openly.

Emily Mortmain had been a disagreeable woman all her life, and old age had intensified her cantankerousness. Her husband had volunteered for a suicide mission in World War II, and all his contemporaries in the RAF had said how heroic he was, since he was still young and had so much to live for. He had smiled heroically, and said nothing. Her daughter had emigrated with her family to Australia many years before, and had opined at the time that Australia's

22

only drawback was that it was not far enough away. As Emily became increasingly unable to fend for herself, neighbors had tried to help, then fellow church members (for Emily was a "good" churchwoman), and then social workers. All attempts had ended in disaster—plates being thrown by or at her, screaming altercations at her back door, even an attempted throttling. When the local vicar lost his faith and left the church, the parish joke was that he had found himself unable to believe in a God who could create an Emily Mortmain.

The members of her family who came to see her off on the morning she left for the home were two nieces and a nephew. Their contact with her over the years had been sporadic, but had never dropped off entirely, for Emily had money, and it was known that her daughter had been ritually cursed by bell, book, and candle and cut out of the will. Who, if anyone, had been cut in was not known, but it was generally agreed that there was no charity with aims unpleasant enough for Emily to want to give it money.

There was no rivalry among the relatives. They knew no one could suck up to Emily Mortmain, because it was not in humankind to be pleasant to her for long enough to gain any favor. None of the three volunteered to drive her to the home, for each feared the inevitable bust-up in the car. They stood by the front gate waving cheerily as she was driven away in a taxi provided by the local social services. Then they gave a muffled cheer and went away to have a drink together and swap "Aunt Em" stories.

Emily was silent on the drive to Evening Glades. One did not talk to taxi drivers. One did not tip them either. A wheelchair was waiting for her in the driveway of Evening Glades, and the resident handyman got her into it and pushed her into the foyer. She did not thank him, and merely stared stonily ahead at Miss Protheroe the manageress when she introduced herself. She maintained her silence when she was taken up in the lift and shown her room, and preserved the same arctic chill when she was wheeled down into the communal sitting room to await lunch.

Miss Protheroe (whose only fault, if she had one, was a

slight tendency to talk to the residents as if they were children) made a special effort to take her round and introduce her to her "new friends" as she called them.

"Miss Willcocks . . . Captain Freely . . . Miss Cartwright . . . Mr. Pottinger . . . Mrs. Freebody . . ."

But she needn't have bothered. Indeed, the introductions died away in her throat. Emily Mortmain had risen from her wheelchair with the aid of a stick, and placed herself in the nearest available armchair. She acknowledged neither the names, nor the tentative (or in some cases appalled) greetings of the other residents. When Miss Protheroe had finished she merely announced, "My room does not have a sea view."

Miss Protheroe, as was quite often necessary in her job, took a firm line.

"The rooms with a sea view are very highly prized here. Mrs. Freebody, Mrs. Johnstone, and Captain Freely have the sea views at the moment, as our residents of longest standing."

Emily Mortmain fixed each in turn with a look of malevolence that seemed designed to ensure that all three rooms shortly became available.

"And when—if—they should for any reason . . . become vacant," said Miss Willcocks, greatly daring, "there is a long waiting list."

Emily Mortmain's face took on an expression of relish, as if she was spoiling for a fight which she had no doubt she would win.

"Lunch in half an hour," said Miss Protheroe brightly.

It was predictable that lunch was not to Mrs. Mortmain's liking. The gravy was too thin, the beef was overdone, and the peas were tinned. She aroused in the others a vociferous and unusual enthusiasm for thin gravy, well-done beef, and tinned peas. This cut no ice with Emily Mortmain, who had all her life adopted the position that anyone who had an opinion contrary to her own on any subject whatsover was either a fool or a degenerate. When the pudding came, a rhubarb tart, she pushed it away. "I can't abide rhubarb."

As she made her way slowly, with the aid of a stick,

toward the sitting room, she shouted to Miss Protheroe, "Remember, I can't abide rhubarb!"

"Funny," said Mr. Pottinger. "I'd have thought rhubarb and Mrs. Mortmain would have suited one another."

"I do *wonder* whether she's going to fit in here," said Miss Willcocks.

That was a matter on which there could be only one opinion, but it was an opinion that was bounced backwards and forwards over the rhubarb tart; it was productive of a satisfactory gloom at things not being what they used to be. This feeling was reinforced when they all trailed back to the sitting room and stood horrified in the doorway. Emily Mortmain had appropriated the armchair closest to the fire.

The comforts of Evening Glades were distributed with a rough-and-ready attempt at democracy. The possessors of the rooms with a sea view did not have the chair closest to the fire, and the person with the first rights to the *Daily Mail* in the mornings was someone else again. The armchair by the fire was Miss Willcocks's by right.

"Tell her!" Miss Willcocks urged Captain Freely, poking him quite painfully in the ribs.

Captain Freely was only just an officer and not quite a gentleman, but he could be quite splendidly officerly and gentlemanly if the occasion called for it. He advanced with the solemnity of Black Rod on a state occasion.

"Mrs. . . . er . . . Mortmain, I'm afraid you don't yet know our little ways here . . . our customs and conventions . . . The armchair you are sitting in is—hmm—reserved for the use of Miss Willcocks here."

The evil black eyes looked at him, then moved toward Miss Willcocks, then back to Captain Freely.

"Switch on the television, will you?" she said. "It's time for *Jacaranda Avenue*."

There was an immediate twitter of protest.

"We don't watch *Jacaranda Avenue* at Evening Glades," said Captain Freely. Then, aware that they had let themselves be sidetracked, he went on, quite severely, "I don't think you quite understood what I just said about—"

"Oh, I understood. Switch on the television."

The other residents stood round aghast. It was at this point that Captain Freely's military training told. Emily Mortmain had taken hold of her stick, and clearly intended to use it to press the appropriate button on the television set. Captain Freely, with great presence of mind, wheeled the set a further two feet away.

"Here at Evening Glades," he said sententiously, "we watch *Coronation Street* and *EastEnders*. We think that that is enough soap opera without adding an Australian one."

"Northern filth and cockney filth," sniffed Emily Mortmain. "At least the Australian program is *clean*."

But Captain Freely, with the nodded support of the other residents, had turned on a wildlife program. Emily Mortmain felt at an unusual moral disadvantage from the fact that she had preferred a soap to this.

"Such a graceful bird," said Mrs. Johnstone, as they watched a flying condor. "One can almost imagine angels' wings."

Such a rubbing in of superior taste drove Emily Mortmain to a suppressed frenzy. Her instinct—for she had all the childishness of the very old—was to get up and change the channel. On the other hand she knew that one of the others—in whom childishness was certainly not absent—would nip over and take her chair. Indeed, Captain Freely had remained standing while all the rest had sunk into chairs, and he hovered near her, no doubt meditating a chivalrous dash to rescue the chair on behalf of Miss Willcocks should the opportunity arise. Emily Mortmain fumed, but sat on.

At 2:30 precisely Emily Mortmain took up her stick and pressed the bell for Carter, the man of all work.

"Take me to my room," she ordered, hobbling towards her wheelchair. "It's my time for a lie-down. Remember that. Half past two is always my time to lie down."

The other residents watched her go in dignified silence, and no one scuttled over to take her chair. Only when the lift had gone up did Miss Willcocks walk over to her rightful place with great, if wounded, presence. She sat down to a little burst of applause, and Captain Freely summed up the general feeling when he said, "We shall have to fight back."

It was generally agreed that, though they would be scrupulously polite to the new resident, it was no use at all relying on good manners or conventional decencies. If the chair by the fire was to be kept for Miss Willcocks, this would have to be done by stratagem. After various possibilities were considered, Captain Freely dragged down from the bookshelves more than a dozen bound copies of *Punch*, dating from the 1920s. He placed them near the chair and declared that at meal times, or when Miss Willcocks took her constitutional, he himself would place these on the chair, which Mrs. Mortmain, with her limited ability to move, would find exceedingly difficult to remove. "I haven't lost *all* my strength yet, thank the Lord," he declared. It was agreed that for the moment the television would remain at some distance from all the chairs, however inconvenient this was for those with poor eyesight. It was also agreed that the morning paper would be kept for Mrs. Freebody in the office until she called for it after breakfast. Thus was the strategy conceived, and the mere discussion of the measures gave the old people an agreeable sense of having taken part in a council of war.

"Just like the Home Guard," said Mr. Summerson, the oldest inhabitant, "planning what to do when Jerry landed."

But of course Jerry had not landed, and it was typical of Mrs. Mortmain that by the next day she had decided to fight on a completely different front. What had most rankled about the skirmishes of her first day had been (not that she admitted it in these terms to herself) that she had allowed herself to be put at a moral disadvantage. Her insistence on the Australian soap when the others (*apparently*, and so they *said*) preferred to watch a wildlife program was, in retrospect, unwise. It was imperative to regain the moral initiative.

The following day was warmish, and Mrs. Mortmain affected not to have seen the piled copies of *Punch* on the chair by the fire. She took an armchair over by the bookcase, the farthest from the television, and she turned it away from the despised screen. She fortunately found among the

stock of books a volume of sermons which had been the
comfort of a previous resident, now gathered to the bosom
of the Lord. This she opened and ploughed doggedly
through, whatever program was on the television. She was
not spoken to by any of the residents, but if addressed by
Miss Protheroe or Carter she would read aloud the passage
she was at, ostensibly to mark her place.

"Would you prefer carrots or greens with your meat loaf,
Mrs. Mortmain?"

" ' . . . the ungodly shall perish in a sea of tormenting
fire.' What precisely do you mean by 'greens'?"

This ploy was gratifying to her sense of superiority, if in
the long run monotonous. For the rest, too, it was a respite,
and they found that life at the Glades could go on pretty
much as normal, almost as if Mrs. Mortmain had not been
there. This, though, was not Emily's intention in the long
term. Having regained the moral heights, she was impelled
once more to assert her presence.

Sunday provided many opportunities. Breakfast was no
sooner over than Emily Mortmain demanded to know when
the transport would be leaving for church.

"I'm afraid there is no transport for church," said Miss
Protheroe, with a tired—almost desperate—kind of bright-
ness. "Those who can get to church, and want to go, of
course . . . go. The rest of us make do with the television
service. And of course, the vicar comes and gives us our
own special little service once a month."

"Incredible! Quite incredible!" Emily Mortmain surveyed the other residents, who were deep in the *People*,
the *News of the World*, and the *Sunday Telegraph*. "It's
news to me that the Lord intended his day to be consecrated
to the reading of newspapers!"

"It's news to me he ever said anything on the subject of
the *News of the World*," said Captain Freely cheekily. But
he felt on dubious moral ground. It was difficult to imagine
a God who would approve of the *News of the World*.

Mrs. Mortmain had a taxi summoned, and was driven in
solitary state to and from the nearest Anglican church. If
any of the other residents had attended the service they
might have noticed that she ignored on principle all the

changes that had occurred in the Church of England forms of worship over the past two decades or so. Change was, to Emily Mortmain, synonymous with degeneracy. When the vicar shook her hand at the church door, she informed him that next time he came to Evening Glades, she wished to see him. "Alone," she intoned. "In private."

The vicar didn't see how he could refuse. Though thinking it over afterwards he didn't see why he should have accepted either. But Emily caught him on the hop, and he said that since she was a new resident at Evening Glades, and a new parishioner, he would come along especially to see her later in the week. Emily nodded to him curtly, and let the taxi driver wheel her away.

Mrs. Mortmain made a great thing of this approaching interview with the vicar. She said nothing about it directly to the other residents, but she communicated quite effectually through Miss Protheroe.

"The vicar will be calling to see me on Thursday," she announced on Monday at lunchtime. "Make sure that he is brought *straight* to my room."

And again on Thursday at breakfast time.

"When the vicar calls we must be *absolutely* private."

The rest of the residents, as they were meant to, wondered.

"She has the sort of obsession about secrecy that afflicts some prime ministers," said Captain Freely acutely.

The vicar, when he came, found the whole interview profoundly depressing. He was a well-meaning man, verging on the ineffectual. His depression took the form of wondering why so many deplorable people were attracted by the Christian religion. He listened to her demands that he insist on the banning of television on Sundays at Evening Glades, that the home should cease subscribing to any Sunday newspapers, that regular churchgoing by the able-bodied be a condition of acceptance, and so on and so on, and his heart sank.

Yes, he was on the governing board, he said, but no, he didn't have that sort of power. And in fact he had no wish to start dictating to a group of old people how they should spend their spare time. Did we really want the Christian religion to seem so negative and coercive? he wondered aloud.

All this was not unexpected to Emily Mortmain. She knew that Church of England vicars these days lacked fire in their bellies, had no relish for a fight. To her, religion was essentially belligerent: a fight against moral laxity, atheism, other sects, and anyone who happened to disagree with her on any matter whatsoever. Emily Mortmain would have fitted in perfectly in Northern Ireland.

But Emily was not in the least disappointed in the vicar's response, for she had not hoped for anything better. The whole business merely provided her with the opportunity for one more skirmish on this particular front, before she switched tack and tried out something completely new. It was a *casus belli*, and when it fizzled out she would find another, equally good. Certainly she had no intention of telling the truth about the interview.

At lunch the next day, when everyone was discussing the previous evening's episode of *EastEnders* and the amorous activities of Dirty Den the publican, Mrs. Mortmain announced, "At least we shall soon have an end to Sunday television. That's an abomination that will be swept away."

"I beg your pardon?" said Miss Willcocks.

"*And* Sunday newspapers. I've spoken to the vicar, and he will be pressing the governors very hard indeed on the issue. It's high time we had a more godly atmosphere in this place. And this is only a beginning."

She ended with an expression of triumph in her voice. The table gazed at her stonily, and then returned to their meals in silence. Silence was one of their weapons these days, though it seemed unfortunately to give Emily Mortmain the impression that she had won.

Only when she went up for her afternoon lie-down at 2:30 did they break out in protest.

"Well, really! What *does* she think she's doing this time? A ban on Sunday television! We might be living in the Victorian age!"

"I believe that even the Queen watches television on Sundays," said Miss Willcocks. She had in fact no information whatsoever on this point, but she was inclined to bring the Queen in to support her position, rather as Emily Mortmain brought in the Almighty.

"And a ban on Sunday newspapers!" said Mr. Pottinger. "It's only on Sundays that the papers are *any good*!"

"Let's be a bit calm about this," said Captain Freely. "Is she just trying to work us up?"

They thought for a moment.

"We do *know* most of the governing body a little," said Mrs. Johnstone. "They come here and talk to us, and they all seem quite kind. They don't appear to be religious fanatics."

"Quite," said Captain Freely.

"On the other hand," said Miss Willcocks, "Evening Glades was founded to be run on Church of England principles."

"Contradiction in terms," said Captain Freely robustly. "No, the fact is the woman's just trying to make trouble."

"I do think it's hard," exclaimed Mrs Johnstone. "One comes to a home like this, at the end of one's life, for *peace*! 'Sleep after toil, port after stormy seas,' as somebody said. Or is that death? Anyway, you know what I mean. A quiet, orderly existence, without too much responsibility, and without *rows*. This woman seems to thrive on rows, unpleasantness, and bad feeling. I do think it's *hard*! And it will go on like this as long as she's here."

"There is one advantage in being old," said Miss Willcocks pensively, into the silence that followed.

"What's that?" asked Mr. Pottinger.

"One has very little to lose . . . If only one could hit on a plan . . ."

Emily Mortmain died in her room, some time on Sunday afternoon. After lunch she had sat with her back studiously to the television, while the rest watched a film they had all been looking forward to, which gripped their attention. At 2:30 precisely, before the film had ended, Mrs. Mortmain had rung to be taken upstairs, as was her habit. At 4:45 Miss Protheroe had taken up her tea and toast and had discovered her dead.

The doctor, from the beginning, was very unhappy indeed. Though it appeared that the body was face down into the pillow, there were clear signs, or so the doctor thought, that it had been turned over after death. Deliberate suffocation is a difficult death to prove, and he thought the best thing would be to have a word with Miss Protheroe, to discover if, for instance, there could have been an intruder.

"Quite impossible," she said. "The domestic staff were off, and the kitchen door was locked. I was working in my office off the hall, with a perfect view of the front door. No one came in or went out."

"I see." The doctor shifted from foot to foot. "I wonder what the old people were doing."

Miss Protheroe shot him a quelling look.

"I will find out, tactfully, if you really think it worthwhile. I will tell you what I learn if you would be so kind as to return tomorrow."

When he did come back she was in triumphal mood.

"It was totally satisfactory. They were all—*all*—watching the film until 3:15. Then four of the ladies played whist, Captain Freely and Mr. Jones played chess, and the other six played *Trivial Pursuit*—a new game with us, but very popular. They were all in the lounge, or in the conservatory just through the door, and they were there all the time, until some time after I discovered the body. No one left even for a moment."

The doctor began his shifting-from-foot-to-foot routine again.

"That would be most unusual, not to leave even for a few minutes. Old people's bladders—"

"No one left even for that." Miss Protheroe got quite commanding. "In any case, how long would this . . . what you suggest . . . take?"

"Quite some time," admitted the doctor. "There was comparatively little obstruction . . . up to ten minutes."

"You see? And how much strength would be required?"

"Oh yes, certainly it would require strength."

"You see? These are *old* people, doctor. Even Captain Freely, though active, is no longer strong. It's quite impossible."

The doctor's voice took on a wild note.

"Perhaps two of them," he suggested. "Or all of them in relays."

Miss Protheroe rose in wrath.

"Doctor, that is as disgraceful as it is absurd. A joke in extremely bad taste. To suggest that all of my residents, respectable old people, should gang up to kill a new-comer—"

The doctor was young, and saw he had gone too far.

"Yes, yes, of course. I was merely theorizing, getting too fantastical. Point taken, point taken."

And he signed the certificate.

Miss Protheroe sensed the excitement in the residents after the death of Emily Mortmain, but there was nothing unusual in that. After any death in Evening Glades there was always excitement, even a sort of exultation: I have survived, she has gone under. Always there was an attempt to disguise it too. Now Captain Freely, if he realized she was in the room, would mutter, "Terrible thing, terrible thing," and the rest would cluck their agreement. Miss Protheroe was not deceived. They were pleased and excited, and if these emotions were more intense than usual, this was not surprising, in view of Emily Mortmain's character. Even her relatives, after the funeral, had seemed cock-a-hoop.

Amongst themselves they did not talk about the death a great deal, and to outsiders, of course, it was a matter of no importance. Only Miss Willcocks mentioned it, in her weekly letter to her niece (letters which generally remained unread, or even unopened). Miss Willcocks's treatment of the matter, it must be said, was not entirely honest:

Here we have been greatly upset by the death of Mrs. Mortmain, a new resident. Death is always upsetting, and particularly so in this case, as we had not had time to get to know her. It quite spoiled our Sunday, which up to then had been extremely enjoyable, with a quite thrilling game of Trivial Pursuit, *and before that a most entertaining film on television. Did you see it? It was* Murder on the Orient Express—so *amusing, and with such a clever solution . . .*

Jan Burke is the author of the Agatha-nominated Irene Kelly series, including Bones, Liar *and* Hocus. *Burke's short stories have won the Macavity and the* Ellery Queen Readers Award. *Her favorite Agatha Christie novel is* The Man in the Brown Suit, *which inspired the title of her short story in* Malice Domestic 9. *You can learn more about her books and stories at http://www.janburke.com.*

The Man in the Civil Suit

Jan Burke

I have a bone to pick with the Museum of Natural History. Yes, the very museum in which the peerless Professor Pythagoras Peabody so recently met his sad, if rather spectacular, demise. I understand they are still working on restoring the mastodon. But my grievance does not pertain to prehistoric pachyderms.

If the administrators of said museum are quoted accurately in the newspapers, they have behaved in a rather unseemly manner in regard to the late Peabody. How speedily they pointed out that he was on the premises in violation of a restraining order! How hastily they added that he had similar orders placed upon him by a number of institutions, including the art museum, the zoo, and Ye Olde Medieval Restaurant & Go-Cart Track! When asked if he was the man named in the civil suit they filed three days ago, how rapidly the administrators proclaimed that Professor Peabody was no professor at all!

Oh, how quickly they forget! They behave as if the Case of the Carillean Carbuncle never occurred. A balanced account of recent events must be given, and as one who knew the man in the civil suit better than any other—save, perhaps, his sister Persephone—I have taken on the burden of seeing justice done where Pythagoras Peabody is concerned.

Although Pythag, as his closest friends—well, as I called him, because frankly, few others could tolerate his particular style of genius at close range—although Pythag never taught at a university or other institution, it is widely known that the affectionate name "Professor Peabody" was bestowed upon him by a grateful police force at the close of the Case of the Carillean Carbuncle, or as Pythag liked to call it, 300. (Some of you may need assistance understanding why—I certainly did. Pythag explained that the first letters of Case, Carillean, and Carbuncle are Cs. Three Cs, taken together, form a Roman numeral. I'm certain I need not hint you on from there, but I will say this was typical of his cleverness.

Need I remind the museum administrators of the details of 300? This most unusual garnet was on display in their own Gems and Mineralogy Department when it was stolen by a heartless villain. True, the museum guards were in pursuit long before the ten-year-old boy left the grounds, and after several hours of chasing him through the halls, exhibits, and displays—including a dinosaur diorama, the planetarium, and the newly opened "Arctic and Antarctica: Poles Apart" exhibit—while conducting what amounted to an elaborate game of hide-and-seek, they caught their thief.

Unfortunately, the Carillean Carbuncle was no longer on his person, and he refused to give any clue as to its location. This was, apparently, a way of continuing the jollification he had enjoyed with these fellows. Not amused, the museum called the police. The boy called in his own reinforcements, and his parents, in the time-honored tradition of raisers of rogues, defended their son unequivocally and threatened all sorts of nastiness if he were not released immediately. The boy went home, and the Carillean Carbuncle remained missing.

Enter Peabody. Actually, he had already entered. It was Pythag's habit to be the first guest to walk through the museum doors in the morning, and the last to leave at closing. He made himself at home in the Natural History Museum, just as he once had in the art museum, and in the zoo. (The trouble at Ye Olde Medieval Restaurant & Go-Cart Track occurred before we were acquainted, but Pythag once hinted that it had something to do with giving the waiters' lances to the young drivers and encouraging them to "joust.")

I have said I will give a fair accounting, and I will. Pythag was a man who knew no boundaries. His was a genius, he often reminded me, that could not be confined to the paths that others were pleased to follow. I know some stiff-rumped bureaucrats will not agree, but if he were here to defend himself, Pythag would undoubtedly say, "If you don't want a gentleman born with an enviable amount of curiosity to climb into an elephants' compound, for goodness sakes, rely on more than a waist-high fence and a silly excuse for a moat to keep him out."

Likewise, he would tell you that if your art museum docent becomes rattled when a gentleman with a carrying voice follows along with a second group of unsuspecting art lovers, telling them a thing or two the docent failed to mention to his own group, well then, the docent stands in need of better training. Pythag enjoyed himself immensely on these "tour" occasions, tapping on glass cases and reading aloud from wall plaques to begin his speeches.

He soon varied from the information in these written guides, however. He often told visitors that when x-rayed, the canvases beneath the museum's most famous oil paintings were shown to be covered with little blue numbers, a number one being a red, two a blue, and so forth. This, he claimed, was how the museum's restoration department could make a perfect match when repairing a damaged work of art. He also claimed to be such an expert as to be able to see the numbers with his naked eye, which, he said, "Has quite spoiled most of these for me."

The art museum director, Pythag declared, would soon be under arrest for the murder of Elvis—the director's supposed motive for the killing being to increase the value of his secret, private collection of velvet portraits of The King. (I understand the We Tip Hotline, tiring of Pythag's relentless pursuit of this idea, blocked calls from the Peabody home number.)

I'll wager a tour with Pythag was much more interesting, if less enlightening, than one taken with the regular docents. The art museum, however, was unwilling to offer this alternative. It seemed a little harsh to tell him that he, and not the director, risked arrest if he returned. As Persephone argued when she came to fetch him home, how could anyone in his right mind fault a person for being *creative* in an *art* museum?

Please don't bother to mention Pythag's exile from the Museum of Transportation. Pythag would tell you that a velvet rope may be seen by a man with panache (and if he could have withstood one more *P* in his moniker, panache would have been Pythag's middle name) as less a barrier than an invitation to step over it and into the past. He went into the past by way of an eighteenth-century carriage, as it happened, and ever seeking the most realistic experience possible, Pythag had to bounce in it a bit. "I promise you," Pythag told the irate curator, "the King of Spain bounced when *he* rode in the dratted thing."

Perhaps you have already seen from these examples that Pythag was the perfect man to consult on the matter of the missing carbuncle. Who was more qualified to determine what a clever boy, let loose in a museum, might do? Indeed, I readily admit that for all his genius, Pythag's enthusiasm sometimes led him into rather childish behavior. I concede that he was subject to bouts of stubbornness over silly things, bouts that made him not much more than a child himself at times.

On the very afternoon the carbuncle was stolen, for example, he *insisted* on staring into the penguins' eyes in the

Antarctic exhibit, convinced that each penguin retained on his retina a memory of its last moments. If he could catch the reflection of this last recollection, he decided, he could experience the thing itself—it would be, he said, "Bird's eye *deja vu*." This was one of those times when, were I not courting Persephone, I would have been tempted to leave the exhibit without him. Nothing I said would convince him that memory resides in the brain rather than the eye. He utterly rejected my claim that these were not the penguins' actual eyes, but glass reproductions, and rebuked me loudly and in horrified accents for suggesting such a thing.

But as Persephone was most appreciative of my willingness to watch over her brother and accompany him to public venues, I did my best to overlook his occasionally irritating behaviors. Persephone, brilliant and far less given to acting on impulse than her brother, told me that restraining orders were a small price for Pythag's genius, but she'd just as soon not be asked to pay any larger prices for it.

Thus I made an effort to distract him from the penguins by mentioning his beloved mastodon. (Pythag had a fondness for all things the names of which begin with the letter *P*. His attachment to the mastodon puzzled me, and I wondered if he was taking on the letter *M* as well, until I noticed that he constantly referred to it as the "proboscidean mammal.") Pretending to be struck by a sudden inspiration, I muttered something to the effect of, "an elephant's ancestors might also 'never forget,' " then asked Pythag if he thought there might be some memory retained in the eye socket of the mastodon. The ruse worked, and soon we were off to the Prehistoric Hall.

Here he was again distracted, this time by the sight of several policemen carefully searching for the carbuncle. Pythag managed, in his inimitable way, to quickly convince a detective that he was an official at the museum. He induced the fellow to follow him to the planetarium—not a bad notion, for the young thief had most certainly visited this facility during his flight.

The carbuncle being ruby in color, Pythag's theory was based on meteorology. "Red sky at night is a young rogue's delight!" he shouted as we ran after him. He believed the boy might have been planning to alter the color of the light in the planetarium projector. With the help of the policeman, he hastily disassembled the rather costly mechanism, but alas, it was not the hiding place.

At my suggestion that they both might want to quickly take themselves as far away from the results of their work as possible, Pythag made one of his lightning-like leaps of logic, and announced that "Polaris was beckoning." We sped back to the polar exhibits.

Here Pythag had another brainstorm, saying that there was something not quite right about the Eskimos, and delved his hand into an Inuit mannequin's hide game bag. In triumph, Pythag removed the carbuncle.

On that day, you will remember, he was the museum's darling. Pythag's new policeman friend, perhaps distracting his fellows from the disassembled projector, extolled Pythag's genius in solving the mystery of the missing gem, and proclaimed him "Professor Peabody," by which address the world would know him during the brief remaining span of his lifetime.

Not many days later, tragedy struck. Having dissuaded him from climbing atop the mastodon skeleton's back, and seeing that he was again entranced by the penguins, I felt that it was reasonably safe for me to answer the call of nature at the Natural History Museum. But when I returned from the gents, Pythag was nowhere to be found.

I heard a commotion at the entrance to the exhibit, and rushed toward it, certain he would be at the center of any disturbance. But this hubbub was caused by the bright lights and cameras of a cable television crew from the Museum Channel. The crew was taping another fascinating episode of *Naturally, at the Natural.* This particular segment focused on a visit by the museum's newest patron, Mrs. Ethylene Farthington. Mrs. Farthington was possessed of all the right extremes, as far as the museum was concerned: extremely elderly, extremely wealthy, and extremely generous. Add to this the fact that she did not choose to meddle in the specifics of how her donations would be spent, and you see why the director of the museum thought her to be perfection itself.

Her progress through the polar exhibits was regally (if not dodderingly) slow, but none dared complain. For reasons that do not concern us or any other right-thinking person, Mrs. Farthington was fond of places made of ice, and her sponsorship of this exhibit was but the beginning of the largesse she was to bestow on the museum. That day, she was on her way to sign papers which would finalize her gift of a staggering sum to the museum. She would also sign a new will, supplanting the one that currently left the remainder of her enormous estate to her pet tortoise, and establishing in its stead a bequest for the museum. Apparently, there had been a falling out with the tortoise.

So taken was I by the sight of the frail Mrs. Farthington gazing at the *faux* glaciers, I nearly forgot to continue my search for Pythag. If I had not chanced to glance at the opposite display, where I saw a familiar face among the penguins, I might not have known where to look for him. The face was not Pythag's, although the clothes were those of the man who now asked me to address him as "Professor." No, the face was that of an Inuit mannequin. How careless of Pythag! Everyone knows Inuits and penguins do not belong in the same display!

I did not for a moment imagine that Pythag was cavorting about the museum in the altogether. He had decided, undoubtedly, to expand upon his experience with the hide bag, and bedeck himself in the clothing and gear of the Inuit.

I was a little frightened to realize that I knew his mind so well, even if gratified to see that there was one rather usual member of the Inuit family represented in the display. I had no difficulty in discerning which of the still figures was Pythag, and had I never met him before that day, I doubt I would have failed to notice the one apple which seemed to have fallen rather far from the Inuit family tree. There are, undoubtedly, few blond Inuits. Besides, none of the other mannequins blinked.

Otherwise, he was remarkably doll-like, clad in all his furs, and I was unable to fight a terribly strong urge to enjoy a few moments of seeing Pythag forced to be still and silent. How many times since that day have I told myself that had I foregone this bit of pleasure, disaster might have been avoided!

When I turned to see if anyone was watching before bidding him to hurry away, I was vexed to espy Mrs. Farthington and entourage approaching the display. There was nothing for it now but to wait until the group had passed on to the next display. But as if taking a page from her tortoise's book, Mrs. Farthington was not to be hurried, and stood transfixed, perhaps on some subconscious level perceiving what Pythag had perceived so recently—that something was not quite right about the Eskimos.

Pythag was masterful. Even under this prolonged scrutiny, he—as the saying goes—kept his cool. Or would have, were it not for the television lights. The heat they generated would have made puddles of the exhibit if any of the ice and snow had been real. Instead, it made a puddle of Pythag. He began to perspire profusely.

I do believe he still might have carried it off, had not Mrs. Farthington chanced to look at him just when he felt forced to lift a finger to swipe a ticklish drop of moisture from the end of his nose.

Mrs. Farthington, startled to see a mannequin move, clutched at her bosom and fell down dead on the spot.

The tortoise inherited.

When his friends in the police department refused to pursue a criminal case against him, Pythagoras Peabody was sued by the museum.

Persephone was not pleased with me.

This last was uppermost in my mind when I strolled alone through the museum the day after the civil suit was announced, and my own suit of Persephone rejected. Had I not loved her so dearly, I might have been a little angry with Perse. Her brother was a confounded nuisance, but she blamed me for his present troubles. I should have kept a closer watch, she told me. Had *she* deigned to accompany him on his daily outings? No. Monday was the worst day of the week, as far as she was concerned. That was the day her lunatic brother stayed home. I decided to give her a little time with him, to remind her of my usefulness to her.

One would think I would have gone elsewhere, now that I had the chance to go where I pleased, but there was something comfortable about following routine at a time when my life was so topsy-turvy. So I returned to the museum.

Standing before the great mastodon, I sighed. It had been Pythag's ambition to ride the colossus. Could it be done? To give the devil his due, that was the thing about going to a place like this with Pythag—he managed, somehow, to always add a bit of excitement. I mean, one really doesn't think of a museum as a place where the unexpected might happen at any moment. Unless one visited it with Pythag.

Why should Pythag have all the fun? I overcame the hand-railing with ease.

It was not so easy to make the climb aboard the skeleton, but I managed it. I enjoyed the view from its back only briefly—let me tell you, there is no comfortable seating astride the spine of a mastodon. Knowing that Pythag would be nettled that I had achieved this summit before him, I decided that I would leave some little proof of my visit. I made a rather precarious search of my pockets and found a piece of string. Tied in a bow about a knot of wires along the spine, it did very nicely.

The skeleton swayed a bit as I got down, and the only witness, a child, was soon asking his mother if he might go for a ride, too—but in a stern, Pythag-inspired voice, I informed her that I was an official of the museum, repairing the damage done by the last little boy who climbed the mastodon, a boy whose parents could be contacted at the poor house, where they were working off payments. Although we haven't had a poor house in this city in a century, she seemed to understand the larger implications, and they quickly left the museum.

As anticipated, Persephone called the next day.

"Take him," she pleaded. "Take him anywhere, and I'll take you back."

"Persephone," I said sternly.

"I know, and I apologize, dearest. I will marry you, just as we planned, only we must wait until this suit is settled.

I won't have a penny to my name, I'm afraid, but the three of us will manage somehow, won't we?"

"Three of us?"

"Well, I can't leave poor Pythagoras to fend for himself now, can I?"

And so once again, I found myself in the Museum of Natural History with Pythag at my side. He had donned a disguise—a false mustache and a dark wig. A costume not quite so warm as the Inuit garb, but no less suited to its wearer.

He began teasing me about my recent setback with Persephone. If he was an expert at devising troublesome frolics, Pythag's meanness also derived benefit from his ingenuity. When he told me that Perse would never marry me, that she had only said she would so that I would continue to take him to the museum, I felt a little downcast. When he averred that she would keep putting me off, always coming up with some new excuse, I found his Pythagorean theorem all too believable.

I had experienced such taunting before, though, and I rebuffed his attempts to hurt and annoy me by remaining calm. Outwardly, in any case. The result was that he became more agitated, more determined to upset me. At one point, he said that she would never marry me because I was dull, and lacked imagination and daring.

"Really?" I said, lifting my nose a little higher. "As it happens, *Professor*, I have done something you haven't dared to do."

His disbelief was patent.

"I've climbed the mastodon," I told him.

"Rubbish," he said.

"Conquered the proboscidean peak."

"Balderdash!"

"Not at all. There's a little piece of string, tied in a bow on his back to prove it."

It was enough to do the trick. He climbed, and it seemed to me the skeleton swayed more than it had the day before. As I watched him, and saw him come closer to my little marker, it became apparent to me that I had tied the string at a most fragile juncture of supporting wires.

It was a wonder, really, that I hadn't been killed.

The thought came to me as simply as that. One minute, Pythag was astride the spine, asking me to bring him a piece of string, so that he might tie his own knot. I imagined spending the rest of my days nearly as tied to him as I would be to his sister. All my life, protecting treasures of one sort or another from a man who thought rules were only for other people, never himself.

"You must bring my own string back to me," I said. "That is how it's done."

And that was how it was done.

I was horrified by the result, and remain so. Mastodon skeletons are, after all, devilishly hard to come by. Persephone is convinced that the experts there are actually enjoying the challenge of reassembling the great beast.

The museum, no matter what it may say to the papers, is considering dropping its civil suit, hoping to extract a promise from Persephone not to pursue a wrongful death action against them. We are mulling it over.

I say *we*, because Pythagoras was mistaken, as it turns out. His sister will marry me. I confessed all to her, of course. Persephone merely asked me what took me so long to see what needed to be done.

Persephone and I are indeed well-suited.

Kate Charles, a former Chairman of the U.K. Crime Writers' Association, is a keen member—and observer—of the Church of England, which is reflected in her Book of Psalms novels and such mysteries as Unruly Passions. *She was inspired to write this story by her new vicar (though she declines to say in what way), and it is dedicated to him with great affection (though she hopes he will never read it).*

The Murder at the Vicarage

Kate Charles

I would be lying if I said that I didn't think there was something wrong that Monday morning when I arrived at the Vicarage. Not that I suspected what it was, of course. But Father Luke had always been a man of regular habits, and one of his habits was to spend the morning in his study, the curtains open so that he could enjoy the views over the rolling countryside while he worked at his desk.

On that morning, the curtains were drawn. I noticed it at once; noticing things is part of *my* job. Still, at that point I wasn't unduly alarmed. Father Luke might have been called away to an emergency in the parish, or varied his routine for any number of reasons.

So I opened the front door with my key, calling out to Father Luke as I did so. There was no reply. The door of his study, to the side of the entrance hall, was ajar; I tapped lightly at the door, then pushed it open and stepped inside. "Father?"

The study was empty, or at least uninhabited. In the curtained dimness it seemed to me that everything was in its usual place: the blotter lined up precisely with the edge of Father's highly polished Queen Anne desk, his heavy gold fountain pen capped atop it. A tidy pile of correspondence, the accumulation of the weekend, awaited my attention beside the typewriter on the little side table.

Briskly I crossed to the window and pulled the curtains open, flooding the room with late summer sunshine. The light glinted from the gold pen, from the surface of the antique desk, from the black bakelite telephone. And from something else, catching the corner of my eye as I turned. Something out of place in the neatness of the study. Just visible, protruding from behind Father's favorite wing-backed leather chair.

On the red Turkey carpet. Father's spectacles. Father's polished black shoe. Father.

I screamed.

The next few minutes were, I admit, something of a blur. Alone in the Vicarage, I did the things that one usually does in these situations: rang the police, made myself a cup of strong tea—laced with plenty of sugar—and waited for the police to arrive. I sat at the kitchen table as I waited, trying not to think about what I'd seen.

Impossible, of course. The monstrous image blotted out every other thought. Father. Father Luke.

I want to make something quite clear from the outset. I am not one of those sad spinsters who attach themselves to the clergy—married or single, be they ever so unprepossessing—because they have nothing else with which to occupy themselves, or through some exalted idea of clergymen as more than mere mortals. My father was a vicar, so I grew up with the phenomenon. Even when my mother was alive it happened, and after she died they swarmed round my father like bees round a honeypot.

It was never like that for me. Perhaps, strictly speaking, I could be defined as a spinster, it is true that I have never married. But it's not because I haven't had the opportunity. I was engaged to be married, in fact, but my fiancé was killed in the war—a pilot, shot down during the Battle of Britain. Fully fifteen years ago now since poor Reggie died, and in that fifteen years I've had other chances as well. A succession of my father's curates, among others—all of them wet, none of them worth a second look. And besides, I enjoy living on my own, in my cozy house, with no one but myself to please.

I have a full and fulfilling life: Margo St. James, author of popular whodunnit novels. Scarcely ever off the best-seller lists. By far the most famous inhabitant of our little village; some might even say that I've put Nether Deepwell on the map.

But I digress.

It was some time before the police arrived. We have a constable in Nether Deepwell, but he was at that moment enjoying his annual holiday at the seaside with his family. That meant that the police had to come from Deepwell Green, all of six miles away.

Two of them, and they were just like characters out of one of my books: thin, ferret-faced Inspector Sharpe, and the pencil-licking Sergeant Dove. I'd never seen either of them before, but they knew who *I* was, all right; as I said, my fame goes far beyond Nether Deepwell.

They were suitably deferential, and from the beginning they never treated me like a suspect. I'll give them that.

Steeling myself for the hideous sight, I took them into the study and showed them what I had found. For a long moment they just looked; I'm afraid that I had to avert my eyes.

"Hmm," said Inspector Sharpe. "What do you make of it, Sergeant?"

The sergeant folded his arms and looked solemn. "Killed by a blow to the head. Blunt instrument." Since the blunt instrument was still present, this was scarcely a great leap of deduction, but stating the obvious was probably Sergeant

Dove's role in the partnership. "An iron," Sergeant Dove went on. "Killed by a blow from an iron." He chewed his cheek. "Looks like a domestic to me, sir. I think we need to talk to the vicar's wife."

Inspector Sharpe glanced in my direction, questioningly. I shook my head and swallowed. "There's no wife," I said. "Father Luke wasn't married."

No, Father Luke wasn't married. He'd come to Nether Deepwell on his own, just a year before, and moved into the large old Vicarage outside of the village, beyond the church. The previous vicar had been very much married—a callow boy with a growing family of badly behaved children and a shrew of a wife, filling the Vicarage with prams and familial clutter and emptying the church of its congregation.

Father Luke had turned things round. He had brought order to the church, introducing a moderate amount of High Church ritual. Many of the congregation had been suspicious at first, but they'd soon grown used to the incense and the candles. And he had brought order to the Vicarage as well, turning it into a calm sanctuary for a single man. Everything just so, in the large gracious house and the extensive gardens. A beautiful house for a beautiful man.

Yes, Father Luke was beautiful. A far cry from unprepossessing. Golden-haired and silver-tongued. About forty years of age, so there was a maturity about his beauty which made him all the more attractive—those few endearing lines at the corners of his blue eyes, crinkling when he smiled.

Not that he smiled all of the time, like one of those shallow, smarmy evangelicals. His smiles were rare, and genuine; they transformed his rather austere beauty into something breathtaking. They were worth waiting for.

Inspector Sharpe was still looking at me speculatively. "A housekeeper, then?" he postulated. "Someone who lives in?"

I shook my head. "You know how difficult it is to get servants these days." Twenty years ago this vicarage would have been staffed by half a dozen at least; the war had changed all of that. "Father Luke lived alone," I said.

Sergeant Dove took out a dog-eared notebook and—I swear he did—licked his stub of a pencil. "What, exactly," he asked, "was your role in the . . . err, household?"

That was a fair question. I breathed deeply and attempted an answer. "I helped Father Luke with some of his paperwork."

"His secretary, then," the Sergeant supplied.

"No, not that." My voice was perhaps sharper than I'd intended, but the word was so prosaic, so menial. I needed to make him understand. "It was more than that. Father Luke . . . well, he wasn't very adept with the typewriter. And in my line of work"—I gave him a self-deprecating smile—"it's essential to be a good typist. So I offered to help him out with his correspondence and that sort of thing." That was how it had started: a few letters, perhaps once a week. There had been no question of payment; one of his smiles was payment enough, and I always received one. *I don't know what I would do without you, Margo.*

It had escalated from there. *My handwriting is so terrible*, he'd said, though it wasn't at all. *And my eyesight isn't what it was. I find it so difficult to read my sermons when I'm in the pulpit.* So I had begun typing his sermons for him. He preferred to dictate them to me, sitting in his favorite chair as I typed.

My mother had always typed my father's sermons, and helped him with his letters. Doing that for Father Luke had been not a duty but a pleasure, bringing us closer together. Once a week became twice, and before I knew it I was coming to the Vicarage nearly every day: Monday, Wednesday, and Thursday mornings for letters and other paperwork, and Friday mornings to type his sermons. Indispensable. I'd even learned to produce a passable version of his signature to save him from the task of having to sign all of his letters.

"Did you ever do any of his ironing?" Inspector Sharpe interposed into my thoughts.

My reply was definite, my tone icy. "Certainly not."

"There must have been a lot of ironing. All of those

vestment things," he suggested. "Surely he didn't do it himself?"

It didn't take a writer of whodunnits to understand what he was getting at. I had no choice, really, but to tell him. "I think that the person you need to talk to is Stella Clulow," I said slowly. "Miss Clulow. Lilac Cottage, in the village."

Stella Clulow—or Stella Clueless, as I think of her to myself—is a relative newcomer to Nether Deepwell. Her origins are shrouded in mystery, and I never have discovered why she came to our village. Gossip has it that she wanted to be a nun, but was turned down by every Anglican order in the country. She has a certain reputation for holiness, and seems to be one of those women who devote themselves, vaguely, to good works.

"Vague" is an appropriate word to use in relation to Stella. "Vacant" would also do, or even "dim." But the most descriptive word of all is "bovine."

Her eyes are huge and brown. Her temperament is placid. And the workings of her mind are as laborious and transparent as a cow chewing its cud.

I had been aware of Stella, as one is in a village like Nether Deepwell, from the time of her arrival. For instance, I knew that she had organized—disastrously, as it happened—one of the church fetes, and then there had been some great kerfuffle over the flower rota. But our paths had scarcely crossed until one day just after Christmas last year.

It was typical of Stella that our first encounter occurred because she'd got muddled up about dates.

I was at the Vicarage that Wednesday, as usual, and when the doorbell rang, Father Luke was on the phone, so I went to the door.

Stella stood on the doorstep, her arms heaped high with a tangle of white linen; she was as surprised to see me as I was to see her, and dropped half of her burden.

"Father Luke is expecting me," she said, gathering up her lost items, then added, as if some explanation were necessary, "I always come on a Saturday."

"But this is Wednesday," I pointed out.

It transpired that Christmas had confused her. She explained it all to me as I helped her in with her load.

She always collected Father Luke's laundry—his shirts, his albs, his surplices, and so forth—on a Sunday evening, after Evensong, and took them home with her to run them through her mangle. On Saturday she brought them back, and ironed them in the scullery of the Vicarage. At first she had tried ironing everything at home, but had discovered that by the time she transported it back to the Vicarage, it needed ironing all over again. "And look," she moaned. "I've managed to drop Father's best alb, and it has mud on the sleeve."

I ran it under the cold tap in the scullery while she volunteered her feelings about her labors. "I just wish I could do more for Father Luke," she said. "But he insists that this is enough."

"Oh, does he?" I turned off the tap and faced her.

"He's so . . . so *spiritual*, don't you think?" Her brown cow eyes shone. "It's such a privilege to be able to help him, in my little way. And ironing his things," she added shyly, fingering an item which propriety prevents me from mentioning, "it makes me feel closer to him."

I said that I supposed it would.

The coldness of my voice—quite deliberate, that—didn't discourage her from going on, her tone becoming even more confidential. "I asked Father Luke, once, why he'd never married. I thought that maybe he believed that priests *shouldn't* marry. You know—what's that word?"

"Celibacy," I supplied. "Clerical celibacy."

"That's it. But do you know what he said? He said that he just hadn't met the right woman. Yet." Her face glowed as she wrestled the first of Father Luke's shirts onto the ironing board and plugged the flex of the iron into the mains.

While I was lost in my memories, the police surgeon arrived to examine the body. Inspector Sharpe seemed to accept me as part of the furniture, and didn't ask me to leave, so I remained, though I kept my face averted from the proddings and pokings of the surgeon.

It was when, with the help of the two policemen, he

rolled the body over, that I heard a gasp of surprise. "I say!"

Involuntarily my gaze moved to the floor. Father Luke was now lying on his face, and from his back protruded the handle of a wicked-looking three-pronged gardening implement.

"He's been stabbed!" stated Sergeant Dove, characteristically. "Stabbed in the back!"

Inspector Sharpe turned to me. "Have you ever seen this tool before, Miss St. James?"

I nodded, remembering. "Or one just like it."

"And where have you seen it?"

"It belongs," I said, "to Annabel Marston-Moretaine."

I'd run across Annabel Marston-Moretaine, with that very tool in her hand, one sunny Wednesday in the spring. I had taken the short-cut through the churchyard, and came round the side of the Vicarage to find Annabel on her knees in the herbaceous border that runs along the south side.

Annabel Marston-Moretaine. Spinster sister of the local squire, Ralph Marston-Moretaine. A horse-faced woman sporting roan-colored hair with all the style of a horse's tail, and rather a lot of teeth. I suppose, to be fair, that she has the usual number, but their prominence and size suggest otherwise. She dresses badly, as women of that class often do. And she has the raw red complexion of a country-woman who enjoys outdoor pursuits.

I do *not* enjoy outdoor pursuits, so I don't know Annabel well. She rides to hounds, and is mistress of the local hunt; her dahlias usually take first prize at the county agricultural show. But our paths have crossed often enough through the years that we're on a first-name basis.

"Annabel!" I said, surprised to see her.

She buried the three prongs of her tool in the soil, wiped her face on her sleeve, and grinned at me. "Taking advantage of a jolly good day, don't you know," she said. "Yesterday was absolutely foul. I usually come on a Tuesday afternoon, but there was no question of that yesterday. And I mustn't get behind."

"You come here regularly, then?" I echoed.

"Oh, yes." She rocked back on her heels. "What would the dear old thing do without me? He doesn't know one end of a dibber from the other."

"But I thought that Father Luke took care of the garden himself."

Annabel laughed. "Not a chance. He'd pull up all of the flowers and leave the weeds. No, I've had to take the garden in hand, and I must say that I think I've made a jolly decent job of it."

"Indeed you have," I had to admit.

Her face softened in an uncharacteristic way. "Mind you, he needs a bit of taking in hand himself."

"Oh?"

"To put not too fine a point on it, he needs a wife."

In my pocket, my hand clenched into a fist; I tried to keep my voice light. "Did you have anyone in mind?"

She gave a little chuckle. "Oh, I reckon I'd do quite nicely. Right sort of class and all that. I mean, who else is there in Nether Deepwell?" She rubbed her hands together to get rid of some of the soil, and inspected her empty ring finger with a speculative look. "Just a matter of time, I should think. Do you know, I asked him once why he'd never married. And he said that he'd just not met the right woman. But I dare say he could be convinced otherwise."

"He seems a confirmed bachelor to me," I couldn't refrain from saying in a strained voice.

"Oh, we'll see about that." Annabel Marston-Moretaine laughed her cheerful braying laugh and retrieved her three-pronged implement from the soil.

My whodunnits are well known for their complicated and ingenious plots. In fact, I've sometimes been compared by reviewers to the great Mrs. Christie herself. I suppose it's not too surprising, then, that the police seemed to regard me as more than just a witness, more than just the person who had found the body. They treated me almost as a member of their team.

The day after that horrible, harrowing morning, still in shock, I received a telephone call from Inspector Sharpe. "I just wanted to update you on the case," he said.

"You don't suspect *me*, do you?" I said in an attempt to sound light-hearted.

"Good Lord no, Miss St. James." The inspector paused. "I thought you might like to know. The postmortem has established that the vicar died some time on Sunday evening," he went on. "They can't be more precise than that, I'm afraid. But they've turned up something . . . um . . . unusual."

I suppressed my revulsion and fell back on the language of my books—words which were robbed of their emotive meaning by their very familiarity. "Did he die from the blow to the head, or from the stab wound?" I asked.

"Well, that's just the thing. It might have been either, or it might have been. . . . something else," the inspector told me.

"Something else?"

"It would seem that at some time shortly before he died, the vicar ingested a caustic and poisonous substance."

"I don't understand."

The policeman elaborated. "Something called oxalic acid, apparently. Also known as salt of lemons. A household poison, used in cleaning."

"Eunice Empy," I said without hesitation.

There was a pause on the other end of the phone. "Could you spell that for me, please, Miss St. James?"

I complied.

"And that would be *Miss* Empy?"

"Yes," I said. "Miss Eunice Empy."

Friday mornings were, as I've said, the time set aside for the typing of Father Luke's sermons. He would write out his rough notes on Thursday evening, and dictate to me the following morning. We were always finished by lunchtime.

On the Friday before Holy Week, though, it took much longer, as he had several different addresses to deliver during the coming week, and it was well past one o'clock when I typed the last full stop on his sermon for Maundy Thursday.

"Well done, Margo," said Father Luke as I pulled the

final page from the typewriter with a flourish. "I don't know what I would do without you."

I allowed myself to feel some pride in this, and my heart beat a bit faster when he leaned over to take the page from my hand, favoring me with one of his wonderful smiles. Our eyes met, and so did our fingers.

Just then, though, the phone rang, and while Father Luke answered it, I excused myself silently to go upstairs to the cloak room to freshen up after our long session.

I went to the basin and splashed some cold water on my face. Then I turned and found that I was not alone in the room.

My companion was Eunice Empy, on her knees. But she was not praying: she was leaning over the edge of the bath, polishing the gold taps.

I'm not sure which of us was the more surprised. Eunice, probably, as I was beginning to get used to this sort of thing. But nevertheless I was the one who went on the offensive. "What are you doing?" I asked.

"Polishing the taps," was her reply—she must be related to Sergeant Dove, as I come to think of it. She proceeded to give me a discourse on the subject, explaining that she was using a solution of oxalic acid to remove every water spot and bit of lime scale. "Not many people know that oxalic acid is the very best thing for gold taps," she said. "Poisonous, of course—so you have to be careful. Especially since it looks so much like epsom salts. But it was a little trick I learned from Mother."

She said the name with a sort of reverence. Eunice's mother had died, at an advanced age, only the year before, closely following her father to the grave. Her parents had been the center of Eunice's life: once, in the dim reaches of the past, she might have had some sort of life of her own, but no one—including Eunice—remembered back that far. She had lived with them and cared for them as they had grown older and more infirm, doglike in her devotion to her crotchety and difficult progenitors.

I looked at Eunice now. Kneeling on all fours, she really did resemble a dog—an unkempt, overweight dog. Her untidy grey hair hung in lappets over her ears, and her eyes were trustingly raised to me. "Do you do this . . . often?" I asked, suppressing the urge to pat her on the head—or perhaps deliver a sharp kick to the ribs.

"Every week," she said. "Every Friday afternoon. I give the Vicarage a good going-over. Not that Father is untidy— far from it—but it's such a large house." She leaned over and breathed carefully on the cold water tap, then gave it one last wipe with her cloth. "There. Looks perfect."

"But why?" I couldn't refrain from asking. "Why do you do it?"

She didn't understand the question. "It needs doing. And you certainly couldn't expect Father to do it. The poor dear man," she added in a more confidential tone, her jowly face going all soft and dreamy. "All on his own. He needs someone to look after him."

"But he just hasn't met the right woman," I supplied.

Eunice missed the sarcasm in my voice. "That's right! That's exactly what he told me. Of course," she added shyly, her doggy eyes downcast, "he might have met her, and just not realized it yet."

The next call from Inspector Sharpe came a few days later. I won't go into the agonies of memory and regret that I suffered in that period; suffice to say that I wasn't able to concentrate on my work, wasn't sleeping well, and that my mind was working overtime, as I waited for news of an arrest.

The Inspector didn't waste time on preliminaries. "I thought you might want to know," he said. "The toxicology report has come back from the Home Office. And the vicar was poisoned."

"You told me that," I reminded him. "Oxalic acid."

"Oh, it was more than that. Poison mushrooms, in fact. Death caps."

I closed my eyes. "Deirdre Harling," I said. *"Mrs. "*

By the time I encountered Deirdre Harling one evening at the Vicarage, I was no longer surprised at the phenomenon. I was now used to the sad spinsters who flocked round Father Luke, and found them pathetic rather than anything else.

Deirdre Harling, though, was a different matter. She was by far the most dangerous of the lot. More dangerous than the rest of them put together.

She is, you see, a clergyman's widow, and younger than that description would suggest. Her husband was an army chaplain, killed in the war, so she's been on her own for over ten years. Still, she isn't yet forty, and attractive with it. More attractive than a clergyman's widow has the right to be, and with an unsuitably frivolous and romantic name.

Deirdre Harling is sleek and pretty, in a feline sort of way. A triangular face, slanting green eyes. Lithe, slim. Not dumpy like Eunice. Not badly dressed like Annabel. Not dim like Stella. Dangerous.

And Deirdre Harling was clearly very much at home in the Vicarage kitchen. She unpacked her basket on the table, stowed a few things in the fridge, then slid a pie into the Aga. "Steak and mushroom," she said. "Luke's favourite."

Luke. Not Father Luke, but just plain Luke.

"Men *do* seem to like steak," she went on complacently. "They need their meat. My late husband was just the same." The look she gave me said, *you wouldn't know about such things.*

"I don't suppose that Father Luke thinks too much about food," I said severely. "His mind is on higher things." I listened to myself with horror: those words could have been spoken by Stella Clueless.

"Oh, you'd be surprised." Deirdre showed her small pointed teeth in a smug smile. "Underneath that cassock, he's a man like any other man."*And I should know*, her smile invited me to conclude.

I was shocked at my response, which could best be described as murderous. I wanted to punch her, to throttle her, to make that smug smile disappear from her face.

Instead I clasped my hands together, by force of will, and said through clenched teeth, "A man who needs a wife."

"Oh, exactly," purred Deidre. "I couldn't have put it better myself."

*   *   *

We buried Father Luke today. I got through it some-how—through the funeral and the committal and the cold meats in the church hall.

The police were there as well. Inspector Sharpe and Ser-geant Dove. They haven't made any arrests yet. It seems that there is a problem: the pathologist has yet to determine the cause of death.

What *did* kill Father Luke? Was it the poison mushrooms which he'd eaten, baked into a steak and mushroom pie? Was it the oxalic acid, given to him in the guise of epsom salts to settle his stomach when the effects of the mush-rooms began to be felt? Was it the stab wound by the gar-den implement, with the resultant loss of blood, or was it the trauma inflicted by the blow to the head with an iron?

Which of them will hang for it? Deirdre Harling, Eunice Empy, Annabel Marston-Moretaine, or Stella Clulow? They can't hang them all, though if intention to commit murder is a hanging offense, all four of them deserve to hang.

I have cooperated fully with the police, have told them everything.

All except for one little thing.

It was my fault.

If anyone should hang, it's Margo St. James.

I didn't mean for it to happen, of course. It all went horribly wrong.

After my encounter with Deirdre Harling, I could think of little else except poor Father Luke, surrounded by women with designs on him. And then, the following week, after another long typing session, Father Luke and I had the conversation that started me down the path that ended with his death.

This time there was no phone call to interrupt us, as our hands touched. Father Luke sighed and looked at me. "Ah, Margo," he said. "You're such a help to me. Such a tower of strength. It's so difficult, being on my own."

"Why have you never married?" I heard myself asking him.

He shook his head, and his eyes slewed away from mine.

"I've never met the right woman," he said softly. "But perhaps it's not too late."

Not too late. I passed the rest of the day in a daze of happiness. He *did* need a wife, and he had recognized in me—I was sure—the one who could give him all that he required. Who could be all things to him. No longer would he need those hangers-on, those designing handmaidens.

I, of all of them, was worthy of him. I alone. He knew it, and I knew it.

But how to get rid of them?

It was then that I hatched my plan. As I've said, I'm well known for my plots, and this one seemed to be a masterpiece. Foolproof.

Except that I wasn't dealing with just one fool, but with four. Or was it five, or six?

Together they looked after Father Luke very well: Eunice cleaning the Vicarage, Stella doing his laundry, Deirdre preparing his meals, Annabel looking after the garden. Together they equalled one wife.

The only reason that this domestic menage had worked, I realized, was that each of the handmaidens was unaware of the existence of the others. Each thought that she was the only one on whom he relied for his survival. Each had hopes that she would prevail in the end and banish his bachelor status.

What if they were to meet, and discover that it wasn't so?

I sent each of them a note, typed on Father Luke's typewriter and signed with my own passable imitation of his signature. The notes would ensure that they would each turn up at the Vicarage at the same time on a Sunday evening—a time when he would not be there. Then the truth would be out.

They would all find out about Father Luke's little game. And in disgust they would all desert him.

Leaving the field open for the one who was worthy of him.

But it didn't happen that way.

Instead, they killed him. I don't know whether they

planned it together, or whether each of them took it upon herself to do it.

Once the police sort it out, one of them will hang for it.

And me?

My punishment—my penance—is that I shall have to live with the guilt for the rest of my life. The guilt. And the regret.

I loved him.

My love killed him.

It wasn't supposed to happen like that.

Marjorie Eccles, winner of the Styles Award from Agatha Christie Ltd., has written suspense novels and has had short stories broadcast and published in magazines and anthologies, including the Malice Domestic *and the British Crime Writers' Association anthologies. She writes the Gil Mayo series of police procedurals featuring Superintendent Gil Mayo and his assistant, Abigail Moon, which are set on the edge of the Black Country, where she lived for thirty years.*

Peril at Melford House

Marjorie Eccles

It was nearly six months since I'd last visited my elderly aunts, Marigold and Lydia, at Melford St. Bede, and I was rather ashamed of the fact that it had been so long. I'd been so occupied with practicing and studying for my final exams—not to mention returning my engagement ring to Freddie—that it only belatedly occurred to me I hadn't seen my family since Christmas. I'd gone home to stay with them at Melford House and we'd spent the holiday as cheerfully as one could in postwar Britain, with shortages of everything still apparent, and food still rationed, despite the war having ended three years ago.

Lydia met me at Leverstead station with the car which she had, as usual, parked outside the station entrance, blocking the narrow High Street with lofty disregard for all traffic regulations. She seemed to feel she had a special dispensation to park wherever she wished, confident that the police would recognize the car and not make a fuss. And of course they could hardly fail to recognize it—a prewar Baby Austin which Jimmy Cole at The Garage had resprayed a cheerful, bright yellow to her instructions—and naturally, they wouldn't make a fuss, knowing the car belonged to Miss Crowe from Melford St. Bede. Since the war, people no longer doffed their caps to the gentry, Jack was as good as his neighbor, but here in the small town of Leverstead, just as in Melford village itself, people had long memories, and the Crowe family were still kindly regarded for their benevolence and their participation in local affairs. Even my grandfather, Nathaniel Crowe, irascible and autocratic as he was, had been respected during his lifetime, if not loved. It was only behind his back that Melford House had been referred to as "Old Crowe's Nest."

By the time Lydia had wedged her stout, tweed-costumed body behind the wheel and we had stowed my cello and my bags alongside a great deal of shopping and a large, ungainly parcel from Postleford's, the butcher's, there wasn't much room left in the tiny car.

"Shove that parcel to one side," Lydia ordered, in her abrupt way. "Only sausages, and bones for Hector." The statement was accompanied by a large wink, from which I understood the parcel also to contain something from under the counter to supplement the human rations, dragooned from Bert Postleford, or obtained in exchange for a hot tip for the two-thirty: Lydia was mad about horses, hunting, and racing, and her little flutters were a byword in the family. "Wonderful to see you, Vicky!" she added gruffly, attacking the engine and setting us off with a kangaroo jump.

I glanced at her in surprise. My Aunt Lydia was not one to voice her emotions so openly. Her straight, iron-grey hair was cut short and brushed back from her face in the same old-fashioned, uncompromising style she'd worn for years, but I fancied the set of her chin was a little less determined than normal. As we climbed the hill toward Melford I realized she was driving her car even more erratically than was her wont—which was to say I thanked the Lord above that we encountered no other vehicle.

Melford St. Bede is a lovely village standing on a hill overlooking a deep valley, and the road from Leverstead winds up through the woods that clothe the hill. We were nearly at the top, where the road takes a sharp right turn, when Lydia stopped the car and switched off the engine. I was happy that she pulled in to the side first and didn't simply stop in the middle of the road, as she was quite likely to do.

"Vicky," she began, "something you should know. I've moved back to the Grange."

"Goodness!" The Grange belonged to Lydia, a largish house in the center of the village, with stables attached where she kept several hunters, but she'd returned to Melford House to live with Aunt Marigold since Marigold's stroke the previous year. She had seemed since then to accept the arrangement as more or less permanent. The Grange, though not the stables, had, in fact, been on the market for months. "But why? What about Aunt Marigold? Why didn't you let me know? And what—"

"Whoa there, old thing," she said, much as she would have addressed Winston, her favorite horse. "One question at a time."

"Well," I said, more calmly. "Which one would you like to answer for a start?"

"First one, I suppose," she answered after a moment's pause. "You asked me why. Why I went back to the Grange after Christmas. That was when *he* came."

"When who came, Aunt Lydia?" I asked the question gently, and took her capable hand in mine, because it was, incredibly, trembling. A tear, even, rolled down her weatherbeaten cheek.

"Why, Malcolm Deering. Nurse Wilcox's stepbrother." Her voice hardened, and she brushed the tear away angrily. "But of course, you haven't met him yet. Suppose you'll be like everyone else—especially Marigold—and think he's charming! Butters her up shamefully and she just laps it up, thinks he can do no wrong. Then I had an offer for the Grange, but when it came to the point I couldn't face the thought of actually selling it. Then Marigold became impossible so I went back home to live. Realized my mistake too late! Only thing to do now, I suppose, is go back to Melford House and stay with Marigold until all this is cleared up. Oh, Vicky, if only your mother had still been alive! Always the one who knew the right thing to do, you know. But you're so like her, I'm sure you'll be able to help."

My mind reeled, trying to sort all this out. My mother, Grace, I should explain, was the youngest of the three Crowe sisters by many years, the only one who had married. Though Marigold, I had always suspected, had had her moments when she was younger, even accounting for the exaggerated stories of what she liked to think of as her colorful past. My mother had fallen in love with my father, a penniless young academic; when the war came, he was chagrined not to be able to serve in the forces because of his poor eyesight and had to be content with a job in the Air Ministry. We lived in a flat nearby but soon the Blitz started and despite my protests, I was sent away from the dangers of London to live with my mother's family at Melford St. Bede. Two months later, both my parents were killed when a bomb dropped on our flat and demolished it, and Melford House became my permanent home. I was fourteen years old, and I would never forget the love and kindness shown to me by my aunts during this terrible time—and even, in a less demonstrative way, by my grandfather.

Not that it was all sweetness and light, living with my relatives. My grandfather, as I have said, was an old curmudgeon, and tight-fisted at that. He enjoyed tyrannizing over his little empire and, as far as his two elder daughters were concerned, had seen off one suitor after another as not being good enough, or rich enough, though perhaps he also realized that neither of them were really cut out to make good wives. Lydia was too devoted to her horses and dogs, and Marigold to herself. My mother, his youngest and his favorite, had been allowed to go her own way with only token objections.

As for the aunts . . . they had a great deal of affection for each other, but they could scarcely have been more different and, needless to say, their temperaments often clashed. Their squabbles were usually short-lived, due no doubt to their very wise decision after Grandfather died to keep separate establishments, but there was always some on-going drama between them—which I believed they enjoyed as adding a little spice to life. Marigold was the elder, though only by about eighteen months. She was devoted to the arts, especially to music, and I had her to thank for encouraging me to work for a scholarship to the Royal College of Music, as a first step toward making music my career. She was no mean pianist herself, and she also painted. Before the war, as she never let anyone forget, she had been in with the Bloomsbury set, numbering Virginia Woolf among her friends; she had even, at one time, until stopped by my grandfather, attempted to surround herself at Melford St. Bede with arty types, rather fancying herself as another Lady Ottoline Morell, I suppose. She had always been delicate, and was still very pretty, rather vain, and perhaps a trifle shallow.

Whereas Lydia . . . plain, blunt old Lydia, she was the one who'd worked untiringly during the war with the Women's Voluntary Services, taken charge of the billeting arrangements for evacuees, and done her stint as a fire-watcher. When the war ended, she went back to occupying her time with her horses, her dogs, and riding to hounds. Lydia in hunting pink was a sight to make strong men quail. She'd always been formidable, and to tell the truth there were times, as a child, when I'd been more than a little afraid of her. At the same time, she was eminently sensible, so that her attitude now was all the more disturbing.

"Oh, that woman!" she declared now, cutting into my thoughts. "What a snake in the grass she's turned out to be!"

I presumed she was referring to Nurse Wilcox, which didn't altogether surprise me, since she was not a woman I naturally warmed to. She had been taken on following

Aunt Marigold's stroke about a year ago, a voluble, irritating woman of about thirty-five, bossy as nurses are, with an enormous appetite, and always demanding endless pots of strong tea. She had sandy hair and a mole on her chin, from which sprouted a single, black hair.

Perhaps it was the thought of tea which made me say now. "Let's go on to the Grange, and you can tell me all about it. I'll even have a cup of bonfire tea with you." (My childhood name for her favorite smoky Lapsang Souchong.) "You shouldn't be living there all on your own . . . I can stay with you just as well as at Melford House—"

"Lord, no! Wouldn't do at all. I'm quite all right, and Marigold's expecting you, and besides . . ." Her voice faltered to a close. She really was quite unlike her usual, confident self.

"Besides what?"

"I want you there to keep a watching brief."

"A watching brief?" I tried not to laugh. "You've been reading too many of those thrillers." Gory pulp fiction with lurid covers constituted Lydia's bedtime reading, but they'd never before affected her clear thinking.

"Maybe I have," she said quietly, "but you can't put everything that's been happening down to my imagination. Nor to accidents, as Marigold insists. Something's going on, Vicky."

"Good heavens! What sort of things?"

"They're trying to kill Marigold."

There was a long pause. Had it been anyone else but Lydia, I might have thought this a leg pull. But a sense of humor was never her strong point. I reminded myself of her age, and her addiction to crime fiction. "Aunt Lydia! Isn't that going a bit far?"

"Ha! Maybe you won't think so when you hear what I've got to say. For a start, there was Benjie, and that finnan haddock Wilcox sent up for Marigold's supper. Shows what a fool the woman is, not to have listened when I told her how Marigold hates smoked fish. She fed it to Benjie and an hour later the poor cat was stone dead."

"He was very old, and he *was* ailing," I reminded her gently. When Marigold had written to me, mourning his death, she'd said he was 17, which she reckoned was 119, in human terms. Be that as it may, he'd certainly been around for almost as long as I could remember.

"That's what everyone said. All the same, wish I'd obeyed my natural instincts, had him down to the vet to see just what he *did* die of. She knows about poisons, that woman. She's supposed to be a nurse, after all. And it all began after Malcolm appeared on the scene, just after Christmas. Marigold should never have allowed him to stay, lounging about, doing nothing. Think they're on Easy Street, both of them."

"If that's so, wouldn't killing Aunt Marigold defeat the object?"

She gave me a baleful look. "Not now that she's changed her will in his favor!"

"What!"

"Thought that'd make you sit up! As you know, through your grandfather's will Melford House goes to me after she dies, and there's nothing she can do about that. It's falling to pieces, going to rack and ruin because Father was too mean to spend anything on its upkeep and Marigold really has no interest—but I don't mind about that." Her face reddened. "Fact is, I *should* mind frightfully if it were to go out of the family."

I knew how much she loved the old house, though it wasn't a sentiment I could share. It was the dreariest old place imaginable, a hideous Victorian brick edifice, all high chimneys and unnecessary gables and turrets on the outside, and inside full of dark corners, gloomy, allegorical stained glass, and heavy old oil paintings of dubious artistic worth. It had been built and furnished by my great-grandfather, who had been too busy making money from the manufacture of boots and shoes to acquire any taste, and had remained largely unchanged ever since.

"She can't touch the house, but she can leave her money where she wants—and she's left it all to Malcolm Deering! 'Fraid she's cut you right out, left you without a penny, old girl!"

This was a shock, but not the disaster Lydia seemed to think it would be. Money for its own sake had never appealed to me. "I've quite enough as it is, Aunt Lydia . . . certainly more than most of my friends. After all, Grandfather did leave me something—"

"A pittance!" she interrupted. "Mere pittance! Because he meant me and Marigold to leave you something as well, don't you see?"

I vaguely recalled that Marigold, as the elder daughter, had come into the bulk of the Crowe fortune, such as was now left, but I'd never given it much thought. If asked, I would have supposed Marigold would leave her money to some artistic foundation or other, and Lydia to some charity for retired horses. But I was astonished that Marigold, who was quite sharp underneath all the fluff and frivolity, could have been so utterly foolish and uncaring of her sister, so taken in as to make a will in favor of a stranger, a young man virtually unknown to her, however much he flattered her. When I met Malcolm Deering half an hour later, I found it even more unbelievable.

But for the moment, Lydia was continuing with her story. "There's more, Vicky. Only two days ago Marigold was nearly killed by one of those finial thingummys falling off the roof, though there was only the lightest breeze. Remember what happened when one blew down that time before? Shattered a York stone paving slab, no less! The rest should have been removed or made safe there and then. She was lying out on the terrace in a deck chair—only missed her by the purest chance."

"Aunt Lydia. Just supposing anyone would try to climb out there on to the roof to push it over, the chances of getting it to fall in exactly the right position must be remote."

"Ah, but it is *possible* to get out there. You know that, don't you?"

And of course, I did. In a famous escapade, when I was about eight, I suppose, I had scrambled out of an attic window on to the roof with my cousin William, where we crouched behind one of the false gables and dropped tiny pebbles onto the grownups who were drinking cocktails on the terrace below. We nearly fell off the roof with helpless laughter, which was how we were found out. Poor William took the brunt of the punishment because he is seven years older than I am and should have known better, they told him. Each of these false gables, of which there were many, was crowned by a heavy stone finial in the shape of a foliated fleur-de-lys. Lethal, if it fell on anyone's head. But even if the one above the terrace had become loose enough to push over . . . "It's too much of a coincidence, Aunt Lydia."

"Not when you remember the fish—and the rabbits."

"Rabbits? Was there some poisoned rabbit stew as well?"

"You're not taking this seriously, Vicky!" she admonished, poking me with a sharp finger. "Well, maybe this'll convince you. Yesterday, when Marigold was taking a stroll in the old rose garden, dear Malcolm was out potting rabbits in the copse, or so he *said*." She plunged her hand into her capacious pocket and showed me what she explained was a spent bullet. "First time I've ever known anybody go after rabbits with a revolver!"

I confess that one did rather take me aback. "Does Malcolm own a revolver?"

"There's Father's. Never got rid of it," she added unnecessarily, because at Melford House no one ever threw anything at all away, even unto the third and fourth generation.

"Well, he obviously missed," I said lamely.

"Only just. She imagined it was a wasp zinging past her head, thought there must be a nest in the gazebo. A wasp! Went out and looked when she told me and guess what? Found the bullet, of course." She went on rather hurriedly, "Bad business all round—and unnecessary, too. They've only to wait, after all, but they won't want to do that, in case she changes her mind again."

"Aunt Lydia, what do you mean, *they've only to wait?*"

"Prepare yourself for a shock, Vicky. Marigold . . . her heart, you know. Doc Crampton's an old fool in some ways, but I suppose he knows his job. Says it can't be long before she cashes in her chips. Any day, in fact. Mind you, the best doctors have been wrong before now. She may go on for years."

I was as saddened to hear this as Lydia evidently was, despite her gruff words, although it wasn't unexpected:

Marigold had never fully recovered from that stroke. I really couldn't imagine what Melford House would be like without her—or even how Lydia was going to manage without their constant sparring. "Know she can't help it," Lydia added, starting up the car. "Best sister in the world, matter of fact, but one can't help thinking it's made the poor old thing a bit gaga." I could think of nothing sensible or comforting to say to this and we drove the last couple of miles in silence.

"Anyway, it's not just me, Vicky," she said, as we at last turned through the gates at Melford House and bucked up the potholed gravel drive. "Your cousin William thinks there's something fishy about that pair, too, yet he keeps telling me not to worry, everything will turn out right. Can't understand him. You should talk to him—he's joining us all here for dinner tonight."

"Oh, then if William agrees with you, it *must* be so," I answered tartly. "But you're wrong if you think he'll talk sensibly to me. He still treats me as though I'm twelve years old, with a brain to match."

William (he of the pebbles thrown from the roof) was actually my second cousin twice removed. We'd always been the best of friends, but since he'd been demobbed from the navy, and had gone back into his father's solicitor's firm, he'd changed for the worse. He wasn't fun any longer, though I suppose he could be excused, in a way. His father suffered from gout, an acutely painful and disabling condition which seems to provoke amusement in everyone but the sufferer, and consequently, William had had many of the decisions and worries of the firm thrust on to his shoulders. He'd become pompous, at least when it came to advising me what I should, or should not do, especially regarding my engagement to Freddie Fergus. He'd been right about Freddie, as it so happened. He'd turned out to be just as ghastly as William had predicted, and though I'd given him the old heave-ho several weeks ago, I'd seen no reason to inform William of this fact and give him the satisfaction of saying "I told you so."

Why Lydia thought I'd be charmed by the man who came to the door to greet us as we drew up before the house, I cannot imagine: I loathed Malcolm Deering on sight. There was something just too good about his wavy hair, his mustache, the silk cravat tucked into his shirt neck, and his Errol Flynn smile. He was older than I'd imagined he would be. According to his sister, Nurse Wilcox, he'd flown Spitfires in the war and been decorated for bravery, all of which I felt was an unlikely story, despite his handlebar mustache and his tedious use of RAF slang. "Oh, jolly d!" he said, when we were introduced. Apparently, he'd had a nervous breakdown due to the traumatic effects of the war, and needed a long rest to recuperate. I didn't believe a word of it. It seemed to me he was basically unintelligent. I was more than inclined to agree with Lydia that he and his sister had found a cushy number at Melford House, and were trading on the fact.

But . . . just supposing it was true? That he had been brave and audacious? Not all heroes look like heroes. Did that mean he would also have the audacity to carry out these attempts on Aunt Marigold's life?

"You'll see a big change in her," Lydia had warned, but as it happened I did not. I was never to see my Aunt Marigold before she died.

She was resting in her room when we arrived and slept on and on. It was only when Nurse Wilcox went in to rouse her to get ready for dinner that we realized why she hadn't put in an appearance. Yet another accident. And this time, it had been a fatal one.

"I'm not one to give in to hysterics, I'm sure," the nurse said, after a third cup of fiercely strong tea had revived her somewhat, "but it fair gave me a turn when I went in and saw what had happened. Not that I didn't warn her. I told her that great heavy portrait was downright dangerous, right over the bedhead—nasty old thing, begging your pardon, glaring out of that ugly frame! What would happen if the cord gave way? 'Good heavens, Nurse, that's my grandfather. He's been there as long as ever I can remember and he's never fallen!' she said, which didn't seem very logical to me. But then, that's what she was like! Not that you'll get me to say anything against her, she was one of the best patients I've ever nursed. Fussy about her food but then, there's many a nurse would be glad if that was the only thing to complain of in their patients, *I* can tell you! Caught her right on the head, that frame did, but the doctor says even if it hadn't, the shock of it falling like that would have killed her, and I'm sure he's right."

"Damn poor show, all the same," Malcolm Deering said, walking across to the window and looking out over the lawn with what I couldn't help thinking was a sickeningly proprietorial air. Perhaps he didn't know that the house, if not Marigold's money, was now Lydia's.

It was at that moment that William arrived from Leverstead, having been informed by telephone of what had happened. He came into the room and I forgot that my relations with him had been on the cool side lately. Those nice, steady brown eyes sought mine immediately. "Vicky."

"Oh, William!"

He put his arm around my shoulder and its clasp was oddly comforting. He included Lydia with an outstretched hand. At the moment, he wasn't being at all pompous.

Nor was he later, when he gave his father's apologies for not being there in person, and said to us all, "He's given me permission to inform you of the contents of Aunt Marigold's will. I think you, Nurse Wilcox, and your brother, should hear it too. It's soon told. She leaves one or two small bequests to various people. A pension for life and the tenancy of his cottage to Gornal, her old gardener. A legacy of a thousand pounds to you, Vicky. The rest of her entire fortune goes to you, Lydia, to pay off the mortgage on the Grange and to help with running Melford House as you wish it to be run. The house now, of course, belongs to you." He paused. "Oh, and in a codicil, she leaves fifty pounds each to Nurse Wilcox and Malcolm Deering for their kind attention to her over the last few months."

The faces of Malcolm and his sister were a study. Lydia went brick red. It was news to me that the Grange was mortgaged—but after all, those stables of hers didn't run on fresh air, and it was well known in the family that her regular racing wagers more often than not demonstrated the triumph of hope over experience. But her embarrassment at her finances being made public was coupled with another expression I couldn't put a name to.

"I think that's a very fair and straightforward will," concluded William, shuffling papers briskly together.

"Fair! A miserable fifty! That's a calculated insult, considering—" began Malcolm, only to be stopped by a vicious look from his sister. He subsided but his languishing blue eyes were now smoldering with anger and resentment.

"Fifty pounds more than you deserve!" muttered Lydia.

"Oh, so that's what you think?" said Nurse Wilcox. "Well, Miss Crowe had every right to leave her fortune as she wished, I'm sure. I've known patients to have stranger fancies than she had before she died, but all the same . . ." She glared at Lydia, then me.

"All the same what, Nurse Wilcox?" asked William.

"She gave us to understand she'd changed her will, entirely in favor of my brother. She said she was very fond of him. She said . . ." She paused in a curiously knowing sort of way, trying to stare us down. The black hair on her chin trembled visibly. She seemed about to say much more, but only added, "She said he was like her own son."

"Fine thing for a chap to find out he's been left nothing at all," Malcolm put in. "After all a chap's done for her." His vacuous face brightened. "That's it! There must be a will that supersedes this."

"Be quiet, Malcolm!" Nurse Wilcox said sharply. He opened his mouth, looked at her, then decided to shut it.

"I assure you," said William stiffly, "this was Miss Crowe's last will and testament, to which the codicil was added only last week when you, Mr. Deering, drove her down to my father's office."

"She told me herself, in person, she was leaving every penny to me!"

"There's a world of difference between saying what you're going to do and doing it," William answered dryly. I had no difficulty in going along with this, knowing Marigold quite capable of such dissimulation—deceit, if you like—in order to keep Malcolm and his sister dancing attendance upon her. But, if they had thought they were to benefit when she died—and Nurse Wilcox must have been aware of Marigold's critical state of health—why make those murder attempts at all? Lydia would be bound to contest a will made in Malcolm's favor and allegations like that would not have improved their chances of success. They were an unpleasant pair, but I didn't think the sister, at least, was stupid.

Wilcox said threateningly, "You haven't heard the last of this!" just at the moment that a nasty, horrid thought insinuated itself into my mind and, as I looked at Lydia and finally identified the expression I had failed to recognize before, strengthened and grew, I felt rather sick.

An hour later, on the terrace, I found the opportunity to give my somewhat gabbled explanations to William, who listened with gratifying attentiveness until I'd finished. "What you're trying to say, Vicky, is that *Lydia* staged those 'accidents'?"

"Well, she could have." It was the last thing I wanted to believe but it seemed horribly clear to me: Marigold had thought it wiser to let Lydia, as well as the nurse and her brother, believe that she'd made Deering her heir, for the simple reason that she knew Lydia well enough to realize she'd have been quite unable to keep up the sort of pretense she herself had done. And Lydia *had* believed what she'd been told—the result being those "accidents"—a blundering attempt to make Marigold see the precious pair for what they were and presumably to persuade her to revoke that unfair will.

It occurred to me William was not exactly looking as bowled over by my theories as I thought he would be, and I saw that, as usual, he'd got there before me. "I'll admit the same thing did occur to me," he said, "but that finial just happening to become conveniently loose enough for Lydia to push over? No, that won't wash! It had probably been balanced there for ages, and some freak movement of the breeze finally toppled it. Mind you, I'm not saying it might not have given her the idea for a series of so-called accidents . . . poor old Benjie snuffing it, Grandpa's revolver being fired and the spent bullet being found—"

"It did," interrupted a sturdy voice behind us. We turned to see Lydia stumping out of the drawing room, via the

French windows. "Damn fool thing to have done, though it seemed a good idea at the time to try and make Marigold come to her senses where that pair were concerned. Did nobody any harm. Except old Benjie, of course—but that was a kindness. Should've been put out of his misery months ago, according to the vet, only Marigold wouldn't hear of it."

"But the picture?"

"Nothing to do with me, not that! You don't believe I would've done anything that might *hurt* old Marigold? She wasn't even in the garden when I fired that bullet, and I knew nothing on earth would make her touch that finny haddock."

I was convinced she was telling the truth. Lydia might have been foolish, but she would never have done anything that could actually have killed her sister. "No, I'm sorry I even thought it. Of course I don't believe that." But I couldn't help thinking her schemes had planted a more sinister intention in someone's head.

"I've had a look at that picture," William said. "From what I could see without touching it, I'd say it's impossible to tell whether the cord had simply rotted over the years and finally given up the ghost, or been helped on its way by being teased and pulled apart to the last strand. If it had been doctored, it had been cleverly done. What's more, there's not so much as a speck of dust on the picture."

Even in the best-regulated households, of which Melford House was certainly not one, and never had been, even in the days of a sufficiency of servants, this was unusual. As everyone knows; when a picture has been hanging in the same place for years, dust inevitably accumulates behind it, so this one had obviously been taken down and cleaned before it fell, which had to be suspicious in itself. "No fingerprints, then, not a shadow of proof," I said.

And just supposing the cord had been tampered with, wasn't that an incredibly haphazard way to try to murder someone? The picture could have fallen at any time, when Marigold had not been in bed—or even in the room— though perhaps that was just the point. If it hadn't succeeded in killing her, it would just have been put down to another narrow escape. If it had succeeded, good. Sooner or later, if these "mishaps" continued, one of them had to be fatal.

"There'll have to be an inquest, won't there, and I suppose there's no doubt the verdict will be accidental death? That pair are going to get off scot free."

"Well," said William. "I'm not so sure about that."

And, with the air of having saved the best until the last, he pulled a long envelope from his pocket. "When Marigold made the codicil to the will last week, she left this letter with my father, not to be opened until after her death. It follows on from certain inquiries she'd asked us to make."

If he expected to surprise us, he succeeded. "What inquiries?" Lydia asked.

"About Malcom Deering and his sister. You couldn't understand, Lydia, why Marigold should be so taken in by Deering, but the truth was that she wasn't. Right from the first, she suspected him—with good reason, as she explains in this letter. She asked us to instigate inquiries, though neither my father nor I knew just why, until we read this." He tapped the envelope and asked abruptly, "How much do you know, Aunt Lydia, about Marigold's life when she lived in London?"

It was some time before she answered, and when she did, I thought she had already guessed where his questions were leading. "More than enough. Rackety sort of company she kept, called themselves arty to justify acting as they pleased, without thought for anyone else."

"She had a particular friend called Gayton Bulmer?"

"*Friend!* She actually told you about *him?*"

"In this letter, yes."

"So you also know about—" Lydia broke off, studied the carpet, then looked up. "Oh, well, water under the bridge now, but a terrible thing at the time. To have a baby and not be married . . . the shame, the disgrace." She sighed deeply. "Poor Marigold. You're telling me they were blackmailing her over that?"

"More than that. Deering was claiming he was that child."

"What!" She gave a snort of derision. "Ridiculous!"

"Well, as you know, the baby was given up for adoption. Nurse Wilcox, who, incidentally, is no more Deering's sister than I am, but someone who nursed him just after the war in a hospital for nervous disorders, came across a photo of this Gayton Bulmer, and spotted what she thought was a quite extraordinary likeness to Malcolm Deering. She also found out that Marigold's friendship with Bulmer had been rather more than that—"

"Found out! By listening to village gossip, no doubt, and snooping around among Marigold's private affairs, for I'll tell you one thing. My sister never kept any photo of that rotter on display! Not when he'd damn near ruined her life. Died just before the war, and good riddance!"

"Be that as it may, Wilcox brought Deering here as her stepbrother, on the pretext of his nervous exhaustion due to the war. Marigold let them stay here at Melford House, dancing to her tune, giving them promises of more to come in her will, while she took steps to discover their backgrounds. She let them think she believed Deering's claim to be her son but, as she makes clear in this letter, she knew from the first that was quite impossible."

"Of course she did!" Lydia declared sturdily. "She had the baby adopted, but that didn't mean she'd forgotten him. Always kept track of him. He joined the army when war broke out, and was killed in the western desert. Broke her heart."

There was a silence.

"So why set up that business with the picture?" I asked.

"Yesterday morning, my father sent up details to Marigold of what our inquiry agent had established regarding Deering's real identity. I believe she confronted them with what she now knew to be the truth, and they realized time had run out. They could have faced charges for attempting to get money by false pretenses, but remember, they still believed they were to benefit from her will. So they had to get rid of her before she could revoke it."

"The portrait *didn't* fall by accident, then," I said, hating to think of it.

"If it had been prepared, it would take only a sharp tug

when Marigold was sleeping to bring it down. Or—"

"Or it could have been lifted down and Marigold clobbered with it," Lydia finished. "Especially if she'd been given something to make her sleep like she did. Well, a post mortem will soon find *that* out."

We fell silent, each of us unwilling to face the prospect ahead, though thankful that, one way or another, the two miscreants were not going to get away scot free. Presently, Lydia left us to go and see to her horses, and William and I were alone. When he took my hand and pulled me to him, I didn't object. In the circumstances, it was very good to feel the warmth and comfort of his arms around me.

"And now," he announced masterfully, "about that ass Fergus. You're not going to marry him, Vicky. I won't let you."

"Oh, you won't? And why not?"

"Because you're going to marry me. You've owed me that ever since you let me take all the blame for throwing those pebbles from the roof."

"In that case, it's about time I paid my debt, isn't it?"

In this story, Teri Holbrook introduces some shady characters who would feel entirely at home in Christie's Bertram's Hotel. Holbrook is the author of the Edgar- and Agatha-nominated Gale Grayson and Katie Pru series. Her next book, The Mother Tongue, *is due out in 2001. She lives in Atlanta with her cartoonist husband Bill Holbrook and two children.*

Drawing to a Close

Teri Holbrook

I don't know what made me start sketching the events in the parlor of the Ravendaw Hotel. Maybe it was the way the woman (I named her Sassy) breathed her *H*s—hard, as if every time she said one she flounced. Without knowing her true hair color, I made her a blonde. Back home the only women with blond hair were also liable to wear red shoes. I figured they'd probably bring an attitude to their *H*s as well, so I drew Sassy a pair of high-heeled shoes and penciled them a hotsy-totsy red.

My chair was a wingback, and it faced the hotel's mammoth fireplace. I couldn't see the expanse of the room behind me, but in the beginning anyone who came in could have seen me if they'd bothered to glance beneath the chair to where my knee-socked legs reached the floor. By the third day, I had taken to crossing my feet underneath me, so that I sat like a child in the big chair with my sketch pad on my knees. Someone would have had to walk around to notice me, for I was very still. No one ever did. This led to my first conclusion: If I ever became a criminal, I would make sure I was the kind that paid attention.

I had only been in England for a month when I came to London and the Ravendaw. Mama had sent me to spend the summer with her aunt Suzie, an elderly woman with hair like blue hydrangeas, and after four weeks Aunt Suzie had finally agreed that a young woman might be allowed to visit London on her own as long as she lodged at the Ravendaw. Mama liked Aunt Suzie because, among other things, she agreed with my parents' assessment that I should pursue literature in my college studies, not the awful trade of cartooning I had fallen in love with my freshman year. At the collective hands of my relatives, I had endured lectures, logic, even a lengthy letter from an old family friend. This friend had tried her hand at professional cartooning in New York City, and I could see her stern glare right on the page. "1951," she wrote, "still finds cartooning the province of barrel-chested, cigar-smoking, ink-fingered men. And if you want to draw for comic books of the suspense and crime and horror variety—which, let's be honest, is where a lot of the future is—you gotta have a female victim and an eye for muscles and gore. Men assume women can't do that. If I had to do it over again, would I spend so many years banging against the closed doors of comic book publishers? Maybe. But I'd bind my breasts and walk with my legs apart."

Recalling the last line made me glance at my knees, poking my skirt out as I sat in the wingbacked chair. That was another thing Mama hated about cartooning: I tended to do it splayed out like a starfish, my arms and legs pointed in all directions. An oil painter, she'd lamented, even a pastel artist—either one would have been preferable to the manly art of cartooning. It was a peculiar distinction, in my view. Male eyes aren't the only ones that can exaggerate.

I stretched and thumped my pencil against my tablet. It was 9:30 A.M. and Sassy hadn't been by today. Usually, she arrived in the parlor by 8:45, an admitted discrepancy in my portrait of her. I would expect a woman with blond hair and red shoes to sleep in, not come downstairs at a responsible hour in clothes crisp enough to hiss and wearing perfume that could crush air. But that's exactly what she had done for the past three days. On day number one, I had just listened. On day number two, I began to draw. On day number three, I filled in the colors. Now I wanted action. I sketched boxes on one page, then on another. I had no way of knowing if Sassy in action was going to be a four-panel gag or a whole comic book.

The hiss came first, then the perfume, curling up under my chair and to my nose like kudzu on the prowl. It was a sensuous smell ("Sensuous smell!" I could hear Mama say. "Cartooning taught you that!"), and I had figured out on the first day that Sassy was neither married nor already engaged in a disreputable relationship by the way she lathered on the perfume, like she had to make her purpose clear. Since the rules for this game were that I couldn't look behind me, I never knew how her message was received. Did the man find her enticing? Did she annoy him? One thing was clear: he kept coming back.

I didn't have a name for the man. He talked in whispers and murmurs, and he didn't have an aroma strong enough to navigate the parlor. He was colorless and formless to me; I couldn't see his hair, the cut of his clothes. On paper, he was a rectangle, taller than Sassy. I suspected that he dressed well, only because the Ravendaw Hotel had been, before the war, a place of some prestige, and although now somewhat shabby, I had gathered from Aunt Suzie that the patrons still had a privileged air about them. Still, he was without details. He could have been the hotel chef or the doorman. The only thing I knew for sure was that he made himself available to listen to Sassy's humpfing *H*s every morning. If he was here on holiday, he wasn't sleeping in, either.

I heard a whisper, then an exasperated cough. I glanced

at my watch and scribbled 9:34 in the upper corner of the sketchbook.

"Is that all?" No *H*s, but Sassy made the question flounce anyway.

Whisper. Murmur. Definitely a male murmur. Idly, I drew a line down the middle of the rectangle. At least I knew he wore pants.

"Not good enough, is it? Not good enough at all."

Sassy had red fingernails, and since her arms were crossed, they were tapping her own biceps ("Biceps! Women don't have biceps! That cartooning . . ."). She wore grey today, but it was a shiny grey fabric, expensive, a dress with a cinched waist. I tried to make the cloth shiny, but it looked dirty instead. Shoot, I thought, and I pulled a lavender pencil from my box and changed the color.

"We're going to have to reconsider this. This isn't working out."

What wasn't working out? As I shaded the dress, I thought about all the things Mama said didn't work out— engagements, pregnancies, church committee meetings, vacations. She had wrung her hands for weeks before I finally boarded the airplane for New York to start my trip to England. "It isn't going to work out," she fretted. "Something will stop you from going—a flat tire, a gall bladder attack. And then . . ." She had pressed her apron to her mouth. And then, and then. We all knew what her "and then" was. A fate worse than death. A career as a . . .

"Maybe we just need to kill her."

I started to object that while Mama was irritating I really didn't feel inclined to kill her when I realized what I had heard. The pencil paused above the paper. I waited for the man to respond.

He said his first audible word.

"Yes."

YES? I almost yelped. I had to force my arms and legs from spilling out of the wingbacked chair.

"Yes," Sassy said. "I think maybe we just need to do that."

Suddenly I knew her dress wasn't lavender at all. It was black, which wouldn't look good in the funny papers, but that couldn't be helped. And she wasn't flouncing her *H*'s, she was chopping them, like a helicopter chopped waves, like a knife chopped onions. And my heart pounded, like her little knife of a voice was mincing its way across the room to me.

But when she spoke again, she was still at a distance. "We need to plan it out."

More manly murmurs.

"Good," Sassy said. "I'll be there."

The hissing sound moved away, but I waited a full three minutes, body shaking, before I twisted in the chair and peeked over the back. The room was empty. I scrambled to get my supplies together. I had to tell someone what I had heard.

I hurried to the front desk where a man in a dark blue suit shuffled through a card file.

"Please," I said. "I just overheard something terrible. A woman in your hotel is in danger."

The front desk clerk looked at me oddly, his eyes settling on my hair before drifting down the top of my dress. I knew I hadn't groomed myself according to Aunt Suzie's specifications—my hair had received only a quick brush through, no lipstick to brighten my face, and my top blouse button had come undone so that the collar rolled under like a folded pie crust. I nervously ran my hand over my hair and buttoned the button. It wasn't enough. The clerk looked at me skeptically.

"I'm sorry?"

"A woman is in danger," I repeated, slower. "I overheard two people in the parlor saying they were going to kill her."

He laughed and returned to his card file. "You're American, aren't you? 'I'm going to kill you'—it's a common phrase. Never heard it in the States?"

"Yes, I've heard it and that's not what they meant. I was sitting in one of the chairs in front of the fireplace where they couldn't see me. They didn't know I was there. I overheard what they said."

His look was stern. "Where is your mother, Miss . . . ?"

I felt my face grow flushed, but I battled on. "My mother is in Georgia and I am not a child. I'm telling you I overheard two people discussing murder. Here, in your hotel. Are you just going to ignore me?"

I could tell by his expression that he desperately wanted to, but instead he picked up the phone and turned his back. After several seconds, he hung up and faced me.

"Security's gone until Wednesday."

"Wednesday? Your hotel is going to be without a security guard for two whole days?"

He gave me the same peeved look Aunt Suzie did when I asked why she didn't have any cream for our coffee. "Not so long ago, the war," Aunt Suzie had said by way of explanation. "You Americans are very fortunate."

"We can always call the police if the need arises," the clerk said.

"The need has arisen," I said.

"I don't believe so."

I slapped my sketchbook on the counter and flipped it open. "See, I've been drawing them. There's two of them, a man and a woman. Here's the woman," I pointed to Sassy "and here's . . ." I looked at the rectangle with the line drawn down the middle. My face flushed again.

The clerk studied the woman. "No one here looks like that. I know everyone by looks if not by name."

"The thing is I've never actually seen them."

If I had been a gnat about to hit his bumper he couldn't have been more disdainful. "What?"

"I've never actually seen them." My voice quivered. "The chair faces the fireplace, you see. I've just been sketching my impressions."

"Impressions. Without seeing them. Damn fine. I've got work to do."

"But I heard them. I honestly did." I was stammering now, stupid. "Someone here is going to die, and if it happens, you'll blame yourself."

I could hear the cracking in my words. He was hunched over the card file, making it clear that he was now going to ignore me. I closed my sketchbook and turned away.

"Perhaps you just heard an impression of their conversation," he said quietly, but when I glanced back at him, he picked up the card file and disappeared into a room to the side of the counter.

I didn't know what to do. I wandered back to the parlor. Empty. Then into the dining room to stare at men and women drinking tea and eating dry toast, but none seemed to be my man and woman. Surely Sassy wasn't the portly matron with tea dribbles on her bosom, or the thin, nervous schoolteacher-type brushing breadcrumbs into her hand and hiding them in her sweater pocket. Sassy was both more refined and bolder than either. And the man—not as elderly as the great-grandfather by the window nor as young as the teenager bussing the tables. They were not there. I could tell by the plainness of the air and the unemphatic drone of the voices.

A waitress in a frilly penguin dress walked up to me. "Can I help you, miss?"

I hesitated for only a moment. "I'm looking for a couple. A man and a woman. They're usually in the parlor earlier in the mornings, but they came by later today and I missed them. You don't happen to know who I'm talking about, do you?"

"Don't know. Can you tell me what they look like?"

I can tell you what they sound like, what they smell like. I can tell you what's in their hearts and in their minds. But no, I cannot, in any way tell you what they look like.

I gave her a regretful smile. "Thank you," I said. "I'll check somewhere else."

But I didn't know where else to check. In the lobby, in a chair partially screened by a large, frondy plant, I spent an hour watching people come and go, first focusing on any would-be Sassys and her man, and then wondering which of the women passing by might be, right this second, enjoying the final moments of her life. For the most part, the women of the Ravendaw Hotel were joyful, appreciative of this reprieve from the long postwar reality. A little early spring weekend in the city. Nippy, but at least someone else had to worry about the sheets on the beds and the dust under the tables. Someone else made the tea. Someone else washed the dishes.

Someone else. Whoever Sassy was, she was none of these women. She was someone else.

I stood, not knowing what to do. I tried to make a long distance call to Aunt Suzie, although I couldn't begin to believe she would have a helpful suggestion, but no one was home. I wandered outside on the street and looked halfheartedly for a police officer. But I knew what the question would be: What did the couple look like? And I would have to offer up my poor sketchbook and explain that, for four mornings in a row, I had sat hidden in a wingbacked chair, conjuring up their physical bodies based on their perfume and their consonants. No one would believe me. I was an American. I was young. I wanted to be a cartoonist.

I skipped lunch, not hungry, and retreated to my room early to dress for dinner. Dinner was a tasteful affair at the Ravendaw—men in jackets and women in sparse jewelry taking canapes in the parlor, followed by a filling if not complicated meal. I laid out my navy blue skirt and twin set. In the shower the tepid water tapped my back as I evaluated the situation. How long did it take to plan a murder? Could Sassy and her man already have it mapped out? When would it take place? What kind of supplies does one need for a murder, and how late do the stores stay open? It was all so ridiculous. I felt like a fool.

At 7:30 I went downstairs, passing the clerk at the desk who dipped his head my way before giving it a disapproving wag. My face burned. I didn't want to go into the parlor, didn't want to stand in the corner and try to figure out if the way a woman bit into her cheese indicated a certain Sassy-ness. At the parlor entrance I detoured left and retreated to my spot behind the fronds.

The front wall of the parlor was part etched glass and part white plaster edged in gold. Two ornate electric sconces shed a soft light on the dinner guests as they, by twos and threes and fours, made their way to the cloth-covered table inside the room. I could hear their chatter as they entered the parlor, but once inside their sound was muted, and I was reduced to watching their bobbing mouths through the glass.

A couple here, there. A lone man. A trio. A single

woman with a child. They glided into the parlor, the sconce light bathing them, transforming them. I thought of Aunt Suzie and her cream, and wondered if these people came to the Ravendaw Hotel to pretend there had never been days of bombs and sirens and rationing, if they could fool themselves into believing that every man came home, that every family was whole. "You Americans are very fortunate," Aunt Suzie had said, and I knew she was right. The battle in my home was whether or not I worked for EC Comics or taught Shakespeare. How frivolous was my young, untested life.

A man left a woman standing by the wall and made his way to the canape table. He placed six crackers on a small plate, hesitated before a bowl of olives, then spooned up some of them as well. The woman smiled as he handed her the plate.

I couldn't hear their speech, just their motions as the woman leaned toward the man, briefly resting her head on his shoulder. I didn't imagine it, surely, that he reared ever so slightly back, tensed . . . repulsed? If I had brought my sketchbook with me, I would have drawn him repulsed. His rectangle shape would have been tapered, and I would have filled in his slicked back blond hair. He was the man, I was certain. But the woman wasn't Sassy. Blond, yes, and her fingernails were dark with color, and her dress was black, but this woman was too fawning. Not my Sassy. My Sassy would have taken one look at the plate and sent him back for celery sticks.

So she was the Dead Woman. She was the one who was not to live.

Out of the corner of my eye I saw Sassy. I don't know why I knew instantly it was she. She didn't look anything like my sketch—short-waisted, dark hair, a dress of ugly green. I stared at her as she marched across the room to the couple, a cup and saucer in her hand. Why was I so convinced? Then I saw it—the chop, chop of her strides. Like a helicopter over water. Like a knife after an onion.

I glanced around, frantic. The front desk clerk was gone; no maître d' stood at the dining room entrance. I turned back in time to see her stop in front of the couple. She said something that made all three of them laugh. Then she held out the cup and saucer to the Dead Woman.

I knocked back the fronds and barreled into the room. I elbowed aside the mother with her child, pushed back a man in military garb. When I plowed into Sassy I was going full speed. We both fell to the ground, the hot tea from the cup burning my thigh and arm as it spilled.

For a long moment, silence. Then a sputtering from Sassy.

"What on earth—?"

I stood up, words stumbling from my mouth, me not knowing what they were except that they were apologies. "I'm sorry, I'm sorry," I kept repeating. "I don't know . . ."

The man helped Sassy to her feet. "Are you all right?"

"I suppose I am." She looked stunned, and then, glancing around, focused on the wet tea stain blooming on her green dress. "Oh, Jim. Look. I'm covered."

"Never mind, dear. Tell you what. Let's go home and give you a chance to change. Bev won't mind, will you?" He faced the Dead Woman. "You don't mind if I take Marian home to change? We'll be back before dinner is finished."

"Of course not," the Dead Woman, now Bev, answered. "You two go home. I'll wait until you come back and we can have a nice meal together."

The man turned to me, his expression moving from concern to confusion to annoyance. "Are you all right, miss? Do you need help?"

"No, no. I'm fine. Sorry. Really. Sorry."

My face burned and my breath came in short spurts as I hurried from the parlor. Had I done it? What had I done? Had I foiled a murder? Merely delayed it? And what was this about Sassy-Marian and Jim? They were married? Sassy and the man were *married*?

I started to head for the stairs and my room when I heard Sassy's voice behind me. "You don't mind, Bev? You're being honest with me? We could have dinner another night."

"No, Marian. Truly. Go home and change. I'll wait here. Tell you what. The night's so pleasant, why don't I wait with you while you find a taxi? I could use the air."

The man: "Good idea. This way."

I was at the top of the stairs, having walked slowly, despondently, when I heard the screech of tires, the scream, the horns. I knew before I hit the hotel door and felt the slap of the March air that the Dead Woman had finally earned her name.

I pushed past the crowd that had immediately formed and saw her on the street, her feet on the curb, her black dress pushed up around the torso lodged under the taxi's frame. Blood spattered the fender; a thin red stream beaded on the pavement then snaked toward a storm drain. The taxi driver was in a panic, running around in the street.

"I didn't see her! Can you see how I didn't see her? She fell in front of me! Call an ambulance! Somebody!"

The man Jim stood staring at the body—for I was certain it was now a body—as Sassy-Marian in her green dress clutched him, her face pale. No one made a move to touch the woman. In the distance I heard a whistle, and thought vaguely of bobbies on bicycles coming to save the day. Too late for the Dead Woman. I knelt beside her and touched the vein at the back of her ankle. No pulse. Too late for poor Bev.

Then I stood. And as I did, I smelled the unmistakable scent of Sassy's perfume rising from the corpse.

Months later, back in Georgia, I blew the final eraser crumbs from the rough sketches of my comic book and put down my pencil. I don't know for sure what the true story is. I told the police what I had overheard, but no one was impressed. They didn't even ask me to sign a statement. I pestered Aunt Suzie into calling the front desk clerk and asking whatever happened to the case of the woman who was hit by the taxi. He replied, no doubt tartly, that he wasn't aware of a "case," but if there was one, perhaps it had been placed in the coffin with the woman. Aunt Suzie told me she wouldn't call again. So I was left to my own devices. And this is what I think.

It was indeed Sassy, aka Bev, who met Jim in the parlor of Ravendaw Hotel every morning at 8:45. It was her with her blond hair and red fingernails. (Pity no red shoes; they would have fit her.) And she and Jim were plotting something against Jim's wife, the short-waisted Marian. But she wasn't smart enough to know that Jim and Marian also plotted against her. (She also wasn't smart enough to know one does not wear heavy perfume when one is having an affair, or that one should always check to see who is hiding in the chairs.) I decided that Sassy wanted Jim to divorce Marian; that Jim, a rising politician, and Marian, a rising politician's wife, agreed to put an end to her. The Ravendaw Hotel made a nicely shabby-genteel place for them to meet, concoct, and carry out their plans. Jim, I was sure, was destined to be prime minister.

At least, that's what my comic book says. It goes into the mail—muscular, gory, and with a female victim—tomorrow morning.

This story of literary malice domestic features Gwen Moffat's resourceful spinster sleuth, Miss Pink, who appears in nearly 15 novels including The Lost Girls, Veronica's Sisters, Rage, The Raptor Zone, *and* The Stone Hawk. *Moffat lives in England.*

The Dark Tower

Gwen Moffat

"Susan looks distraught tonight," Beryl Milburn said. "Has she been drinking?"

"Only a couple of sherries," I said stiffly, and then relented. Beryl was old. "She's not happy," I admitted. "We finished the book only this afternoon and when you've lived with a murderer for three months you're shattered. Perhaps I should have allowed her a third sherry."

"But Joyce, Susan's a brilliant speaker!"

"She used to be. Now—"

But Sir Adrian was on his feet. The chatter stopped as if he'd thrown a switch, until someone laughed at the back of the hall—Jackson Stubbs. Even his laugh conveyed contempt. I couldn't think why the fellow had come to hear a lecture on the Golden Age except to ridicule it—and the speaker. The thought of questions toward the end made my toes curl.

Sir Adrian's introduction was fulsome. If I'd written it I'd have mentioned Susan's Gold and Silver Daggers and her Edgar, but perhaps details of her awards would have been the last straw. Her smile was fixed as Adrian burbled on about the debt we owed her, not only for years of en- thralling entertainment but also in reviving the past glories of the Hall "on the proceeds of crime," which produced laughter despite the lack of originality. It was a quote from a feature on her in *The Sun*. Then she was standing, moving forward, placing her notes on the lectern.

I stared at my knees. I daren't catch her eye in case it should throw her. The moment was fraught. She hadn't spoken in public for over six months and now my own confidence had drained away, but that wasn't new. I'd felt for a while that I was losing touch with her. Something was wrong. It could be her age, but she was only forty-four.

"Murder is a serious business," she began, and you could have heard a mouse scamper across the stage. "Mrs. Chris- tie was well aware of that," she went on. "We think of Poirot, with his little grey cells and his tisanes as a figure of fun but not Jane Marple . . ." I let my breath go with a sigh. From Miss Marple she'd progress to Sayers, Al- lingham, Marsh, dealing cleverly with the geniuses of the Golden Age. I relaxed; two sherries was the right allow- ance. I wondered what Giles was doing at this moment, at the exhibition or the symposium that he was attending. Of course, having your photographs exhibited was quite a fil- lip, but it was in a different league from a lecture delivered by your wife, even if it was held in the village hall. It wasn't the place that mattered but her standing. It looked bad not to be here to support her, particularly now. When I'd taken in the tea tray this afternoon she'd been staring down at the river; she felt quite empty, she'd said when I jolted her out of it. You had to obtain a response, force her to speak, to bring her back to reality. She wasn't daydream- ing at these times; she maintained that she simply wasn't *here*—and that it was a delightful feeling. I found that frightening.

She was winding up Miss Marple, about to lead in to Lord Peter. I moistened my lips, prepared to mouth "Wimsey" at her in case she forgot her lines, waiting for the continuity: "Unlike Dame Agatha, Dorothy Sayers was a scholar . . ." and she was saying harshly, "Miss Marple, you see, never trusted anyone; she said that husbands are the only people who can truly hurt you—" I gaped, she caught my eye, hesitated, and went on smoothly. "Unlike Dame Agatha . . ."

Husbands are the only people . . . When did Miss Marple say that? I puzzled over it for the rest of the talk—which went well, as it should. Her voice was rich and creamy, like a luscious dessert. At the end she asked for questions.

They were predictable: where did she get her ideas, how did she start writing—and then I saw her stiffen. Her eyes widened and she nodded towards the back of the hall.

" 'Murder is a serious business'," Jackson Stubbs announced in his assumed rough accent, daring to quote *her*. "So where is the impact of the blows, the spouting blood, the splintered bone? Where's the sex in your Golden Age: the abuse; incest, intimidation, child prostitutes? Where is reality?"

Sir Adrian's lips tightened. He enjoyed battle and he loathed Stubbs, who had rings in his nose and eyebrows. He got halfway to his feet and subsided. Susan was speaking. "Crime writing is a broad field." She addressed us all but she was aiming at Stubbs. "There's room for any number of genres. The cozy is one; there's police procedure and there's the hard-boiled novel. There are readers who like mysteries or characterization; some go for novels of place. Then there are the sex and violence fans. Blood spouts and child abuse happens but portraying them graphically is pornography. We don't need it." She nodded to someone at the side and smiled happily, suddenly beautiful, an image of the time when she, like Adrian, loved a fight.

We went back to the Milburns's place for drinks. I was bursting with curiosity. "When did Miss Marple say that about husbands?" I demanded as Susan sank into an armchair.

"It slipped out," she said vaguely, accepting a generous measure of whisky from Adrian.

"But it's not the kind of thing she would—"

"Christie said it," she snapped, adding more reflectively, "It could be true, present company excepted. Stands to reason: you're most vulnerable to the person closest to you. 'Et tu, Brute?' Is there anything more heart-rending?"

Beryl bustled in, followed by the spaniels who made straight for Susan. Dogs adored her.

"Jackson Stubbs should have been put down at birth," Beryl announced, accepting a drink from her husband. "Manners! The fellow's a lout, attacking Susan like that!"

"He's jealous," I said. "He's a village boy who wrote one porno pot-boiler—unpublished—and thinks he's on a par with an established novelist."

Susan smiled. "We were both village girls, Joyce."

"But I know my place!" Everyone laughed except me. "I'm a secretary," I protested. "OK, it's not so much I know my place but I've found my niche. I know where I'm coming from."

"All right, love." Susan extended a hand. "You're half the team, and I'd be lost without you. If I'd fluffed my lines this evening you'd have got up there and taken over, wouldn't you?"

I nodded. I felt like weeping. Adrian said, "This has been a very emotional day. A new book finished, an important lecture delivered, an attack by the village yobbo—is that the term, Joyce?"

"Low-life," I supplied. "He's low-life."

Beryl giggled. "Joyce, you always have the right word."

"That's how she comes to be my—what?" Susan asked, turning to me like a child.

"Amanuensis?" I hazarded.

"Better than that," she said.

I drove her home. Her little Peugeot was parked nose-in to the bank, in the same position as it had been that time she'd nearly reversed through the rail and into the river twenty feet below. "I'll turn your car tomorrow morning," I said firmly.

She was staring at it. "It's more convenient to park here

than in the stable yard." She sounded listless.

"It's only a light car but if you were to hit the rail harder next time, it doesn't bear thinking about. And suppose you were in the Range Rover! It weighs a ton, the rails would collapse like matchsticks. Really, Susan, you must park at the back or widen this space. Make a proper turning circle."

"It means the magnolia would have to come down."

It was Giles who wanted the magnolia to stay. I made her promise not to try to turn the Peugeot herself and I drove home wondering what had become of her skill. Six months ago she'd been a superb driver: fast, confident, with split-second reactions. Now she couldn't turn in front of her own house without hitting the fence. Which would have been funny if the river at that point hadn't been deeper than a car.

I'd wanted to keep her company for a while but she said Giles would be home shortly. I hoped she was right. I wouldn't put it past him to spend the night with his cronies in Newcastle. Him and his photography! It was this hobby of his that had resulted in Susan's other near-accident, and we never let her forget it: the time she slipped on the Snab and fell in the river. It was sheer luck that she'd hit no rocks and had managed to swim ashore. If the river had been in spate, if she'd hit her head on the way down . . . Giles would have drowned too, trying to save her. He couldn't swim. As it was, he'd tumbled down the side of the crag in such a hurry to pull her out that he was in a worse state than her when they staggered home. And that was all because she'd been trying to help him as he took photographs of a kestrel's nest, something to do with letting go of the rope by which he lowered himself. Apparently she'd got herself into a difficult position and panicked. So what with the crags and the river and the erosion of her driving skills both Giles and I were worried about her. The situation wasn't helped by the position of the Hall itself.

The original Kletter Hall was a pele tower, built in the fourteenth century as a defense against marauding Scots. Nowadays the owners lived in the attached fifteenth century house which was considerably more civilized with its grand staircase, paneling, and gorgeous traceried windows. The place must have cost a fortune for heating alone but then Susan, with her movie and television sales, was a rich lady—and the Hall wasn't mortgaged. Certainly it hadn't cost much; it had been very rundown and the old earl virtually paid her to take it off his hands. What she'd spent on it since was a different matter. It would have featured in any number of glossy magazines if she'd valued her privacy less.

I lived in the lodge at the gates. I'd been with Susan for five years and the thought of moving on had never occurred to me, at least not until recently when I realized that my employer was starting to run out of steam. She'd always been full of drive, of creativeness, of passion, but in the past few months she'd seemed to be breaking up. She wasn't depressed but there were those strange blank stillnesses when she appeared to contract her world like an anemone until she was living inside her own skull. "You're broody," I'd said once, thinking she was preoccupied with an idea for a mystery, that she was plotting, but she only smiled and said something innocuous like what a relief it was not to have to think. As if she had problems with all her money and looks, and her literary success, and a handsome husband.

Giles didn't come home that night. When I rolled up next morning there was no sign of the Range Rover. Susan's car was there but the rear wheels were missing and it was resting on its hubs.

"Have you seen the Peugeot?" I asked, rushing through to the kitchen. "The wheels are gone!"

She was in her dressing gown, drinking coffee beside the stove. She looked frightened. We went to the front door and she let out a gasp. "A thief in the night!" she breathed, and laughed hysterically.

I soon put a stop to that. I fetched the brandy and called the police. I asked where Giles was but he'd stayed in Newcastle overnight. When the police arrived they said someone would fingerprint the Peugeot but we all knew the thief would have worn gloves. If you steal wheels you have another car with you. This was no random theft.

Giles came home before the police left and their manner

changed immediately. They hadn't been disrespectful to
Susan but indulgent. On the other hand Giles was a man,
the squire, and he played the part to perfection with his old
school tie and his BBC accent. And the new Range Rover
at the door. He was polite but dismissive. "Country boys,"
he remarked when they'd gone. He left in the Range Rover
to find new wheels for the Peugeot.

I went to the Milburns that evening. They had a visitor,
a Miss Pink: large, plain and stocky, a typical country spinster. I apologized for the intrusion but I stayed; my mission
was too important for me to be put off by a guest.

"Problems?" Adrian asked, handing me a glass of Tal-
isker.

I sighed. It was a relief to unburden myself. "I don't
know where to begin," I confessed. "Susan seems to be on
the verge of a breakdown, if she's not actually having one.
Oh, she hides it very well, and I've done what I could to
cover for her, even with the police—"

"The police!" Beryl gasped. "When was this?"

I told them everything, starting with this morning and
working backwards. They hadn't known about her nearly
reversing into the river, nor her fall from the Snab. We'd
kept it quiet. Beryl and Adrian were astounded. "She could
have been killed!" Beryl protested. "Joyce, you should have
told us."

"She made me promise not to say anything. And then,
you see, there are the times she goes still."

"Goes where?" Adrian barked.

I explained about Susan's blank times, when she appeared to retreat from reality.

"How does her husband behave on those occasions?"

Miss Pink's interjection startled me. I'd lost sight of her.
Now I saw that it could have been imprudent to talk about
my employer in front of a stranger. "He doesn't know," I
said shortly, and turned back to Adrian. Miss Pink, however, was a determined old bat. "But if her state of mind
has been deteriorating over a period," she insisted, "her
husband has to know. *You* do."

"I'm close to her," I snapped. There was a dead silence.
"I mean," I rushed on, flustered, "he's close too, of course,

but—well, we work together, Susan and me. And I'm a woman."

"He's noticed nothing?" This woman was driving me into a corner. "He was there when she fell off the crag," she pointed out, which was totally irrelevant. That hadn't been one of her blank times, just clumsiness, or carelessness.

"Of course he was there, she was trying to help him take a photograph. The kestrel nests in an awkward place. She'd never have gone there on her own. She's not stupid, just accident prone. That's Giles's term for it. He nags at her not to take risks, to park in the stable yard instead of at the front door, to keep away from the river. He makes no impression."

"What does he do?" Miss Pink asked.

I stared at her. "Do?" I repeated.

"Photography is his main interest at the moment," Adrian told her. "And no doubt he's involved with the estate?" He glanced at me.

"She has a bailiff," I reminded him. I was starting to feel superfluous among these people. I mean, I'm only an employee.

"What are you worried about?" Miss Pink asked gently, and I felt a rush of warmth. She had a heart under the nosiness.

"I'm frightened," I admitted. "And sometimes I know she is. Like this morning when she realized someone—a criminal—had been creeping round the Hall during the night, looking for an open window, and her on her own."

"He wouldn't know she was alone," Beryl objected.

"Where was Mr. Baring?" Miss Pink asked.

"Giles's name is Lawton. They're married but she uses her maiden name because that's the name she writes under." I laughed. "It sends him up the wall when he's addressed as Mr. Baring at parties. He was in Newcastle last night."

Adrian frowned and shook his head. "The Hall isn't the kind of place for a woman to be alone at night," he told Miss Pink. "Isn't it odd," he went on, addressing no one in particular, "that the thief should have come on a night that Giles was absent? Almost as if he knew."

"I never liked Kletter Hall," Beryl said. "That great pele tower looming over the water . . . thank goodness they don't sleep in the solar."

"The solar is sometimes used as a guest room," Adrian told Miss Pink. "It's the top floor of the tower: fantastic place—a drop of fifty feet sheer to the river. We'll walk along the opposite bank tomorrow."

I kept quiet. I knew Susan slept in the solar occasionally. No one else went there. The village women hated the place with its dangerous newel stair, its crumbling walls eight feet thick that were constantly shedding grit from the sandstone blocks. Cleaners entered the tower only when it was used as overflow for large house parties but I had explored it once when I was alone in the house. The massive door was kept locked but Susan kept the key on a hook in her bedroom, so I'd taken it and climbed the spiral stair to the solar.

At first I thought that there'd been some domestic oversight, that Susan had forgotten to give orders for the room to be cleaned after the last house party. Then I saw that the most recent occupant had left toilet articles behind. A little dressing table, ridiculous in that huge space, held moisturizer, a brush and comb. I turned to the unmade bed, realizing that the linen looked quite fresh. The last time I knew this room had been in use was at Christmas, over four months ago. I looked at the ceiling: it was vaulted and grand with cracks that would shed dust, yet the sheets were clean. This bed was in use now.

I lifted the pillow and there was a bottle of Temazepam, the label printed with the name of Miss Susan Baring and the date only a month old. I took the bottle to the window and held it to the light. There were three tablets left. I thought about it, leaning against the window. It moved and I threw myself back into the room. The window was tall and relatively modern, with leaded panes but side-hung, and the catch had not been fastened. I pushed it open and looked down.

The drop could have been a hundred feet but I knew it

was only fifty. I was deeply shocked. Here was Susan, sleeping in this room, powerful tablets on hand—"avoid alcohol" it said on the label, and Susan liked malt whisky. I knew that she slept with her window wide open in summer and winter. She hadn't even troubled to fasten this one. I pocketed the tablets.

Next morning when I was alone with her I set about approaching the delicate subject of sleeping arrangements. She guessed I'd been in the tower because she smiled and said she occupied the solar now and again when she was sleeping badly. Then she changed the subject so obviously that I was left wondering if there were another reason why she should choose to sleep apart from Giles. There was nothing I could say, of course, but I hung on to the tablets. I was bothered about that window.

The morning after I'd unburdened myself to the Milburns I told Susan that Sir Adrian wanted his guest to see the pele tower. She said that he could walk the river path any time, he knew that. There was no invitation to see the interior of the tower. "You should go for a walk yourself," she told me. "You don't get out enough." I went to telephone Adrian.

There are several footbridges across the river, one just below the Hall, and this was where we met that afternoon. I was amused to see that Miss Pink had managed to find some appropriate clothes: Levis, even stout boots, and she carried binoculars. Evidently a bird watcher.

The woods were at their best: drifts of bluebells under the silver birches, primroses on the banks. Across the river rhododendrons and azaleas splashed the shrubberies of the Hall with carmine and lemon. And then, sombre, without color, the great sandstone cliff of the pele tower loomed above the water, in black shadow beyond the bright young leaves of beeches on our side of the river.

"You have to come here in the morning," Adrian told Miss Pink. "Then it's full in the sunshine and you can see the detail of the window moldings." He went on to describe the interior, turning to me. "I'm sure Susan will allow us to go over it?"

I said I was sure she would. He hesitated but he'd sensed

my stiffness so he drew Miss Pink's attention to the proportions of the great solar window which did look rather
fine, providing you didn't know that those tall casements
were side-hinged, their sills far too close to the floor. I
looked down at the black water, at the shape of a huge
boulder just below the surface, and I shivered.

"Cold?" Adrian asked, concerned.

"A goose walked over my grave."

Miss Pink was preoccupied with the tower. "A long way
to fall," she murmured. "What a wealth of bloodshed this
place must have seen in its time. Wealth? Wrong word."

"We fantasize," I confessed, "about producing an historical novel, I mean. Living here we're steeped in history."

She was intrigued. "Why don't you do it?"

"She says it's too bloody—excuse me—too bloodthirsty.
This was the Debateable Land: raids went on for centuries
and the atrocities were appalling, on both sides: English
and Scots. No way could she deal with those." Especially
now, I thought.

"The horrors were balanced by great loyalties, no doubt."

"I'm certain of it," I assured her, adding firmly, "I'd discover them. I do the research, you see; she hasn't the patience. And why should she have it? She's the creative one,
I'm the—what are they called? The painters who filled in
the corners after Raphael and such had done the figure?"

"Apprentices?" Adrian ventured. "I think you'd find that
Susan thinks of you as rather more than that."

I found myself blushing. "Let's walk on. Maybe we'll
see the kestrels."

The spaniels were with us, rampaging through the bluebells as we strolled the river path, barking and racing ahead
as we approached the Snab. "Rabbit?" Adrian wondered.
"Can't be a hiker, this is all Susan's land."

It was Giles, looking remarkably exotic in his Spanish
riding hat with its broad flat brim. It was hardly suitable
for scrambling about the Snab, but he was attached to it
and I had to admit that he looked every inch the grandee.
All he needed was a quirt and spurs. He was introduced to
Miss Pink; I half expected him to kiss her hand. He was
carrying the Leica that Susan had given him for Christmas,

and on the ground was his camera case that would be full of lenses and goodness knows how many filters and other odds and ends. Hanging down a gully was an orange rope that had been passed round the trunk of an oak tree. He explained that the kestrels' nest was out of sight but by roping down the gully to a ledge at the side he could get into a position to take pictures of it.

"Abseiling?" Miss Pink asked uncertainly. She must have picked up the term from television, where celebrities were always swarming down sheer cliffs in aid of charities.

"I don't bother with technical terms," Giles said off-handedly. "I just slide down the rope, and then pull myself up again."

"Is this where Susan fell?" I asked.

He hesitated. "Yes. Yes, it is." He inhaled with a gasp. "I don't like to remember it." He looked at Miss Pink, his face full of contrition. "She let go of the rope."

"Oh dear." She was shocked. "Why did she do that?"

"Well, you see, the gully's slimy." He gestured and we saw that it looked very slippery with rushes trampled into the black soil. "She must have slipped and shifted her handhold so she was holding only one half of the rope. Her weight pulled the whole thing round the tree trunk."

We all looked from the tree and the doubled rope to the river some thirty or forty feet below. "It was very fortunate that she could swim," Adrian said, "and that she didn't hit her head on the way down. It's not a clean fall."

Giles shook his head as if to rid himself of the image. I realized that he must have seen her fall and would have expected her to be killed. It didn't bear thinking about.

From the far bank a raptor started a shrill scolding. "Damn!" Giles exclaimed. "I've used all my film. I was about to go home for more now that the sun's on the nest."

The only way to view the nest—apart from roping down that lethal gully—was from the opposite bank. We left Giles to run down to the Hall while we strolled upstream to cross by another footbridge and come back through pastures on the far side.

"Why is it called the Snab?" Miss Pink asked as the crag

came in sight, the pink rock fiery in the full glare of the sun.

"It's archaic," Adrian said. "But whether it's Norse or Middle Flemish no one seems to know. It has to mean a steep place."

"It's that all right," I said, eyeing the rope hanging down the gully, looking curiously sinister with no one around to indicate its function.

"How many chicks are there?" Adrian asked, and I saw that Miss Pink had her binoculars up. She moved them a fraction. "Three," she said, adding, "I wonder if he should be photographing so close. He could do it quite well from here with that long lens."

"I wouldn't be the one to put it to him," I said. "I'll mention it to Susan." I remembered how much she'd lost confidence. "Maybe," I amended.

Miss Pink shot me a glance. A kestrel came in to the nest while above us its mate set up its alarm. "Let's move," Adrian urged. "We're bothering them."

We strolled on and Miss Pink asked about Giles's photography. Did he sell his work? It was just a pastime, I told her. He was passionate about it, at the moment. It wouldn't last. He had these short-lived enthusiasms. "Such a beautiful camera," she said wistfully, surprising me. Few old ladies would recognize a good camera.

I telephoned Susan from home to ask if she needed me tomorrow, Saturday, and when she didn't, I said I'd go in Monday morning as usual. Then there was nothing to do except cook myself a meal and watch television.

I was late going to bed, having watched *Thelma and Louise* for the third time, so I was still bleary-eyed at ten the next morning. Miss Pink came to the door, bright as a button and much amused to find me drinking coffee in my pyjamas. She had been out by eight o'clock (the Milburns were early risers), had photographed the pele tower in the morning light, but the kestrels' nest would have to wait until this afternoon, she said. It was still in the shade.

"You never went down his rope!" I exclaimed.

"Oh no, of course not. Too close to the nest. Anyway, the rope wasn't there. I didn't go up that bank of the river either, but this side, through the pastures. Incidentally, Adrian's coming over this morning to ask Susan if he can show me the pele tower."

I was relieved. If Susan refused—and she wouldn't want the Milburns to know that she and Giles slept in different rooms—it wasn't I who would have to convey the message.

Miss Pink turned down an offer of coffee and left. I showered and had just finished drying my hair when a police car stopped at my gate. I remembered the wheels that had been stolen from Susan's Peugeot. It was the same sergeant on the step.

"Great!" I said. "You found them?"

"Good morning, miss." He was solemn. "Found what?"

"Why, the wheels that were stolen."

He shook his head, eyeing me fixedly. "We haven't come about that. Is Mrs. Baring alone at the Hall?"

"Miss Baring," I said automatically. "What d'you mean, alone? She's married, she just uses her maiden name. We told you that when you were here—" I realized I was babbling.

"Where would you expect her husband to be, miss?"

"There. At the house." His odd form of words hit me. "You mean he's not there? You've come—oh God, he's had an accident—" But it was too early; people don't have accidents in the *morning*. "He was out last night," I said dully.

"Was he, miss?"

"No. I'm asking you. Was he out last night? Look, tell me. Has he crashed the Range Rover?"

"He's had an accident, miss. We'd like you to come up to the Hall with us. We have to inform Mrs.—Miss Baring."

"You're telling me he's dead."

"Yes, miss."

I shook my head and tried to breathe deeply. "Shut your door," he said, avuncular now. "And your windows."

"We don't have crime here," I said inanely.

"You may be gone for a while."

*　　*　　*

Susan took it how I thought she would. She went into one of her blank moods. Giles hadn't crashed the Range Rover; his body had been found by a fisherman about half a mile downstream of the village, snagged on a partly submerged tree. His wallet was still in his back pocket and the police had traced him by his driving license.

Beryl came across to stay with Susan while I went to Carlisle with the police. Someone had to identify the body. It was Giles all right, curiously pale and rigid, all the charm gone, a dead shell. I was glad the police drove me back to Kletter; I was too shocked to have driven myself. I didn't like Giles but I didn't dislike him either; he was part of the furniture, something I accepted like the Range Rover or the pele tower, but like them he was a fixture. He left a gap.

On the way home I was asked about his movements the day before, but I could tell the police nothing after we met him at the Snab in the afternoon. "Except I know he went back," I said. "He left his rope hanging down the gully and it's gone this morning. He must have gone out—" I stopped, then resumed. "The Range Rover. We didn't look in the stable yard. Maybe he didn't go out after all."

The Rover was in the yard. And then other things started to come to light. A village boy, playing with chums on the river bank, came home wearing a Spanish hat, the label identifying it as the one Giles had bought in Mexico. A farmer found a length of orange rope among debris on a gravel spit in the river. Then, to clinch matters, when Adrian and Miss Pink walked the river path again they found Giles's camera case on the Snab, but the Leica and its telephoto lens were missing.

It was obvious what had happened. He had gone back to the Snab with a new film in the camera and had repeated Susan's mistake: missed his footing on the slimy mud, lost his hold on one half of the rope, and his weight had pulled it round the tree trunk. And he couldn't swim. The camera would be in the water below the gully. And that was where the divers were to find it on Monday morning. Poor stupid Giles. But I couldn't get the thought out of my head that it was poetic justice. Miss Pink had said he was disturbing the kestrels and I wondered if one of them came in close and tipped him with a wing, startling him, making him lose his grip . . .

I suggested this to Susan and she said it could have happened that way. The blank mood hadn't lasted long; when I came back from Carlisle she said she didn't mind having a word with the police. Beryl left but I stayed, no way would I leave her to face them on her own. They wanted to know why she hadn't reported Giles missing but she explained that when he came home for more film he'd mentioned that he was going to see friends in Keswick that evening. Then she went out herself and she'd never known he was missing. When he didn't come home she assumed he was spending the night in Keswick. "He was very responsible about not driving when he'd been drinking."

"They're suspicious," I said jokingly, having seen them out. "You were sleeping in the pele tower, weren't you? That's why you didn't know Giles hadn't come home."

She stared at me. Oh no, I thought, not another blank mood.

"Do you love me?" she asked.

What a question! She amended it. "Are you loyal?"

"Susan, what's got into you?"

She regarded me steadily and I was terribly confused.

"Don't mention the pele tower to anyone," she said. "I know you were in the solar. Did you tell anyone?"

"Never!" I was hurt. "It's nothing to do with me where you sleep—except I wasn't happy about that window."

"Forget it. Now we pick up the pieces and start over. Stubbs may try something but I can deal with him."

I gaped at her. This was a new Susan, or rather, the old Susan with regained confidence. "What on earth does Stubbs have to do with you? I know he's furiously jealous but—"

"I fell off the Snab because a gun was fired. Not at me, nothing so obvious, but near enough to shock me into losing my grip on the rope. Afterwards Giles said I had imagined the gunshot, there was no one about. It was like the time I was reversing the car and hit the fence. Giles was directing me."

"You never even said he was there!"

"How could I?"

"Are you saying that he tried to—that he fired at you on the Snab?"

"No, that was Stubbs. I caught a glimpse of him. It didn't matter if I saw him—they thought I was going to die. Giles was below me, out to the side." She smiled grimly. "Away from the fall-line."

I couldn't take it. I couldn't *believe* it. Giles conspiring with Stubbs to kill her? The shock of his death had sent her over the edge. I decided to watch her closely and I moved into the Hall. She didn't object. I think she was rather relieved.

We had company the morning Jackson Stubbs came to the Hall. The Milburns had business in Lancaster that day and Miss Pink had come across on her own to see the pele tower. I would have expected Susan to give up any form of entertaining until after the funeral (the autopsy had been held, the verdict misadventure), but she seemed quite happy to receive this friend of the Milburns. She asked me to accompany them on the tour, but I would have gone anyway. I trailed behind them wondering how she was going to explain the state of the solar.

We climbed the stone stair and emerged in a room that appeared not to have been used for months. The bed was made, the dressing table bare except for a Victorian toilet set. The casements were closed. Miss Pink opened a window, after a quick warning from me. "Oh my," she breathed, awestruck by the long drop to the river.

We were drinking coffee when Stubbs walked past the drawing room window. I started to get up but Susan was already on her feet. "You stay here," she ordered. "I'll see to this."

Miss Pink sparkled at me. "More visitors?" she asked brightly.

"This," I said, furious, "is the lout who—who's a troublemaker. He thinks of himself as a hard-boiled novelist and he sneers at her because she writes cozies—as Giles called them."

"He was a friend of Giles?"

"Jackson Stubbs doesn't have friends. Anything he does he does for money." I stopped there and considered what I'd said.

Her head was cocked. Stubbs was shouting. "You're not going to get away with it!"

There was an indistinct murmur. I stood up, aware of Miss Pink on my heels. Together we went into the hall. They turned as we appeared.

"He's demanding money," Susan said calmly. "I think he's suggesting I pushed my husband off the Snab."

"Not the Snab," Stubbs said. "He fell from the pele."

"Rubbish!" I was disgusted. "There was the rope and his camera in the water, his camera case on the crag, plain as day."

"She threw the rope in the river and took the camera and the case up to the Snab—at night. He died at night, not in the afternoon."

"How do you know? I asked. "Were you there?"

"I'll tell you how I know." He was vicious. "Because she slept in the tower and I know Giles meant to—" He stopped, eyed us warily and went on. "Meant to stop her doing that because he was afraid what she might do, seeing there was a drop to the river." He turned to Susan. "What did you do? Wait behind the door, hit him when he came in the solar, and push him out the window?"

"You were about to say that the plan was for Giles to throw his wife out of the solar," Miss Pink said, startling me out of my wits—Susan too; she stared at the old girl as if a stone had spoken. As for Stubbs, he was immobile. "How was her fall from the Snab engineered?" she asked curiously.

Susan turned to her. "This fellow fired a shot from a few feet away when I was in the gully. I was so shocked I let the rope go."

Miss Pink nodded. "That was the idea. So there were two lines of attack. You might die in a simulated accident— a slip on the rocks, reversing your car into the river, or, if you fell from the tower, the verdict could be suicide. Your husband would testify that the balance of your mind was disturbed. There was certainly a concerted plot to disturb it."

I bit my lip. I had thought her confused too. "You were scared stiff," I said, full of guilt. "No wonder we—I thought you were losing your mind."

"You were paid," Miss Pink told Stubbs.

"I never did anything." He glowered at her, biting a nail. "Yes, I've been shooting in the woods. But always with Giles's permission," he added quickly. "I've never done anything illegal."

"Apart from stealing the wheels off the Peugeot," I said nastily.

"You're in it too!" He turned on me. "You'll give her an alibi for the whole night."

"Afternoon," Susan corrected, watching him.

"Alibi," Miss Pink repeated thoughtfully. "You were being paid—to do what? You were friendly with Giles: someone will have seen you together, your prints will be in his car, in the solar—"

"No! No way could—"

"Were you to be the killer or the fall-guy? No, you were to be his alibi, *that* was your purpose. Did you blackmail him for a higher percentage when he inherited his wife's fortune? You quarreled and you pushed him in the river."

"Knowing he couldn't swim," I pointed out.

He laughed. "You're mad. Try telling the cops that."

I said, "I'd start by telling them to find the fence you sold the wheels to."

He inhaled deeply. "Right, I'm a thief. You can't involve me in a murder plot."

"Try us," Susan said.

"Miss Baring never slept in the solar," I told him firmly. "No one slept there. And I can certainly account for her movements that afternoon—and evening. And another thing I saw you on the river path with a shotgun the afternoon that she nearly drowned. And I heard gunfire."

"You stole the wheels," Miss Pink said. "You attacked Miss Baring publicly in the village hall. Do you really think a jury would accept your word against hers?"

"It might be an idea to up sticks and leave before the

police reach you," I suggested. "Particularly if you have a record."

He glared at us, thin-lipped. "I'll be back."

"You do that," Susan said. "We wrote the book, remember? Did it never occur to you that it's only the first murder that's difficult?"

Agatha Christie dedicated By the Pricking of My Thumbs *to the "many readers . . . who write to me asking: What has happened to Tommy and Tuppence? What are they doing now?" By the time of her last novel* Postern of Fate, *Tommy and Tuppence Beresford have three children. Their adopted daughter, Betty, is working in Africa and the twins, Deborah and Derek, are married. At the end of the novel, Deborah makes a brief appearance at the Beresfords with her children. Now, years later, Marcia Talley, author of* Sing It To Her Bones, *wonders what the Beresford grandchildren might be doing today.*

Conventional Wisdom

Marcia Talley

It was after eight, yet the day was still dark, the sky a uniform gray that shrouded the earth like a wet sweatshirt. It wouldn't be correct to say the rain fell; rather it hurled itself against the window, beading along the glass in plump droplets. Caroline watched one skitter down the oval pane, swallowing the smaller drops in its path. As her eyes gradually refocused further away, she observed the airport routine going on outside her window. It reminded her of a

silent movie and she amused herself by providing dialog
for a workman wearing ear protectors like bulky head-
phones as he waved the plane forward with laser wands.
Lights reflecting from the terminal building shimmered in
an immense puddle then shattered as a luggage train
splashed through it. "So much for sunny California," Caroline thought. "I might as well have left my bathing costume back in London." She tried to remember whether she
had packed an umbrella. She'd set one aside in her flat,
ready to stuff into her bookbag. She recalled putting it in,
then taking it out again in order to fit in a last-minute paperback. In her mind's eye Caroline saw the umbrella, still
sitting on the hall table right where she left it. "Damn!" she
whispered, turning her head deliberately away from the
gloom outside the window. "Stephen had better be here to
meet me."

"I beg your pardon?" Her seatmate, a scrawny woman
clutching a Marks & Spencer carrier bag on her lap like a
precious object, turned dark, serious eyes on Caroline.

Caroline blushed. "Oh, nothing. I was just hoping my
brother wouldn't be late picking me up. He's flying in from
New York." She sighed. "You can never tell with Stephen.
He might be sitting in the coffee shop reading a book and
have forgotten all about me."

"Don't worry, dear. I'm sure he wouldn't let his little
sister down." She removed her reading glasses and dropped
them into her bag.

"We're twins, actually," Caroline explained. "I'm
slightly older, by a few minutes."

"Twins?"

"But we're not all that much alike." She fumbled for her
purse. "Would you like to see?"

Her companion made encouraging noises so Caroline
opened her wallet and flipped through the plastic sleeves
containing her credit cards. She turned to a snapshot of a
young man with a determined chin, squinting into the sun,
his rather ordinary face split by an engaging grin. A shock
of red hair was combed straight back over his scalp; an
errant strand hovered over his left eyebrow. The woman's
eyes moved from the photo to Caroline's face and back

again. "I see what you mean, although there's a certain resemblance around the mouth."

"That was taken eight years ago when Stephen graduated from university." Caroline closed the wallet and stuffed it back into her book bag. "Stephen takes after our grandfather—they used to call him 'Carrot Top'—while I," Caroline tugged at a ringlet of her own dark brown hair. "I'm supposed to look like my grandmother." Caroline settled back into her seat and waited for the captain to turn off the seatbelt sign. In spite of the disappointing weather, she was anxious to get on with her journey. Anything was better than sitting around in her flat feeling sorry for herself, hoping that something interesting might happen. After the accounting firm she worked for had declared her redundant, Caroline had retreated to Swallow's Nest to be comforted by home cooking and buoyed by her mother's supportive and upbeat attitude. She'd thought about visiting Rosalie in New Zealand, but a visit to her sister was a nonstarter unless one of the jobs she'd applied for actually came through.

"Are you going to *MysteryCon*?" the woman asked.

"Hmm?" Caroline glanced up. The woman pointed. "I couldn't help noticing your bag."

"Oh!" Caroline guessed her bookbag was, so to speak, a dead giveaway. Against the black silhouette of a revolver, last year's *MysteryCon* logo was printed in stark white letters. She smiled. "Yes I am, actually. My brother and I are presenting the Blenkinsop Partners in Crime Award." Noticing the woman's puzzled expression she quickly explained, "It goes to the best crime novel featuring a detecting duo."

"You mean like Holmes and Watson? Or Hart to Hart?"

Caroline nodded. "Exactly."

"I never read mysteries myself," her seatmate stated flatly. "But I watch that Jessica Fletcher on TV." She bit her lower lip thoughtfully. "Blenkinsop! That's a funny name for an award."

Caroline grinned. "Isn't it? It's related to a practical joke my grandmother once pulled on my grandfather. My uncle Derek established the award in their honor." Caroline heard the *ding* of the seatbelt signal and the clicking of hundreds of buckles as passengers leapt up and scrambled for their bags in the overhead compartments. Caroline waited for her seatmate to step out, then snaked down the aisle behind her, through the business and first class sections, past the flight crew muttering their buh-byes, and along the passageway into the terminal.

As she had feared, Stephen was not at the gate, nor anywhere in sight. Caroline loitered for a few minutes near the bank of telephones, shifting from foot to foot, searching up and down the concourse for her brother's familiar face. After ten minutes, she gave up and followed the crowd to the baggage claim area. She watched a bag of golf clubs go three times around on the carousel before her own flowered suitcase eventually appeared. She set it on its wheels, pulled out the handle, and dragged it and herself into the gloom of the San Diego morning.

Caroline's usually cheerful face was still set in a scowl when the blue and yellow SuperShuttle deposited her in front of the Puesta del Sol on Mission Bay. She made her way to the reception desk and checked in. "Are there any messages for me?"

The desk clerk tapped at his keyboard, studied the screen for a few seconds, then shook his head. "Sorry, Ms. Greene."

Caroline shouldered her bookbag and leaned once more against the counter. "Has Stephen Greene checked in yet?"

The clerk executed a few additional keystrokes, then, happy to please her at last, exclaimed, "Oh, yes." He pointed toward the restaurant. "You can use the house phone over there to call his room, or if you prefer, I could take a message for you."

"No, thanks," Caroline said. In the past hour she had dredged up hundreds of four-letter words with which to blister Stephen's ears, but this relentlessly perky fellow seemed only a decade on this side of *Sesame Street*. Certain words beginning with the letter *F* might not be in his vocabulary yet.

Caroline headed toward the elevators, weaving through the lobby crowded with nametagged conventioneers who sat on every chair and sprawled on every sofa, purses, briefcases, and bookbags heaped at their feet. Through a haze of cigarette smoke, Caroline noticed that the lobby was decorated with dozens of Halloween pumpkins, their elaborately carved faces grinning at her from the planters that divided the lobby into more intimate conversational areas. She smiled in spite of herself, feeling immensely cheered. As she passed the last alcove, one pumpkin head stood up.

"Stephen!" Caroline dropped her bookbag, controlling the urge to hit him with it. "Where on earth have you been?"

"Waiting for you, ducks."

"You were supposed to meet me at the airport, you dunce!"

"I thought we agreed to meet at the hotel."

"Airport, Stephen. We said the airport. Honestly, you do try my patience." She pushed her suitcase toward him. Stephen grabbed the handle, then kissed his sister on the cheek. "Sorry for the confusion, love, but all's well that ends well. Have you had anything to eat?

"Nothing to speak of, except for the slop they gave me on the plane."

The elevator arrived and carried them to the tenth floor. "I'll make it up to you," Stephen promised. "Freshen up and meet me in the lobby and I'll feed you a proper meal." He checked his watch. "In thirty minutes." The elevator doors closed leaving Caroline alone in the hall a good two hundred feet from the door with her number on it.

Once inside her room, she pressed a hot washcloth over her face then leaned close to the mirror and examined her gray eyes for puffiness. Satisfied to see little sign of jet lag, she fluffed up her flattened hair with her fingers, applied some lipstick, and returned to the lobby. Having ten minutes to kill before Stephen was scheduled to appear, she registered for the conference, pinned her nametag on her jacket, found a vacant table near the lobby bar, and ordered some tea.

"Hello. Mind if I sit down?"

Caroline glanced up from the *MysteryCon* program booklet she was reading and shifted her chair a few inches to the right. "I'm saving a chair for my brother, but the others aren't taken." The man standing before her wore chinos and a striped shirt under a denim jacket. His lank, yellowish hair was caught back into a ponytail and he carried a backpack. Caroline stole a peek at his nametag—Lawrence Townsend from Alexandria, Virginia.

Mr. Townsend settled himself into the chair and studied Caroline over the tops of his round, steel-framed glasses. "You an author?"

Caroline smiled. "Not exactly. I'm one of the presenters."

Townsend patted his backpack which now rested at his feet. "I'm here to meet my editor."

Caroline noticed no author ribbon attached to his nametag. "Really? Have I read anything you've written?" She smiled brightly.

Townsend gazed at her shyly from beneath long, pale lashes. "I'm not exactly published yet, but I hope to be soon." He leaned over and rummaged in his backpack. "This book, do you know it?"

Caroline groaned inwardly, recognizing a popular self-help book widely advertised on a home shopping channel by its author, the flamboyant Jeremiah P. Jackson. *Write It! Sell It!* screamed at her in raised, red letters from a cover otherwise unadorned except for a head-to-toe shot of the author in an Armani suit, holding a copy of that self-same book and grinning toothily.

"I've read the reviews," she admitted at last.

"It's my bible." Townsend unzipped the breast pocket of his jacket and extracted a small, square notebook. He showed Caroline page after page of neat columns containing notations in infinitesimal print, the columns dotted with checkmarks. Caroline sipped her tea and nodded mechanically while Townsend rattled on about how he hoped to get published by following the author's advice. He'd attended conferences, networked with authors, schmoozed with publishers, and so on and so on. Caroline found herself growing sleepy. If Stephen didn't appear within the next five minutes, she decided, she was going to ditch this bore and eat alone.

"I've written a mystery based on my experiences in the Gulf War," Townsend told her.

"Hmm." Caroline returned to studying her conference program, hoping, vainly, that he'd take the hint.

"Started writing in a foxhole in the desert. Wrote much of the rest on the metro riding to my job at the Pentagon. But then I said, what the hey! Decided to take a leave of absence to finish up. Been living off my savings."

Caroline regarded Townsend with a sudden spark of interest. "Must have been hard on the wife and kids."

"Ex-wife," he said. "No kids." His face grew serious. "I have it all planned out." He turned the notebook in Caroline's direction. "See, here's where I've checked off all the steps in getting an agent.

"I hear it's hard to get an agent."

"Not really. Just followed what the man says in here." He fanned the pages with an ink-stained thumb, stopping about half-way through. "He suggests reading the acknowledgments in books written by authors you admire. They usually thank their agents. Then you come to conferences like this and contrive to meet them." Townsend's eyes swept the bar. "There are lots of agents here right now."

"Clever," said Caroline.

Townsend shrugged. "It's all in the book. Got my agent at *MysteryCon* last year and he sent my manuscript out to several editors. This particular editor's had my book for three months."

Caroline was searching for a reply when she saw, with relief, Stephen's tall figure approaching. She stood. "Well, good luck . . ." She looked pointedly at his nametag, ". . . Larry."

Townsend smiled up at her. "Thanks, Caroline. But I have a feeling this one's practically a done deal!"

Stephen hustled Caroline quickly away from the lobby bar and into the restaurant. "Why were you talking to that kook?"

"He wasn't a kook. Just some guy desperately trying to sell his book."

"I don't know about that, Caroline. He looked rather shady to me. While I was waiting for you earlier, I overheard him talking to someone on the telephone. All very hush-hush and Tom Clancy-ish. 'Meet me in the lobby bar, I'll be wearing glasses and carrying a backpack' kind of stuff." Stephen studied a copy of the menu while they waited for the hostess to locate a table for two. "Wonder whatever happened to the good old days when you wore a red carnation in your lapel and carried a copy of *The New York Times* folded under one arm?"

Stephen carried on with his spy-among-the-fans-and-authors theory. Caroline half-listened until she felt the soft jab of his elbow in her ribs. "Hot-cha!" Stephen croaked. A certain well-endowed writer of American mystery cozies, clad in a low-cut blouse and a tea towel passing for a skirt, squeezed between them. She held a wine glass by the stem between her thumb and forefinger.

"Ha!" Caroline chided. "I'm surprised you notice anything going on around you."

"I'm a man of many talents, my dear. Why just now I've noticed that our wait for a table is over. Mavis!" Stephen grabbed Caroline's hand and dragged her through the crowded restaurant to a table near the window, already occupied by a pair of diners. Caroline observed with pleasure that the table overlooked the bay. Outside the clouds had broken up and bright sunlight was transforming the day into a Kodacolor postcard.

A middle-aged woman, attractive in spite of a thatch of too-black hair, beamed up at Stephen as he bent over the table and kissed the air next to her cheek. "Mavis! Good to see you. And George! How are you doing, old bean? I'd like you both to meet my sister, Caroline. Caroline, George writes those true crime novels our brother Andrew is so fond of reading." Stephen snatched two vacant chairs from an adjoining table and Caroline soon found herself sandwiched between Stephen's friends. She hoped the waitress had noticed their arrival because the sight of the Belgian waffle sitting on the plate in front of George, decorated with fresh strawberries and dollops of heavy cream, was making her stomach rumble noisily.

"How's tricks, Mavis?" Stephen inquired while waving a hand in the direction of a passing waitress. Mavis slapped her forehead, a look of mock panic on her face. "Overworked, as usual. Spending most of my time dealing with the merger and my conglomerate bottom-line bosses. Publishing's a crazy business now, not like the old days." She tapped the contents of a pink packet into her coffee, stirred, and tasted it. "Thank God I've got a capable assistant."

George raised his water glass and said, "To the indispensable Tiffany Carswell!"

Mavis plucked a pair of reading glasses from where they rested on top of her head, settled them on her nose, and peered at her watch. "Can't imagine what's keeping her. She was almost dressed when I left the room." She scowled. "The bean counters strike again, Stephen. Never thought I'd be bunking with my assistant." Mavis relaxed into her chair, enjoying the last of her coffee. "But the girl's a jewel. Don't know what I'd do without her."

"Knows better than to call in sick every Monday like the last one you had?" Stephen teased.

Mavis closed her eyes and shook her head. "Don't remind me!"

A waitress had finally appeared to take their order when Mavis stood and laid her napkin on the table. "Well, it's been fun, folks, but I gotta go. My panel starts at noon. Coming, George, or do you leave me to face the unpublished masses alone?" She departed in a cloud of White Diamonds with the faithful George at her heels.

Stephen picked up the copy of *USAToday* that George had left behind and began reading aloud from the "Money" section. Caroline, who was used to having the news interpreted for her by her brother, munched happily on a piece of dry toast. She was half-way through her California fruit cup, wondering which of the panels she was going to attend, when a large black object hurtled past the window behind Stephen's head, glanced off the flowering shrubbery, and crashed to the terrace below. "My God!" a waitress screamed. "Somebody's fallen!"

Caroline, her stomach in turmoil and her brunch quite forgotten, rushed outside with the other diners and hovered at the edge of the gathering crowd with Stephen's arm wrapped protectively around her. Paramedics arrived within a few minutes and were attempting to revive the victim. From the pool of blood underneath the woman's head and by the odd angle of her neck in relation to her shoulders, Caroline was skeptical. But then, she had never seen a dead person before.

Sirens screamed, followed in short order, by the police. "She was pushed!" a man at the edge of the crowd shouted when the first officer appeared. "I saw him. Up there!" The witness waved a wild finger in the direction of the balcony. Caroline's eyes followed. The balcony stood empty, but hanging plants dangled in ragged tendrils from where they had been torn away when the woman went over.

Two uniformed officers held the crowds aside, making way for the EMT's carrying the victim on a stretcher. Caroline swallowed a sob as they passed. An oxygen mask covered the woman's beautiful, surprisingly serene and unmarked face. The sea breeze ruffled her ash brown hair and lifted the nametag clipped to her jacket.

Caroline shuddered, then clutched Stephen's arm so hard he winced. "Stephen! I've got to talk to the police! Now! I think I know who pushed that young woman and why."

"So that's how it happened." It was after dinner and Caroline sat with Stephen and George in the lobby bar where a jack-o-lantern grinned mischievously from the planter behind her brother's head. Stephen stirred his martini. "Clever of you to notice the nametag, Caroline."

"Well, I knew the person on the stretcher wasn't the real Mavis Grant because we'd just had brunch with her! Tiffany must have thought she'd be doing her boss a favor by giving Townsend the bad news about his rejection. Mavis said when she went to brunch she left her nametag sitting right next to the telephone. So when Townsend called . . ."

George shook his head. "Mavis told me she'd never met the bloke, just talked to him on the phone. She's despondent, poor old dear. Claims it will be impossible to replace the girl."

George stared into his lager, a look of profound sadness on his suntanned face. "Want to know the ironic thing? Mavis said that chap's book wasn't half-bad. Needed a bit of punching up is all. But he was such a colossal pain in the ass—calling her up two or three times a week—she'd decided to give it a pass."

A few weeks later, in Stephen's New York apartment, Caroline took a brown envelope out of a desk and addressed it in a loopy, flowing hand. Stephen observed his sister in silence, watching over her shoulder as she affixed six thirty-three-cent stamps to the envelope. "San Diego Central Jail? Caroline, are you crazy?"

Caroline looked up, a half-smile on her lips. "Paradoxical, really. When 'Mavis' rejected his novel, Townsend flew into a rage. It wasn't part of his plan, you see. But now, think of all the time he'll have to write." She picked up a copy of *Writers Digest* and turned to a page she had marked with a yellow Post-it note. "Here, in the 'Markets' column." She tapped a neatly manicured finger on the page. "It says prison fiction is big these days." She slipped the magazine into the envelope and smiled up at her brother. "I think it's a good idea to encourage aspiring writers, don't you?"

Stephen took the envelope from her outstretched hand, licked the flap, and sealed it securely. "I do. And I'm sure Grandma and Grandpa would thoroughly agree."

An Agatha winner for Best Short Story, Dorothy Cannell alludes to the classic Miss Marple tale, "What Mrs. McGullicuddy Saw," in the title of her story of murder haunting a young bride. The British-born Cannell is the author of the series featuring designer and sleuth Ellie Haskell, including The Thin Woman, How to Murder Your Mother-in-Law, How to Murder the Man of Your Dreams, *and* The Spring Cleaning Murders. *She lives in Illinois.*

What Mr. McGregor Saw

Dorothy Cannell

"You can talk all you want but I don't believe in them," said the young woman with hazel eyes. She was wearing a brown felt hat and standing in a drizzling rain outside the Sea View Guesthouse.

"Believe in what, Eileen?" Her companion, a fair-haired man in his late twenties, more pleasant faced than good looking, retrieved the suitcase deposited by the taxi driver on the curb and drew her gently toward the white-washed steps leading up to the door framed by Victorian stained-glass panels.

"In miracles. That's what you've been hoping for, isn't

it? You think that by my coming back here and facing up to what happened I'll be struck by some burst of heavenly light and find peace at last."

"Well, I wouldn't go that far." A lace curtain at the bay window parted an inch and a blurred face peered out at them. "All I'm hoping, darling, is that reliving the memories of the week you spent here will help you to open up to me. Darling, I'm your husband. We've been married six whole months and you never given me more than the bare bones of the story. Stuff I could have read about in the papers."

"I know, I know." Eileen stumbled on the last step and caught hold of his arm. "You've been so wonderful, Andrew; most men would have run a mile before hooking up with a girl with my history. I can't blame your parents for being scared stiff and threatening to ship you off to India. After all, who's to say that one day I might not go completely off my rocker and . . ." Before she could finish the door opened and they were ushered into a small vestibule with a mosaic tile floor and an aspidistra standing guard in the corner.

"Come on in," a friendly voice welcomed them. "I'm Vera Gardener and I was watching for you. Didn't want you standing out in the wet a moment longer than necessary. A nasty night if ever there was one, but like as not it'll be sunshine tomorrow. We get some lovely days even this late in September." Talking away, Mrs. Gardener, who had run the Sea View for the past couple of years, led them into a narrow hall with a mustard and red carpet runner that accentuated rather than relieved the gloom of brown varnish. But fortunately Mrs. Gardner did much to offset the impression that any of the other guesthouses on Neptune's Walk might have been preferable to this one. She was a soft-spoken grey-haired body who was seldom out of sorts and always greeted arrivals with a warm smile, but as she urged this young couple to hang their damp coats on the hall tree on the staircase wall, she felt just the least bit unsettled. For a moment she couldn't think why. And then it came to her. The girl's face was vaguely, disturbingly familiar. A photo in one of the newspapers—not recently, more like years ago. Those haunted eyes. Mrs. Gardener remembered thinking she'd never forget the look of them, and in a child's face too, poor Godforsaken little mite! Even so, it took another few seconds for the whole thing to fit into place. Such a horrible tragedy! But here she was, back at the scene of the crime, so speak.

"Mr. and Mrs. Shelby. I've got that right, have I?" she said, hoping her voice wouldn't let on that her thoughts were all of a whirl. "If you'd like to sign the guest book, I'll take you up to your room. Unless, that is, you'd like a nice cup of tea first?"

"No." Eileen picked up the pencil from the hall table and fiddled with it before handing it to Andrew. "We'd rather get settled in right away. It is the room directly at the top of the stairs, isn't it? I particularly asked for it when I telephoned. The person I spoke to said it still had the wallpaper with the red roses on it. I—" again she looked at Andrew, "my husband and I—we were quite definite about wanting that one."

"Oh, absolutely," he agreed quickly. "The person who suggested we stay here made a point of saying we should ask for that room. Wonderful view of the sea and all that."

"Well, I must say it is a nice comfortable room. One of the nicest we've got," Mrs. Gardener responded a little too brightly. "A lot of people ask for it specially." This wasn't strictly true. In fact, she'd had guests who made a point of asking not to be put in that room because of its particular associations. To hide her confusion she bent to pick up the suitcase that the young gentleman had put down on signing the guest book, and upon his insisting that he carry it himself, she led the way up the stairs to cross a narrow landing and opened the door directly opposite.

"Well, here we are!" Switching on the light. "Plenty of red roses on the wallpaper." She was not usually a woman to flutter, but after needlessly twitching the rose sateen eiderdown into shape she adjusted a toiletry dish on the dressing table. Meanwhile, the young lady stood two feet away from her like an additional bedpost, so that when she spoke it seemed natural that she should do so in a small wooden voice.

"Our friends, the people who suggested we come to the Sea View, said the place was run by a Mr. and Mrs. Rossiter. But of course it was years ago that they stayed here. At least ten, isn't that what they said, Andrew?" Without giving him a chance to answer, Eileen hurried on. "So would you have been here at that time?"

"No, dear." Mrs. Gardener stooped to turn on the gas fire. "When my husband died and our only son went out to Australia, wanting to make a life for himself as was only right, I fancied I'd like to move to the seaside and bought this place from the Rossiters. That was two years ago last month."

"You must find it rather a lot at times." Andrew had wandered over to the window and now returned to stand by the bed.

"Not too bad really. We've only got the six bedrooms. And I like to keep busy. Keeps me from growing old. Besides, I've got my niece and her husband working for me. And when the season slows down as it does around about this time of year I get to rest up a bit." Mrs. Gardener, very conscious of sounding too bright and breezy, stood with her hand on the doorknob. "Now I'd better leave you nice people to unpack, hadn't I? The bathroom's two doors down to your left. We serve dinner between seven and eight. But don't you worry. We can always heat you up something if you don't want to rush. We often do that for guests coming in late after a day's sightseeing or a hike across the downs. Like the clergyman we've got staying with us now. He always comes this same week. Every September, has done for years, long before I took over from the Rossiters. Set in his ways, I suppose, but as gentle and kind an old gentleman as you could ever wish to meet."

"That's nice," said Eileen.

Feeling more and more at a loss, Mrs. Gardener mentioned that the bathroom was two doors down to the left. Then she retreated downstairs to the kitchen to restore herself with a cup of tea and explain the situation to her niece, who was mashing potatoes in a big saucepan on the draining board.

"You mean this Mrs. Shelby is the little girl—the daughter in the VanCleeve murder?" Nellie, a big, red-faced woman, wasn't often put off her stroke, but she did pause before adding a dollop of butter and a splash of milk to the potatoes. "How old would she have been at the time, Auntie Vera, do you think?"

"From what I remember," Mrs. Gardener sat at the scrubbed wood table brooding over her cup, "about twelve or thirteen. The worst time, if there could be one, to go through something like that. You know how emotional girls can be at that age, worse than boys some of them, even in normal circumstances."

"I suppose," said Nellie. "But what's she like now?"

"Not bad looking, pretty you might say, in a pale, sad-eyed sort of way. But nothing like the beauty her mother was said to be."

"That's not what I was asking." Nellie returned to mashing the potatoes. "I meant does she look loony? It would only be expected, wouldn't it? Coming from homicidal stock. And it certainly doesn't sound normal to me her wanting to spend even one night in that room. You know the Rossiters said they had people say they felt a presence up there—a darkness even when the lights were on. And we've had some of the same talk ourselves."

"A lot of nonsense. It's not like the murder took place there," responded Mrs. Gardener practically. "But if you want to know, I have tried to figure out the mother. What was her name? Evangeline? Something fancy and sort of French sounding. No, I've got it," looking at the pots of geraniums on the window sill. "It was Genevieve. Anyway, fancy bringing the child with her when she made her getaway! Holing up here, waiting to be found out. I'd have had to phone the police."

"Throw themselves on their mercy so to speak?" Nellie looked dubious. "I can't say I've ever gone around thinking of coppers as a bunch of bleeding hearts. But then I've not got money and a posh-sounding name."

"I just couldn't have had it hanging over my head. But we all are made different I suppose." Mrs. Gardener got up to pour herself another cup of tea. "I couldn't have pretended to my daughter that we were off on a seaside holiday when I was looking at those cuts on my hands, remembering my husband grabbing the knife away from me before I hit him over the head with a candlestick." She shook her head. "No one's ever called me a nervous Nellie. But I tell you I'm worried about that girl. She looks so lost, even with that husband of hers standing beside her. What if she waits until he's asleep and turns on the gas?"

"So we can all wake up dead." Nellie tossed a couple of sprigs of mint into a saucepan of peas. "You know Ed's opinion." Ed was her husband, who was currently in the dining room serving up a steamed fish meal to two spinsters of undetermined age but definite ideas on eating delicate fare at an early hour. "He said we should have changed those gas fires for electric ones, just for the sort of reason we're talking about."

"I wonder," Mrs. Gardener stirred a second teaspoon of sugar into her tea, "if the murder would have been splashed all over the papers if Genevieve VanCleeve hadn't been debutante of the year, always being photographed in *The Tattler* and those other high-society magazines. And the husband . . ."

"Gerald, wasn't it?" Nellie took a peek at the Lancashire hotpot in the oven, eyeing with undiminished satisfaction the rich gravy bubbling up through the thinly sliced crust of golden brown potatoes.

"Yes, well, what I was saying," her aunt sat back down at the table, "is that it was bound to make it all the more of a story with him being a highly decorated officer in the war. A real hero from the accounts of it. Badly wounded— losing the sight in one eye and afterwards always being in a lot of pain from other injuries. It's a terrible thing when a man does his duty to his country and ends up the way he did."

"What did the Rossiters think of them?" Nellie closed the oven door and concentrated on the peas. "The mother and daughter, I mean."

"They said they would never have guessed a thing was wrong from how Mrs. VanCleeve behaved the week she was here. The only thing that could have tipped them off something was fishy was that she was a cut above the sort that usually comes. More the type you'd expect to take her holidays on the French Riviera. Nothing flashy about her, just skirts and jumpers, but that look about her that comes from having gone to the very best schools and mixing with the upper crust. They said she was soft-spoken and always very appreciative, told them how much she enjoyed the meals, that sort of thing. The Rossiters weren't much taken with the girl. Said she was a right little madam, but she didn't look like one this evening." Mrs. Gardener closed her eyes and tried to picture what was happening in the bedroom with the red roses on the wallpaper. She hoped that young man with the kind face had his arms around his wife and was telling her that they should take their suitcase and leave. But she had the sinking feeling that the evening was not going to turn out that simply.

Eileen was, in fact, standing in the same spot where Mrs. Gardener had left her. She took off her hat almost in slow motion and let it drop to the floor. She had silky nutmeg brown hair, cut in a bob—not because it was fashionable, but because she never had to do anything to it. Any more than she thought about clothes in general, or in particular the grey wool frock she had put on that morning. She never wore makeup. Not even lipstick. It wasn't indifference. She had made a conscious decision that the world—and that included Andrew—could take her as she was. Someone no one would ever call beautiful, perhaps adding, "Well, you only have to remember her mother and where her looks got her. What girl in her right mind would want to follow in those footsteps?"

Andrew sat on the bed watching her, loving her so dearly, and feeling as he so often did, unable to reach any part of her. It was a mistake, he decided, to have pushed her into coming here. She wasn't going to open up to him. More likely she would shut down even more completely. He was sure that she wasn't even aware that he was in the room. And he was right. Eileen didn't see him. She could hear her own childish voice denouncing the Sea View guesthouse as the horridest place in the world. She saw her mother bending over a suitcase on the bed, lifting out a teddy bear with an arm and a leg missing and propping him against the pillows.

"I don't know why you brought that old thing," she petulantly replied. "I don't sleep with him anymore."

"But I thought you might like to, because of being in a strange place." Her mother's voice came back to her on a breath of salt wind. The window wasn't open now, but it had been on that day long ago. "And I don't want to sleep in the same bed with you, Mummy."

"Eileen, they didn't have a room with two single beds. We'll have to make do. It's something everyone has to do from time to time."

"The wallpaper's horrible. But I don't suppose you mind. You adore red roses."

"Perhaps not this many. But it could be worse. Cousin Aggie has a bedroom with girls on swings on the wallpaper. She said it looked so lively and cheerful in the sample, but after it went up she felt dizzy every time she went into that room. Eileen, dear, I think you would really love cousin Aggie. I spent a lot of time with her on long holidays when I was growing up. And it's a pity I haven't taken you to see her, but Daddy said he would find the journey too much. She lives in Northumbria, which is a trek from London. But she has the most beautiful garden with a wonderful plum tree. And always at least three dogs and a cat. You know how you've always wanted a pet. But Aunt Mary, of course, wouldn't hear of it. And with Hawthorn Lodge being as much her house as Daddy's, her feelings have always had to be considered."

"I don't know why you had to drag me here. You didn't even let me say goodbye to Daddy."

"Dearest, you know it's not a good idea to disturb him early in the morning." Her mother's voice was fainter now; but her own echoed shrilly, accusingly in her ears.

"That's not the reason. Why do you always have to upset Daddy? It was about that Mr. Connors, wasn't it? He's in love with you. Don't deny it, Mummy. And you feel the same way about him. Aunt Mary said you were flirting with him when he came for lunch last Saturday."

"Aunt Mary sometimes gets things wrong. She's not a

very happy person. Mr. Connors is Daddy's friend. And
he's very sad because his wife was killed in a motor accident only two months ago."

"Leaving the two of you free to run away together."

"Is that what Aunt Mary said?"

"I've got ears, haven't I? I heard you and Daddy arguing.
I heard him say that he wouldn't give you a divorce, not
ever! And that if you thought that living with Mr. Connors
would be all romance and flowers you ought to remember
that the rotten cad hasn't a bean to his name."

Suddenly there were no more voices inside Eileen's
head. Andrew's concerned face swam into view. Then she
saw her mother clearly. It was as if walking out of the past
were no more than walking down a hallway between one
room and the next. Now she was sitting on the bed peeling
off her silk stockings. Now she was picking up the old
teddy bear from the floor where he had been tossed and
gazing at him for a long moment before putting him in a
drawer. Now she was seated on the dressing table stool
brushing her waist-length hair. And with every movement
there were lightning red flashes of the slash marks on her
hands and wrists. Outside the room she kept her sleeves
well pulled down and whenever possible wore gloves. But
you couldn't wear gloves when eating. And Eileen remembered the elderly man. What was his name? Something
Scottish. He had been the only person in the dining room
on the first morning that she and her mother went down for
breakfast. Eileen remembered the smell of kippers from his
table. She could see the crack in the flowered teapot sitting
next to the pot of marmalade on their table. And she could
see the man's thin face, silver hair, and grey cardigan. He
appeared to be reading from a little black book, but Eileen
had been sure that he was looking at her mother. But not
in the same way that she had seen other men do. And she
had been seized by the absolute certainty that he was a
policeman pretending to be on holiday.

The clock on the mantelpiece began to strike and Andrew's voice became woven into the silvery chimes, saying
that it was seven o'clock and wouldn't it be a good idea if
they went down for dinner.

"Darling, you need to eat, you hardly took a bite at lunch."

"You're right." She managed a smile for him, before she went quickly out the door and down the stairs. Away from the blood red roses on the wallpaper and the dressing table mirror in which her mother's face hovered as if trapped in moonlight. Or had it been her own? The same hazel eyes, the same gloss of brown hair, the same fine features and pale clear skin. What made the difference between great beauty and what was merely pretty at best? It wasn't the lack of makeup or the ability to wear the right clothes in the right way. Eileen knew with a tightening of her throat that she couldn't go on telling herself that was all there was to it.

The two spinster ladies came out of the dining room as she and Andrew reached the bottom of the stairs. They were dressed in black and looked like women who existed on a diet of boiled fish and kept a rigid time schedule.

"Good evening," Andrew greeted them with his usual kindly courtesy, to which they responded with the most meager of nods before retreating into the sitting room across the hall. There had been a pair very much like them on that other stay at the Sea View. Eileen remembered saying unimaginatively that they looked like a couple of crows.

"Yes, poor old things," her mother had answered with faint smile, "but perhaps they've never had the chance to do more than peck away at life. That could make anyone look sour."

"I hate it, Mummy, when you do that," the petulant childish voice answered.

"Do what?"

"Sound so horribly smug."

"I don't mean to. Blame it on my childhood, Eileen— growing up in a vicarage with parents who knew how to be happy. And then there was dear cousin Aggie quite content to be a bit odd in her purple trousers and enormous sun hats."

"But you don't have the right."

"What right?"

"To pretend to be such a goody-goody. Not with the way

you carry on. Making Daddy so unhappy. Do you want to know what Aunt Mary calls you?"

"No."

"Well, you're going to hear it. She says you're a tart. She says you were never good enough for him to begin with. That your father was just a country vicar and your mother was only good for making jam."

"Aunt Mary is a very disappointed woman, but that's no excuse for you talking about your grandparents that way. I wish they could have lived so they could have known you. They would have loved you so much."

"Yes, like you do, when you're not too busy being nice to Mr. Connors. I wonder if he really was sad that his wife died in that accident? I wonder if it really was an accident . . ."

"Eileen!"

It was Andrew's voice speaking to her now. And she came back to her surroundings to find herself seated across from him at a round table in a corner of the dining room. It was the same table where she had always sat with her mother. It was all the same. The bottle green wallpaper with the burgundy frieze. The mantelpiece crammed with Victorian vases and jugs, barely giving the heavily ornate bronze clock room to breathe, let alone tick. The same swagged and fringed velveteen curtains framed the lace at the window. The only difference Eileen could see was the small vases on all the tables, each containing sprigs of flowers or a couple of roses. There were red roses at their table. One was still fresh. The other was beginning to droop.

There was no one else in the room but them. "Eileen," Andrew said again. "Look at me! Please, darling, take your hands away from your ears."

"I didn't realize." She blinked and let her arms fall to her sides. "I must have been trying to shut out the voices."

"Talk to me instead."

"I can't." She spoke to the roses and somehow her lips kept moving. "I hated her, you see. You can say I was a child but that doesn't change anything, does it?"

"But you must have loved her once."

"Oh, yes I did! We had such wonderful times together

when I was little. She would take me for picnics and bicycle rides and make up stories to tell me at night. It was only about a year before the . . . end that I became so angry with her. Everything she did seemed wrong to me."

"Lots of girls that age feel that way." Andrew reached for her hand, then changed his mind. She was like a bird ready to fly away at the least movement.

"I was at that really plain stage. Gawky, spotty faced. And knew people were thinking, even saying, she'll never be a beauty like her mother. Aunt Mary said I should be glad of that, and the way she kept saying it made me begin to notice things that I never had before. All those letters Mummy got. The flowers that came that she didn't want Daddy to know about—she let him think she had bought them herself. The times she went out for lunch and came back looking the way I felt when I got home late from school for no proper reason."

"It's a pity your Aunt Mary didn't move out and make a life for herself."

"She couldn't. Daddy needed her. He wasn't an invalid exactly. But there were times when he was in pain from his injuries and she was wonderful with him. She would sit with him and put cool cloths on his head and they would talk for hours with the curtains closed about the days when they were children."

"And your mother."

"He didn't want her there at those times. That's what he told me. He said he didn't want her cooped up looking after him. But I began to think she couldn't be bothered to be with him during the bad times. Because she was too selfish. Too eager to be out enjoying herself as Aunt Mary said, with the likes of Mr. Connors. And those women friends of hers who weren't up to any good either. So much for the vicar's daughter, fooling the gullible into thinking she was all sweetness and light."

Now that Eileen had started talking she had trouble stopping. But she did break off when Mrs. Gardener came in and crossed the room to close the heavy curtains before coming over to their table. The proprietress had told Nellie's husband Ed that she would get the young couple's dinner to them, if he'd be so kind as to start washing up some of the saucepans. She had wanted to see if Mrs. Shelby looked any less haunted than on her arrival. Looking at her now she didn't know whether to be reassured or not. There was a little more color in her cheeks but her eyes had a look to them that she couldn't read.

"I was wondering whether you'd like a fruit salad or soup to start off with." Mrs. Gardener felt as though she was trying to jolly along a couple of kiddies who didn't want to eat their dinner.

"Fruit salad, please." Andrew responded without looking at his wife. "But there's no hurry if it's all right with you. We're enjoying sitting here in all this solitude. Have the other guests eaten all ready?"

"Only the Misses Phillips. The other two couples are dining out this evening. And that nice old clergyman I was telling you about earlier said he probably wouldn't be back till after eight.

"Then," Andrew smiled up at her, "if we're not troubling you . . ."

"Not a bit of it. You go on having a nice chat. The Lancashire hotpot will keep just fine in the oven. Even better for letting the gravy have a nice simmer."

Mrs. Gardener returned to the kitchen to inform Nellie that she wished one or other of them was a mind reader.

"That's one of the happy memories I have of when Mummy and I stayed here," Eileen heard herself tell Andrew.

"What is, darling?"

"She said that she couldn't make jam like her mother did, or nurse Daddy half as well as Aunt Mary could when he had one of his bad times, but that being a vicar's daughter she could always tell a clergyman even when he wasn't wearing a clerical collar. I remember she made it sound like a talent for acrobatics or something else terribly clever and we both laughed."

"And were there other good moments?"

"Some. Going for walks and down onto the sand to paddle. It was much too cold to swim. And I liked hearing her talk about her parents and cousin Aggie and what fun it had been collecting eggs from the hen house when she spent holidays with her. But there were always the other thoughts that I couldn't push away. Especially when she spoke about Daddy and how I needed to understand that he got upset and went into rages sometimes because the injury to his head that had caused him to go blind in one eye had affected his mind. She said that he imagined all sorts of things that weren't true. And that he was even jealous of her friends, anyone she was fond of—even cousin Aggie, which was why she had never been able to take me to see her. But that his doctor wouldn't put him in hospital because he had known Daddy for years and Aunt Mary had persuaded him that she could take perfectly good care of her brother at home."

"You didn't believe her?" Andrew asked gently.

"No! I told her if Daddy got angry sometimes it was because of the disgusting way she was carrying on with Mr. Connors. And probably lots of other men besides."

"You loved your father very much?"

"How could I help it? He was so dear and kind to me. We would sit and do jigsaw puzzles together. We both loved them. And he liked me to play the piano for him. Chopin was his favorite composer. Daddy said the music helped soothe his headaches."

"So he did have them?"

"They were the price he paid for being a hero. I told Mummy she made them worse. And nothing she could say made me sympathize with her one bit. I lay awake at night in that bedroom upstairs with the red roses on the wallpaper. In the darkness everything became so clear. Aunt Mary was away the night before we left home. She had gone to stay with an old school friend for a couple of days. Something she did once a year. And our cook and the maid were away also; Mummy had said that they needed a break too and that it would be fun for her and me to take care of the house together. We could even have a try at making jam. But thinking it over, the pieces all began to fit together just like one of Daddy's and my jigsaw puzzles."

Eileen fell silent, to sit as if she were indeed in a dark

room in the middle of the night. But Andrew did not speak. He sat waiting until she took up the thread of memory again.

"She planned it all. Taken advantage of Aunt Mary's absence, got the help out of the way so that she could have a clear field to pack up what she needed to take with her when she ran off with Mr. Connors. He was free. His wife had been conveniently killed in that car crash. But that still left Daddy, who had refused to give her a divorce. Maybe she tried to talk him into giving her one, hoping he would do so without Aunt Mary to back him up; that was somewhat more bearable to think than that my own mother had killed my father in cold blood. I'm not sure how many nights it took for me to face up to the certainty that he was dead. But there was no getting around those cuts on her wrists that she refused to explain. There was the fact that she hadn't let me say goodbye to Daddy and the rush about leaving the house, all the while telling me that we were just going off on a surprise holiday so she and I could get close again. To this sort of guesthouse! The four of us—my parents, Aunt Mary, and myself—had always stayed in hotels before, fashionable ones, where we would always meet people we knew. And then there was the man in the grey cardigan."

"What man, Eileen?"

"An elderly man, with thoughtful, knowing eyes. He was Scottish, with a name like McDougal—no, McGregor. I remember it made me think of Peter Rabbit. He was eating breakfast—kippers—the first morning we came down to this room. He was sitting over at that table in front of the window. I saw him looking at Mummy not just that time, but on other occasions when we happened to be eating at the same time. It grew upon me with a sort of creeping horror that he was a policeman, a detective on holiday, and because of what he was, he knew what she had done. I could see it, the look that revealed he saw right through to her soul. I was sure she sensed it, because I saw her talking to him one day by the staircase, with her head bent close to his. I wondered what lies she was telling him to charm away his suspicions. And it reached the point that I couldn't bear it anymore—the waiting, the awful waiting for it all to be brought out into the open. That my mother had murdered my father and perhaps even conspired in arranging the accident that killed Mr. Connors's wife. I pictured her being taken away to be tried and hanged. And there was nothing I could do to stop it. I didn't know what I wanted to—I just knew that I wanted it to be over, so I did the one thing she had begged me not to do. I slipped away while she was having a rest one afternoon and went down to the telephone box at the corner of the road. I meant to speak to Aunt Mary, but . . ."

"It was your father who answered the phone." Andrew was suddenly aware of how cold the room had grown.

"Yes," Eileen's voice did not wave. "He said he had been worried about Mummy and me because we hadn't been in touch and he had misplaced the address of where we were staying that she had written down for him. But that otherwise he was perfectly well. And he didn't want me to say anything to Mummy about my ringing up, because they'd had a small quarrel and he understood she needed time away to sort out her feelings. So it would be best not to put a spoke in the wheel, just let things take their course and we would soon be back together, just like we were meant to be. It was such a relief, Andrew."

"Of course."

"How could I know?" Eileen asked in the voice of a twelve-year-old girl. "How could I know what I had done? It never crossed my mind that I had become my father's accomplice in killing my mother. But he was there when she and I went for a walk on the downs the next afternoon. He had found out from one of the other people staying here that we always went out around that time. When I saw him, saw the look on his face—the terrible maniacal rage when Mummy walked toward him—I screamed at him to stay away, even before I saw him lift the knife and bring it slashing down on her. She screamed at me to run, but I couldn't move. I just stood there and listened to him shouting that she had got away from him once. But never again. And as I watched her die I kept repeating over and over again inside my head, 'He's ill, he's ill, he can't help it. You're the one who killed her.' "

"He was ill," Andrew reached out and gripped her hands tight, "too ill to be found fit to be tried for murder. He went into hospital, where he should have been all along. And he died. It was the war that killed him, but you did not kill your mother. You were a child doing what you thought was right."

"I was jealous of her. I was willing to believe everything bad that Aunt Mary had to say about her."

"Eileen, you couldn't have stopped what happened."

"He's right." The speaker was a silver-haired man wearing a grey cardigan over a clerical collar. Neither of them had seen or heard him come into the room. "My name's McGregor. Ian McGregor. You probably don't remember me, but I was staying in this house that week you spent here with your mother. And I have returned every year at the same time, hoping perhaps that you would feel called to return and that I would be granted the opportunity of a few words with you."

"I do remember you." Eileen struggled to stand up but needed Andrew's help to guide her out of her chair. "I thought you were a policeman."

"No, my dear, I am as you see." Mr. McGregor tapped at his collar. "A clergyman. Your mother recognized me as such even though I was out of uniform on that occasion. It was at a point in my life when I was feeling somewhat adrift from my life's work. I came here feeling a need that week to escape from the world, and myself."

"And you sensed that Eileen's mother was also escaping," Andrew said.

"Not that." Mr. McGregor shook his head. "I saw in her face a look I had witnessed on the faces of some of the men and women with whom I had talked and prayed in my work as a prison cleric. People on whom the sentence of death had been passed, and who had found within themselves the peace that passes all understanding. Your mother, Eileen—if I may call you such—had fully accepted the inevitability of what lay in store for her. She wasn't afraid to die. What she feared was that her young daughter wouldn't learn to live. I made several attempts to see you, but I found it impossible even with my connections to be apprised of your whereabouts.

"I went to live with a cousin, Agatha, and she guarded me like a dragon until I married Andrew."

"But somehow I was always certain that I would see you again. I believe that your mother intended I should." Mr. McGregor smiled, looked upward, and bade them good-night. "Perhaps I will see both you young people at breakfast," he said before exiting the room.

"I thought he was going to say in church. A nice man," said Andrew.

"Yes." Eileen plucked the two roses from the vase on their table. "Would you mind if we took a walk? I know it's dark, but there's a sliver of moon and I'd like to go out to where it happened on the downs."

Andrew took her hand. They were unpegging their coats from the hall tree when Mrs. Gardener came out of the kitchen.

"Going out for a breath of fresh air?"

"Yes," they replied.

"Well, don't get wet. It looks like it might come on to rain again."

"It doesn't matter," said Eileen.

"No, I don't suppose it does." Mrs. Gardener stood in the doorway watching what she had come, in the space of a couple of hours, to think of as her young couple walk arm-in-arm down the road. Then she closed the door and went back to the kitchen to tell Nellie that things were going to be all right. She could feel it in her bones.

"I still don't believe in them—miracles, I mean. But I wish," Eileen looked up at Andrew, "that I had that man's pure unclouded faith."

"It would be a good thing to have," he agreed. The Sea View receded behind them into the mist, so that if they had looked back all they would have seen was a glimmer of light shining through a chink in the curtains of an upstairs window.

"But I believe in you, Andrew. I believe in us. That's a beginning, isn't it?"

"Yes." He smiled down at her, tucking her arm more securely into his. "It most certainly is."

In this first short story featuring Ian Rutledge, Charles Todd's shellshocked sleuth, Todd shows Rutledge in action as a "trench detective" during World War I and features some familiar Christie titles. Rutledge novels include A Test of Wills, Wings of Fire, Search the Dark, *and* Legacy of the Dead. *Todd, who lives in Delaware, has been nominated by the British Crime Writers' Association for both the Creasey Award for Best First Novel and the Dagger for Best Historical Mystery.*

The Man Who Never Was

Charles Todd

Private Romney had been a troublemaker.

The story was, he'd served in every unit the army had fielded, in the fervent hope that one day, somewhere, he'd finally get himself shot and be sent home, leaving the war to be won without him.

Gas had finally gotten him, not a bullet, catching him before he'd managed to drag his mask on. Or someone cut a hole in it—that was the popular story circulating in the trenches, where death no longer shocked. Men had seen such horrors that they were inured to sights that had bent them, new recruits, double with bouts of helpless vomiting.

The task of sorting through Romney's personal belongings fell to Rutledge.

He took the box and stared at it with distaste. Next to writing to the families of the dead, telling comforting lies to the parents and wives of men who had died screaming, he hated the necessity of looking through the remnants of a life. Letters, photographs, the trophies of love and war. One soldier had kept the silk scarf of a downed flyer, encrusted with blood. It was odd what men considered important when their lives were on the line.

The first item he came across in Private Romney's box was a packet of French cigarettes, never opened. A blue scarf knitted by inexperienced fingers, with lumps and missed stitches. A small volume of poetry—Keats. Rutledge was surprised. Romney hadn't struck him as a reader of books, much less verse. It showed a very different side of what had been a bristly, uncomfortable personality. Under the poems was a packet of handkerchiefs, daintily embroidered with entwined initials.

Rutledge set them aside and pulled out a long flat book. A leather portfolio, he realized, opening it. Inside he discovered that it was filled with sketches. Done by a talented, observant artist.

Intrigued, Rutledge began to thumb through them, half ashamed at this violation of privacy but driven by fascination.

These were not watercolors of a Saturday afternoon along the Thames, gay with boaters and blowing skirts and clouds like billowing sails. Instead, they were a kaleidoscope of war.

A cholera ward in Cairo, with the title "Death on the Nile" written in fine copperplate beneath it.

Half a dozen Malays struggling to haul a water wagon out of the mire, their backs bent with their effort, muscles taut and hard. "The Orient Express," it was called.

Rutledge turned the pages, reading titles and studying the artist's mordant view of hell.

"Ordeal by Innocence." A band of refugee children

trudging down a rain-wet road, faces strained with hunger and exhaustion.

"Death Comes as the End." A rotting corpse, hardly recognizable as human.

"Pale Horse." The bleached bones of a dead horse, white in the sunlight.

"The Call of Wings." A flight of planes high in the clouds, where, unseen, a red tri-plane lurked like a giant, tawdry feathered bird of prey.

"The Moving Finger." A line of heavy artillery, black against a lurid red sunset.

"The Secret Adversary." A French general, stiff and arrogant in his great coat. Unbending and uncaring as he sent men to their deaths.

An oddly skilled artist, adept at capturing not beauty but horror.

The figures were well drawn, with a fierce vitality, even in death, as if more than imagination had gone into their creation.

Rutledge laid them aside and found, at the very bottom of the box, a small packet in oiled cloth. He opened that and inside there was a collection of photographs. Looking closer, Rutledge realized suddenly that they were all the same man. Hair parted differently, with or without various styles of mustache, with or without spectacles. And with each photograph were identity papers in as many names.

Stunned, Rutledge spread them out and studied each of them.

Who the hell was Private Romney—the man shipped from unit to unit because he couldn't fit in? Or—didn't want to . . . ?

Rutledge, a trained policeman, considered the matter.

A spy. It was the simplest and surest solution.

But was it?

Was there more to the mystery of Private Romney that he had overlooked?

He went back to the handkerchiefs and examined the embroidery again. In the delicate, flowery script it was difficult at first to be sure, but he persevered. JMB entwined with PDS.

Lifting out the knitted scarf again, he saw that along one edge was incorporated a line of something. They looked like green three-legged figures wearing large white hats, but after a time he convinced himself that they were Welsh leeks, worked with more love than skill.

And Romney was not a Welsh name. Still, it was possible that the needlewoman herself came from Wales and wanted to remind him of that.

The book of poems was well-thumbed. As if it had been read over and over again. Or—used as a code? If someone possessed the key to the pages and words or letters, numbered references could easily be deciphered.

Without the book such numbers would be useless— seemingly unimportant.

He went through the sketches one more time.

"Ten Little Indians." A handful of Indian troops lounging in front of a tent, teeth white in dark, smiling faces. At their feet were ornately carved Kashmir chests.

And then, almost lost in the war scenes was a tiny cameo in the center of a page. It had been given the title, "The Thumb Mark of St. Peter."

There was an exquisite Gothic church tower standing stark above the broken walls, like the fragile thumb of a destroyed hand.

It wasn't a ruin of this war, but of another—the Franco-Prussian conflict of 1870 to 1871, where Bismarck had created out of Germany and her Prussian rulers a formidable power in Europe.

Rutledge had seen a photograph of this same church in the London office of David Trevor, an architect and Rutledge's godfather.

Eglise Saint Martin in Lorraine.

A once-beautiful building that had been the pride of its village.

Corporal Hamish lifted the flap of the tent Rutledge had borrowed.

"We're moving up, sir," he said.

"Yes. I'm coming."

Romney was dead. Spy or not, he was dead.

Let it be.

*   *   *

The next morning, as Rutledge was walking down the line with Sergeant MacLaren, he asked him what he knew about the late Private Romney.

"Not much, sir. A funny bloke. Kept himself to himself, if you know what I mean. The only time I saw him join in was when the colonel came. He drew a likeness of him that had the lads silly with laughing . . ."

He broke off.

"Why didn't I see this?"

"Begging your pardon, sir, it wasn't fit to show an officer. Droll, but indecent, like."

Rutledge nodded and didn't press.

"Romney was a good scavenger, sir," MacLaren offered instead. "If we needed anything, he could lay hands on it. Never saw his like, to tell the truth. Most scavengers can talk the teeth out of mummy."

A scavenger. Had Romney in fact stolen the things in his box? The book of Keats? The scarf and handkerchiefs? The sketches—

A desolate need to give himself a life? "My wife embroidered these for me . . . my daughter knitted that scarf, the last Christmas I was home. Ma was Welsh, you see . . ."

Foraged from the living—or the dead?

Rutledge considered that.

A spy—a lonely man with no roots to comfort him in the long watches of the night. Who was Romney?

It was a puzzle.

Instead of sending the box back where it could be posted to any next of kin, Rutledge held on to it for another week.

And he asked the soldiers who had served with Romney what they knew—or guessed—about him.

The answer was, bloody little.

To Rutledge's surprise, he found that Corporal Hamish MacLeod had known Romney better than most. The corporal was intent on getting close to men he was going to lead to their deaths.

"I didna' like him," Hamish said. "But he was a good enough soldier, for all his troublemaking. Loud and unruly, not a man you'd sit down with, still, he fought well enough.

No malingerer. He'd taunt the Huns sometimes, when we needed to pin down where the outposts were located. Called out, pretending to be one of their own. Or made them angry enough over what he said to curse him back."

So Romney had spoken German . . .

Rutledge said, "Have you ever seen him draw—sketch— anything of that sort?"

"No, sir, except for once or twice, drawing a caricature of an officer." Hamish looked away. "No harm in that, it kept the lads' spirits up."

Which told Rutledge that one of the caricatures had been of him. "No, no harm. Did he have any family?"

"Romney? No, sir. Said he was an orphan from Mill Spring House. Never got mail that I ken. A lonely man."

Rutledge nodded. Lonely—or by choice alone?

But if Romney had told Corporal MacLeod and others that he was an orphan, why the ordinary touches of the scarf, the book, the handkerchiefs? An orphan would have no need to spin a life. Or if he had spun one, out of scavenged goods, why would he then admit to anyone that he had no family?

It was a tangle that Rutledge threaded his way through from time to time, pondering the mystery of a man who was dead.

He told himself to send the box back down the lines, where it could be sent to anyone listed as next of kin, or thrown on the rubbish heap.

He found he couldn't bring himself to do it.

Other men died, and he handled their pathetic possessions and sent them back. Yet the box from Private Romney remained beside his own, like a constant reminder of death.

There came a night when the guns were blessedly still and the stars were real, and there was no whisper of war in the soft air. A promise of things to come, silence. He had learned to distrust it, knowing it foreshadowed a great battle.

He sat in the tent with his candle, surrounded by papers. He stared not at them, but at the box standing beside his rough-hewn chair.

Something had to be done about Romney's belongings,

once and for all. He, Rutledge, was no longer a policeman. It wasn't his duty now to come up with proof of anything, answers to any questions, reasons for any actions. He was a soldier, would die a soldier. Let it be . . .

But he couldn't. He took out the photographs and identity papers and went through them slowly, carefully, looking at each photograph and each matching set of papers.

It was frighteningly simple, he began to realize, to create multiple identities for yourself.

Romney had walked into army recruitment stations all over Britain, and eager recruiters, well aware of the slaughter mill in France, took a man at his word. I am this person, I worked at this job, I was employed by this firm, I was born and reared in this town, I was the son of these parents . . .

And slowly but surely, Romney had been trained for war—but never sent to war . . .

Something had gone wrong. But what had the recruiters learned about this man of so many names and faces, that each time had sent him posthaste back to the civilian world?

And the whole process had begun again.

Who was Private Romney?

Why had he so badly wanted to come to a war that did not want him?

Rutledge found himself writing to Sergeant Gibson, who was too old for war and one of the finest investigators that Scotland Yard had ever found.

If Sergeant Gibson couldn't find anything out about Romney, there was nothing to find. And Rutledge would be back with his first theory. That this man must have been a spy.

The letter went out that morning, before the shelling started and living became a hardship that men fought for as fiercely as they fought the human enemy.

It was nearly a month before a reply came from Gibson.

Rutledge tore open the envelope and looked at the first words. He could feel his stomach knot with what followed.

Private Romney had never existed. Nor had Ennis, Smyth, Thomason, Frane, or any of the other identities created by the fertile imagination of a madman.

Behind these shadowy figures, Gibson had painstakingly uncovered the reality of one Gerald Heinrich Taylor-Brach. He was half German and half English, born in London to a German father in the diplomatic service and an English mother. A second son, Martin, had been born in Berlin. Reared in both languages and both countries, the brothers had made their choices early in life. Gerald considered himself an Englishman, while Martin had seen himself as thoroughly German. Martin had in fact been caught in 1915 spying for the Fatherland and been shot. But Gerald had not been in the war—he had been in a private asylum in Sussex since 1910.

A model patient, until Martin died in front of a firing squad. After that, Gerald had been hell bent on serving England. He had escaped so often that the private hospital had finally sent him home for private care, refusing to be responsible for such erratic behavior. Yet it was not his madness that had repeatedly kept him out of the army, it was his blood kin. Divided loyalties was the official view, according to Gibson. Untrustworthy.

Sergeant Gibson had ended, "I don't know how this will help, but it's all I have."

It was enough.

Rutledge understood it very well indeed.

Gerald had persisted until—this time as Private Romney—he had finally gone off to war.

A man who had a heritage he dared not claim, a man who wanted desperately to fight and be wounded to prove *his* courage and *his* patriotism. A man who had made no friends. Unable to cope in the normal world, invariably raising the hackles of officers and comrades alike with what they saw as his infuriating behavior, he'd been labeled a troublemaker. A pariah. A man no one wanted, not even his own country.

Heeding his instincts, Rutledge went back to the sketch book one last time before sending the box home. He turned the pages, seeing war as Gerald had seen it, recognizing the humor and the talent and the humanity of a man who was hopelessly lost in a welter of madness.

He came to a sketch he'd passed over many times before.

A scene so common in this war that he had taken it for granted. Now he saw it very differently.

Drawn in vivid detail was a soldier lying just beyond the wire, his gas mask half on, half off, as if he'd died trying frantically to drag it into position.

But for the first time Rutledge saw two other things: the small, delicately wrought penknife lying on the ground almost concealed in the shadows by the left hand, and the face that had seemed before to be any soldier's. Rutledge recognized it now. It was very like the first of those false identity photographs, when Gerald must have looked most like himself. No mustache, no spectacles, just a simple side parting to his hair.

He read again the title that was so beautifully written at the bottom: "Absent in the Spring."

Romney had found a way to die in the spring. Without knowing which day it would come, but knowing that surely it would come. And that the Germans would kill him as surely as the English had killed his brother. He had been a good soldier, and yet nothing had touched him. He had miraculously survived gas, shells, machine gun fire, while others had fallen all around him. With a knife-torn gas mask, there was no turning back—nor any way of knowing when the next gas would move so softly, so quietly, across the muddy fields of death.

Romney had only to wait. And waiting, he had sketched his own epitaph. A body lying in no man's land who was no man any one knew.

*Ann Granger cooks up a little culinary crime in this tribute
to Agatha Christie's genius in murdering characters by a
complex timetable. Granger is the author of the Meredith
and Markby crime series, published in hardback by St.
Martin's Press and in paperback by Avon, including* Call
the Dead Again *and* A Word After Dying.

Murder At Midday

Ann Granger

"I've put you down for the savories," said Clarissa
Hooper. She smiled in her bright, encouraging way.

Daisy wiped her hands nervously with a rag, smearing
the paint more freely. She wondered why, when Clarissa
smiled, the smile never reached her eyes. Clarissa's large,
protruberant, pale blue eyes were as blank as a dead fish's.

Daisy said, "I'm afraid I'm not much of a cook."

"Nonsense!" retorted Clarissa, as Daisy had known she
would. "You can throw together something, can't you?
Anybody can."

Daisy said, "I can't," as firmly as she could, but it was
useless. Clarissa merely gave a jolly laugh as though Daisy
had made a joke. An idea struck her. She needn't actually

make the savories, whatever they might be. She could buy
some in the nearest bakery. What difference would it make?

As if she could read Daisy's mind, Clarissa continued.
"The important thing is that everything should be homemade. Elderly people enjoy homemade food. Last year
some people brought baker's goods and we don't want a
repeat of that! We want this party to be a success!"

The "we" irritated Daisy. She also wanted the party for
the village old folk to be a success, but by "we" she suspected Clarissa meant "I." Clarissa used "we" as royal per-
sonages do—to indicate both the person and the majestic
office. Clarissa, as chairwoman of the village women's in-
stitute, behaved very much like the all-powerful ruler of a
pocket principality. To argue with her was not only useless,
it was made to feel like treason.

Reluctantly, Daisy asked, "What sort of savory?"

"Good question." Clarissa nodded approvingly. "We
don't want everyone bringing the same thing. That's why
I've made a list. Mrs. Forbes is in charge of sandwiches.
There are three of you making savories. One person is
bringing cheese straws and another is bringing mushroom
vol-au-vents. So I leave it up to you. Perhaps something in
the pastry line?"

"Pastry!" gasped the horrified Daisy, but Clarissa was
already gathering up her various belongings.

"I must be on my way. I've got to call on the vicar before
I go home and I've told the girl to have my lunch ready at
one sharp."

Despite these words, Clarissa didn't go, but fidgeted with
her capacious bag, eyeing Daisy thoughtfully all the while.
"You don't have any family, do you, dear?" she asked unexpectedly.

To this rather impertinent question, Daisy replied that she
had an aged uncle who lived by the seaside.

"Then you'll have expectations," said Clarissa, even
more rudely, thought Daisy. What business was it of Clarissa's? Nor had Daisy any expectations of curmudgeonly
Uncle Frederick. He had twice informed her that she wasn't
to build up her hopes on his account! He was, in addition,
in robust good health despite being well into his eighties.

But she'd mistaken Clarissa's interest. "I have a nephew," she began and then hesitated unhappily. Lack of confidence was unlike Clarissa. Daisy realized the woman wanted to talk something over but didn't know how to begin.

"Yes?" Daisy encouraged.

"I've helped him many times in the past for my poor late sister's sake." Clarissa rushed into speech. "But in the end I had to put my foot down. I wrote and told him it was time he stood on his own feet."

"Where does he live?" asked Daisy, though she didn't really care.

"In London, where he works for an an insurance firm. Naturally, he knows that when I die, he'll have everything, but until then he's got to live on his salary. I've told him so."

Clarissa recalled the reason she was there. "So you'll see to the savories? I'll call by tomorrow and collect them. Two dozen individual servings will do!"

"*Two dozen*—" But Clarissa had swept out, cutting short Daisy's outraged squeak. Through the window, Daisy saw her mount her bicycle and pedal away to bully the vicar, a mild-mannered man known to be in awe of Mrs. Hooper.

Daisy sat down with a bump on the nearest chair. She couldn't remember the last time she had made pastry. She didn't think it was a very good idea to start now. The elderly—for whom these delights were intended—probably had false teeth. False teeth gummed up with Daisy's pastry. She could imagine the scene. The village elderly were vociferous in complaint if things weren't to their exacting standards at their annual summer garden party held in a paddock adjacent to the back of Clarissa's property. Daisy wasn't in the first flush of youth herself any more, but that didn't necessarily make her sympathetic to the village old folk who were never so happy, she'd found, as when finding fault.

She realized the paint had dried on her hands. The painting on which she'd been working when Clarissa had arrived stood in its half-finished state on the easel. Daisy sighed. Clarissa never bothered to ask if you were busy. She always barged in and started talking, oblivious to how inconvenient it might be. Daisy glanced at the clock. It was ten minutes to twelve. Clarissa had arrived at eleven and harangued Daisy for fifty minutes. The morning was completely ruined. It was impossible to restart work now. Daisy went to wash her hands and hunt for a cookery book.

The kitchen was occupied by Mavis Potter, who was about to put on her coat and sneak off early. Being as impecunious as only an artist can be, Daisy couldn't afford proper domestic help. She was reduced to employing Mavis, mornings only. Mavis was fifteen, a slapdash worker, inclined to cut corners. But she was prepared to work for very little wages.

"I'm all done, mum!" announced Mavis perkily. In readiness for the walk home she had applied scarlet lipstick unevenly to her mouth.

Daisy wondered whether she ought to say anything about the lipstick, which she didn't think was really suitable for a fifteen-year-old. Moreover, she doubted Mavis was "all done." Mavis's work was invariably half-done. But after Clarissa's visit, she couldn't be bothered to argue with the daily help. So she said, "Very well, Mavis."

Mavis clattered noisily away.

As it was almost lunchtime, Daisy made herself a sandwich and took it and the cookery book into the garden to enjoy the sun. Rose Cottage was on the outskirts of the village. Daisy had leased it from an old lady, a well-known and respected village resident, who had retired to the Caribbean for her health. The pretty cottage garden faced the road and people passing by frequently stopped to admire it and to chat over the hedge.

Daisy settled down in the shade of an apple tree. She took a bite from her sandwich and gazed dismally at the closed book. It was all very well for Mrs. Forbes to promise sandwiches. Mrs. Forbes's maid would prepare them. Daisy suspected that the providers of the cheese straws and mushroom *vol-au-vents* would have similar help. There was no question of asking Mavis to cook anything. Daisy would have to do her best. On impulse she flipped open the book, resolved to try and make whatever was on the page at which it opened. If it was a disaster, and it was almost certain to be that, she'd have to buy from the bakery after all and explain to Clarissa. It would be humiliating but unavoidable.

Pigs In Blankets was the wording at the head of the page. The name appealed to Daisy, who read on to find out what these delicacies might be. They were, it appeared, a sort of sausage roll. Pigs in blankets it would have to be.

A metallic rattling attracted Daisy's attention. She looked up and saw Clarissa bicycle past, coming from the direction of the vicarage. The rattle was caused by a loose mudguard on the bicycle's rear wheel. No doubt she was on her way home to lunch prepared by her excellent cook. Clarissa waved cheerily at Daisy who waved back, feeling guilty. She got up and returned to her kitchen. The clock on the wall there told her it was twelve-thirty. She checked her store cupboard and found it held the ingredients for the pastry but she hadn't any sausages. The kitchen clock now informed her it was twenty minutes to one. It was Wednesday, which was half-day closing, and the village butcher's shop would pull down its shutters at one for the rest of the day. There was no time to lose. Her abundant greying hair, which she'd pinned up that morning, was falling down again but she had no time to tidy it. Daisy pulled on a wide-brimmed raffia sunhat and hastened out.

Closing the garden gate carefully against stray dogs, she strode along, placing her feet in their sensible flat sandals squarely on the ground, her long skirt flapping at her ankles. The butcher's was at the far end of the already deserted main street. Everyone was at table. Daisy passed Clarissa's rather nice white-washed Georgian house and reflected with resentment that Clarissa would be within, settling down peacefully to her lunch oblivious of any upset she'd caused to anyone else.

Daisy arrived, panting, at the butcher's to find he'd just that moment shut the door and hung the "closed" notice in it. She peered through the glass and tapped urgently. The butcher came to the door to point majestically at the notice, but seeing who it was, opened up the door again. He liked the artist lady who'd taken Rose Cottage.

"I only want two pounds of small sausages!" apologized Daisy.

"Two pounds of sausages it is!" said the butcher.

Perspiring freely in the hot midday sunshine, Daisy set off home again, carrying the wrapped sausages. Halfway down the main street her progress was halted by a shrill scream.

It came from the house to her left, the white-washed Georgian house which belonged to Clarissa. As she stood before it, wondering what she should do, the door flew open and a maid rushed out into the street. Seeing Daisy, she made for her and grabbed her arm.

"Oh, miss! You've got to come. Madam's dead!"

"Pull yourself together," said Daisy automatically, trying to detach the girl's grip. Clarissa ran through maids at a great rate. Mostly they only stayed a month or two before they decided they'd rather work elsewhere. This girl, Daisy saw, was yet another new one. She wondered whether she was given to imagining things.

"Mrs. Hooper can't be dead," Daisy said reassuringly. "I saw her only half an hour ago."

"Oh, she is, she is, and it's horrible!" wailed the maid, clinging even more tightly.

Much against her will Daisy allowed herself to be dragged into the house. As they went, the maid gave an incoherent account of what had happened.

"It's Cook's day off so I had to prepare Madam's lunch—just a salad and a rice pudding. I got it all ready but I hadn't heard her come home, so I went along to the dining room to see if she was there. When I opened the door, I saw her lying there—like that!"

They had reached the door of the dining room. The maid stopped short and pointed at something unseen on the further side of the door.

"I can't go back in that room, I swear I can't!" Tears trickled down her face.

Daisy had perforce to enter alone. It was a small but pretty room from which French windows opened on to the garden. A single place was neatly laid at the well-polished dining table. The chair before it, however, lay upturned on the floor. Beside it sprawled Clarissa, on her back, one hand clutching at her throat around which was a tightly pulled cord. Her pale eyes bulged even more than they had in life and her tongue protruded between her open lips. That she was dead, there was no doubt.

The maid was still hovering outside in the hallway. Daisy returned to her, taking care to disturb nothing on the way.

At least the girl had calmed down now that there was someone else to take responsibility. She was dry-eyed and her expression was more inquisitive than horrified. Daisy was relieved. An hysterical maid on top of everything else was something she could do without. She eyed the girl, a pretty young woman with glossy brown hair. In her black uniform dress and white apron and cap she looked, Daisy thought ruefully, as unlike Mavis Potter as could be imagined. She certainly looked reliable enough to be sent with a message.

"You must go and fetch Constable Wilkes," Daisy said firmly to her. "And also Dr. Partridge."

The maid's bright gaze widened. Her mouth opened and she put her hand to it in dismay. "Is Madam alive then?" she gasped. "I never would've left her if I'd thought—"

"No, I'm afraid Mrs. Hooper is dead. But the constable will want a doctor's opinion. Go along now and whatever you do, don't gossip to anyone on the way!"

"No, miss!" said the maid huffily and hurried off.

Left with the body, Daisy was uncertain what to do. On the principle that it would be best to do nothing, she went outside the house again and looked up and down the street. Not a soul except for the distant figure of the maid, hurrying toward the police house. Poor Constable Wilkes would be sitting down to his midday meal, nicely cooked by Mrs. Wilkes. The news that he had to get up straight away and go out wouldn't be welcome.

A thought struck Daisy. She walked down the path at the side of the house and came out into the back garden. Clarissa's bicycle was propped against the garden shed in which she probably kept it. The garden was mostly laid to lawn and beyond it stretched the grassy paddock which would see the old folks' revels. Daisy frowned. She returned to the house and this time, found her way to the kitchen. It was immaculately clean and tidy, crisp gingham curtains at the open window moving slightly in the warm draft. Clarissa's lunch, which she would now never eat, stood ready. It made a pathetic sight, the ham salad on a tray and the rice pudding—rather lumpy with a burnt skin—being kept warm in a *bain-marie*. Daisy looked out of the kitchen window. It gave on to a small paved area, beyond which was a privet hedge so high that the house was shielded from the back garden.

Much stamping of feet from the front of the house announced that at least one of the two people she'd sent for had arrived. Daisy hastened back to the dining room.

Constable Wilkes, a portly figure with half his tunic buttons undone indicating the haste with which he'd left home, was stooped over the prostrate Clarissa. His red face creased in dismay, he was repeating, "Well, I never . . . well, I never . . ."

He straightened up and took out his notebook and pencil but then appeared at a loss to know what to write in it. Fortunately, Dr. Partridge arrived at that point. He too had been called from his lunch, as shown by the napkin still tucked into his waistcoat. Hot on his heels came the breathless maid with an air of triumph about her now that she'd successfully completed her mission.

"I got them both, miss!" she announced to Daisy.

Partridge knelt briefly by the body. Then he scrambled to his feet and addressed himself to Constable Wilkes. "You'll have to get hold of Inspector Morris in town. This is clearly murder."

"Murder!" screeched the maid, relapsing into her earlier panic. "I'm not staying in this house another minute!"

Once news of Mrs. Hooper's death got around, the village was in turmoil. Who could have done it? She hadn't been a popular lady, it was true. "But you don't go murdering someone because she likes giving orders, do you?" asked Mrs. Potter, mother of Mavis. General opinion agreed with this. Nor could the one obvious suspect, Mrs. Hooper's wayward nephew Gerald, be blamed. The police established immediately that he was at work in the London office of the company that employed him for the whole of that day. In fact, he had not even taken a lunch break because of business involving an important new client. Everyone working at the firm had seen and spoken to him constantly throughout the day.

The police came and went. The case remained unsolved. Rumor had it the police believed the murderer had entered the dining room through the French windows. Possibly he was a thief intent on making off with the silverware. He had escaped the same way, running through the back garden and across the paddock beyond unobserved. The maid's view from the kitchen had been barred by the privet hedge.

The body was released for burial and Gerald Horton, the nephew, attended the funeral looking distressed. He kept his handsome face bowed in sorrow and respect and made quite an impression. Mavis Potter, completely bowled over, declared he looked just like Ronald Colman.

This caused Daisy to become quite cross and declare, "Don't be silly, Mavis, and by the way, I don't think your mother would approve of your spending money on lipstick."

Gerald hurried away immediately after the funeral, much to Mavis's regret. Shortly after that, a FOR SALE notice went up at Clarissa's Georgian house. Mr. Horton had no wish to keep it on and everyone said they could understand that.

Daisy had been interviewed by the police early in the investigation and had given her account of having been called to the body by the maid. They'd written it all down and since then hadn't bothered her again. Daisy had waited, with the rest of the village, for an arrest to be made, as sooner or later everyone believed it must be. When no arrest was made, the atmosphere in the village became tense.

"Mother says we've got a murdering madman among us!" Mavis told Daisy with some relish.

Daisy put on her raffia sunhat once more and walked down the main street. She stood before Clarissa's house, with its FOR SALE notice, for a few minutes in silent tribute, then caught the bus into town. There she went to the police station and asked to speak to Inspector Morris.

"Well now, Miss Winslow," said Inspector Morris politely. "What can we do for you?"

He smiled at his visitor. He remembered speaking to her just after the murder. She was dressed now, as she had been then, in a way Morris categorized as "bohemian." She wore a long skirt, a velvet waistcoat, and a raffia sunhat from beneath which peeped untidy greying curls. She was hung about with a great many bead necklaces and bangles which had a homemade look to them. "Arts and crafts," thought Inspector Morris dismissively. He didn't know why she was here but it was probably to waste his time. She had probably enjoyed the attention she received after the murder and was seeking more of the same.

Daisy folded her hands in her lap and took a deep breath. "May I ask if you are any further on in your inquiries into Mrs. Hooper's death?"

Morris looked distinctly put out at this forthright approach. "These things take time," he retorted testily.

Daisy's courage almost failed her at that point, but she swallowed and went on. "I should perhaps have come sooner but I thought, you see, that you'd have solved it by now. In any case, you wouldn't be interested in *my* ideas. But as you haven't, haven't *yet*—" Daisy tactfully amended her words seeing an alarming reddening of the inspector's complexion "—arrested anyone, I decided I must come and tell you what's been on my mind. I've thought and thought about this since poor Clarissa Hooper died. Indeed, my brain's been buzzing with nothing else. And now I think—I think I know how it was done."

"We know how it was done," said the inspector who'd been listening with growing impatience, his worst suspicions about the visitor confirmed. "With a length of picture cord, could've been bought anywhere."

"No, I mean, I know how they did it—Clarissa's murderers."

"Oh, two of them?" asked the inspector in a dry way. He glanced at his wristwatch. "I'm sure you have a very interesting theory, Miss Winslow, but—"

"There had to be two of them," said Daisy, ignoring his signs of restlessness in her eagerness to explain, "in order for Gerald Horton to have an alibi. He is, you see, the only person with a motive and bound to be suspected. Clarissa Hooper had left him everything in her will. She told me so the morning of her death. She had been giving him money, but she'd recently refused to give him any more. He's a rakish young man who gave her a lot of cause for concern. I dare say he owes a great deal and was desperate when she told him she'd give him no more."

"So who was his accomplice?" asked the inspector. His tone was still patronizing but the look in his eyes had grown shrewder.

"Oh, that girl, that maid person. It's a terrible thing to think that a young woman could commit murder, but she's probably madly in love with Gerald. He's a good-looking young man, and anyone who could persuade Clarissa Hooper to give him money over a period of some years must have a silver tongue. Introducing her into the house wasn't difficult. Clarissa was forever changing maids. All they had to do was wait until she was looking for yet another, and Gerald sent along his young woman."

Morris drummed his fingers on his desk. "As a matter of fact, we've lost trace of that maid. She must have taken a new post. We're trying all the agencies which supply domestic staff." He leaned back in his chair. "But surely, if you're right, Horton and his ladyfriend would be taking a great risk planning to murder Mrs. Hooper in the middle of the day when anyone might come by and see them."

"Not really. You see, it was lunchtime—the one time of day when *nobody* would come by. Midmorning or midafternoon would have been quite a different proposition. People would be moving about. For example, Clarissa was organizing the old folks' party. She came to see me at eleven that morning to discuss it. She asked me to make some pigs in blankets."

"Some what?" asked Inspector Morris, looking alarmed.

"They're like sausage rolls. Actually, she didn't specifically ask for pigs in blankets. She asked for savories, but I decided on pigs in blankets. She left my cottage at ten minutes to twelve to go to the vicarage."

"She did go there," said Morris. "The vicar confirms it."

"That's right. I saw her myself. She bicycled past my cottage at half past twelve on her way back home. Clarissa was a stickler for doing everything in an orderly way. She told me she'd ordered her lunch for one o'clock so I knew that's where she was going.

"I was in a panic because I'm not a very good cook and I hadn't any sausages for the pastries. Also it was Wednesday, half-day closing. But one didn't refuse Clarissa," Daisy said ruefully. "I put on my hat and rushed to the butcher's. It was twenty minutes to one when I left my cottage. There was no one about. It was lunchtime, you see. I passed Clarissa's house. It was all quiet. It didn't surprise me, because on her bicycle, she'd have got there long before me. I calculate it would have taken her less than five minutes to reach her house after passing my garden. So she got home at twenty-five minutes to one. That gave her murderer plenty of time. Remember, Clarissa ate at one sharp. It was the cook's day off. Only the maid was in the house, by her own admission.

"At one o'clock I had reached the butcher's. He'd just closed but kindly opened up again to sell me the sausages. I saw, as I left the butcher's, that his clock read ten past one. I was very grateful to him for staying open an extra ten minutes, just for me. I was passing Clarissa's house when the maid rushed out. You know that bit."

Daisy frowned. "I suppose, with the shock of finding her like that, I didn't really think beyond sending the girl for Constable Wilkes and Dr. Partridge. But afterwards, I got to thinking that one or two things were odd.

"To begin with, the girl had said she hadn't heard Clarissa return. Now, she might not have seen Clarissa because of that privet hedge outside the kitchen window. But she would have heard her bicycle as Clarissa pushed it down the garden because it makes a frightful rattle and the kitchen windows were open. I'd heard it myself earlier and I saw the bicycle leaning against the garden shed while I was waiting for the constable to arrive. The girl had prepared the lunch so that everything would look right. She took great care to tell me, as she was taking me into the house, that the lunch consisted of salad and rice pudding.

Sure enough, I saw ham salad and a rice pudding in the kitchen. I sent the girl for help, as I told you, and that's when the second funny thing happened. The girl had calmed down very quickly—a bit too quickly to my mind! But when I asked that Dr. Partridge be summoned, she looked really dismayed and asked whether madam was still alive. She was afraid, you see, that I'd detected signs of life in poor Clarissa. When I explained it was because I thought a doctor's opinion would be needed—" Here Daisy paused and gave the inspector a nervous smile.

"Quite right," said Morris. "Very clear thinking on your part."

"Thank you. Well, when the girl realized that was why I wanted Partridge there, she relaxed again and went off in very good spirits indeed! So cold-blooded—" Daisy stopped and the inspector waited courteously for her to begin again. "Then I thought of the third odd thing, and really, it's the oddest of all. If Clarissa had asked for lunch at one, she would have expected to see it arrive at one on the dot. Yet when the maid ran out into the street, claiming to have just found her mistress dead, it was well gone ten past one. If the lunch had been ten minutes late in arriving, Clarissa would have been along to the kitchen to find out why!

"So what I believe happened was this. Gerald and the girl had waited for the cook's day off. Gerald made sure to be working in his office all day in full view of everyone. The girl heard Clarissa's bicycle rattle past the house on its way to the shed and got ready for her part in it. Just on one, she went to the dining room. Clarissa was at table, expecting her lunch. I saw from the position of the furniture that she'd been sitting with her back to the door. Hearing the door open, Clarissa would've assumed it was the salad arriving. Instead it was that awful girl, with a length of picture cord. It must have been so easy, Clarissa so unsuspecting . . ."

"Would you like some water?" asked the inspector, as Daisy had turned very pale and broken off her narrative.

"After. Let me finish. I'm almost there. Once she was satisfied Clarissa was dead—it must have been a quick death, for that I'm grateful for Clarissa's sake—the girl opened the French windows to suggest how the killer had got in. After that she ran into the street screaming and grabbed the first person to come along. It happened to be me. Had no one been there, she'd have stood there screaming until someone came out to see what was going on. It was so simple."

Morris heaved a sigh. "It all makes sense, I agree. Between you and me we haven't dismissed Gerald Horton's involvement just because he has an alibi. You're right—he does owe a lot of money. He's a gambler and a very bad one. No doubt someone is pressing him for payment. But we need to find that girl, that maid, if we're to make it stick. As I told you, we're trying all the domestic agencies—"

"Oh no," said Daisy quickly. "Not those. Try the theatrical agencies. I'm sure she's an actress. Such a pretty girl and able to vary her emotions at the drop of a hat, even produce tears!

"Besides," she went on confidentially, "I saw that rice pudding! It was clearly made by someone who'd never cooked such a thing in her life! It looked nearly as bad as something I might make, but then, I have no pretentions to any domestic skills. I tried to tell Clarissa so when she asked me to make the savories, but she wouldn't listen. But such a professional-looking maid as that girl appeared to be should have been able to manage plain cooking."

"It's not something I'd have noticed," admitted the inspector.

"So she was no professional maid! I understand actors leave their details and photographs with agencies. I don't mind how many photographs I have to look at. I'm sure I can identify that girl."

And so it turned out. The girl proved to be a largely unsuccessful actress and—as Daisy had guessed—very much under the sway of Gerald Horton. But not so much that she was prepared to face a charge of murder alone. She confessed everything.

Clarissa Hooper's house stood empty for a long time as no one local fancied living in it. Eventually a couple from outside the area bought it.

While all this was going on, the old folks' party took place, though its location was moved to the vicarage garden. It was very successful. But somehow, Daisy never got round to making the pigs in blankets.

In this story, New Mexico resident Walter Satterthwait features some familiar character types for fans of Agatha Christie and Edgar Rice Burroughs, and provides a colorful answer to the question, "Why are English villages so lethal?"

Author of the Joshua Croft mystery series, Satterthwait was an Agatha Award nominee for Escapade, *the first novel in the rollicking Phil Beaumont–Jane Turner series, set in the 1920s and starring Harry Houdini and Sir Arthur Conan Doyle. In addition to the second novel in the Beaumont & Turner series,* Masquerade, *Satterthwait has received critical acclaim for two other mysteries,* Miss Lizzie *(about Lizzie Borden) and* Wilde West *(about Oscar Wilde on tour in the American West).*

A Mishap at the Manor

Walter Satterthwait

A hundred yards away, their long necks stretched taut, two giraffes elegantly nibbled at the leaves of an elm tree.

"A nasty business, sir," said Sergeant Meadows.

"Nasty enough, Sergeant," said Inspector Marsh. His hands behind his back, he stood staring out at the library's casement window. Hard to believe, with giraffes lolling about outside, that he was still in Devon. "Some sort of an explorer, wasn't he? This lord fellow?"

"Not an explorer, not as such," said Meadows. "More of—well, sir, what you'd call him, I suppose, would be a kind of wild man. He lost his parents in an airplane crash in 1902, and nearly died himself. He was adopted by a tribe of great apes, they tell me. In Africa, this was."

"Africa, eh? Extraordinary. And when did he return to England?"

"Just after the war. From all accounts, he got along well with the old lord, his grandfather. He went into the family business, and took it over when the old man died."

"Publishing, isn't it?"

"That's right. Greystoke Press. Thrillers, crime novels. Trash, basically. But he did very well with it."

"Curious."

"How so, sir?"

"Fellow like that. Raised by apes—"

"Great apes, sir."

"Yes, but still. One wouldn't really expect him to shine at the business side of things. Even a thing like publishing."

"He claimed, so I heard, that the jungle taught him everything he needed to know."

"Not everything, it would appear."

"Excuse me, sir?"

"It didn't teach him how to avoid a bullet, did it?" Marsh's eyes narrowed slightly. A chimpanzee had just capered, screeching, across the formal garden and disappeared behind the chrysanthemums. Remarkable.

"You don't believe it was suicide, then?"

Marsh smiled grimly. "I believe that someone would very much like me to believe that it was suicide."

The sergeant nodded. "You reckon one of the guests did him in."

"Oh, I think so, Sergeant. In a situation like this, a manor house, a weekend party, a dead lord, you can almost always count upon your guests. And didn't you tell me that at night, tigers were set free to roam the grounds?"

"Lions, sir."

"Ah, lions. They're the ones with the manes?"

"That's right, sir. Tigers have stripes, I believe."

"Well, your lion is a largish sort of beast, isn't he? And a carnivore, too, eh? I suspect that they'd prove something of a deterrent to any smash-and-grab passerby. No, Sergeant, I think we can safely focus on the guests."

"They're waiting in the conservatory. Shall we talk to them all at once?"

"No. Individually, I think. Ask Constable Hill to trot one of them in here, and we'll have a go."

The first guest, a Miss Eudora Fields, was a woman in her fifties. She wore a flowered hat atop her curly grey hair, a belted black dress elaborately printed with red fleurs-de-lys, and a pair of sensible black walking shoes. Hanging from her shoulder was a large rectangular handbag. She sat down on the leather-covered divan and carefully arranged the handbag on her lap. Marsh sat down opposite her in a padded club chair. Off to the right, Sergeant Meadows lowered himself to another club chair, his notebook ready.

"First, Miss Fields," said Marsh, "I'd like to thank you for cooperating with us. I know that this must be a trying time for you."

"Oh, dear me, no," said Miss Fields. "No, I'm quite used to this sort of thing."

Taken a bit aback, Marsh said, "Which sort of thing?"

"Murder," she said cheerfully.

"Used to it?"

"Yes. I'm something of a sleuth myself, you see. Only an amateur, of course." She smiled comfortably. "But you've heard, no doubt, of the Lower Wopping Horror."

"I can't say," said Marsh, "that I have."

Miss Fields's smile faltered. "Really? It was one of my most celebrated cases."

"Cases?"

"So I like to refer to them."

"And how many of these 'cases' have there been?"

"Oh, for a time, while I was living in Lower Wopping, there were literally dozens of them. It sometimes seemed that I couldn't leave the house without stumbling upon a corpse. There was Colonel Bedford—bludgeoned in the hydrangea bushes. There was Lady Windham—pecked to death in the aviary. There was Father Elliot, the parish priest—impaled."

"Impaled?"

"On the peak of the church tower. It took me forever to determine exactly how he had got there."

"I shouldn't wonder. And how had he, exactly?"

"A Crane."

"A builder's crane?"

"No, no. Lester Crane. One of the Middle Wopping Cranes. He'd learned, you see, that Father Elliot was in fact Willoughby Rutledge, his nemesis from Eton."

"Ah. But how had he actually contrived to impale this Rutledge fellow upon the church tower?"

"Derek."

"A builder's derrick?"

"No, Derek Crane, his cousin. The two of them used ropes. Hempen ropes. It was a thread of hemp, actually, that did them in."

"Ah."

"And then there was poor Mr. Todd, the barber. And Mr. Norman, the greengrocer. And Mr. Prebbles, the postman—"

"I must say," said Marsh, "that this Lower Wopping of yours sounds a most unpleasant place to live."

"It was dreadful," said Miss Fields. "No proper vegetables. No mail service. No Mass on Sunday. And people are so strange, aren't they, Inspector? Everyone in town—the few who were left—had stopped having me over for tea. As though it were *my* fault that these corpses kept popping up."

"That must have been very difficult for you."

"Unbearable, in the end. I finally gave up and moved."

"To where, might I ask?"

"Upper Wopping."

"And have you been troubled there by this . . . problem?"

"No, thank goodness. This is my first murder in ages. But it's a bit like getting back on a bicycle, isn't it? It all comes back to one." She smiled happily. "I'm very much looking forward to working with you on this, Inspector."

"Yes," he said, and glanced at Sergeant Meadows, who rolled his eyes elaborately. "Now, Miss Fields, I understand that it was you who found Lord Greystoke's body this morning."

"That's correct. At precisely eight-oh-five."

"And how can you be so certain of the time?"

"Oh, I'm always certain of the time. One never knows, after all, when one might stumble upon a corpse. And when one does, precision is of the utmost importance. Consequently, I never open a door or go down a stairway without referring to my pocket watch." She reached into the pocket of her dress, plucked out a gold watch, and held it up for Marsh's admiration. "I synchronize it, on the hour, with the BBC broadcast."

"But I understood you to say that you hadn't been troubled by corpses of late."

"Yes, but old habits die hard, don't they?"

"Of course. But what was it, Miss Fields, that brought you to Lord Greystoke's rooms at eight-oh-five this morning?"

"He had suggested I come round at that time, so that we might discuss my book."

"Your book?"

"An account of one of my cases. The Curious Affair at Middle Wopping."

There was a faint interrogatory note at the end of the sentence, as though Miss Fields were discreetly wondering whether Marsh possessed a familiarity with this adventure.

Marsh, who did not, chose to proceed with his own. "And what was it," he said, "that you found in Lord Greystoke's rooms?"

"May I consult my notes?"

"Your notes?"

"I always take notes when I stumble upon a corpse."

Marsh nodded. "Yes, by all means, consult your notes."

Miss Fields opened her handbag, rummaged through it, and at last produced a notebook identical to Sergeant Meadows's. She flipped through it for a moment. "Yes. I knocked on Lord Greystoke's door at eight-oh-five. Receiving no answer, I tried the doorknob. The door was unlocked. I opened it and proceeded into the room and immediately discovered the body of Lord Greystoke. He was naked except for a bolt of brightly colored material, a loincloth, covering his lower torso."

She looked up. "It passes between the legs and is bound around the waist, so that a piece of the material falls in front and in back. It's an article of clothing sometimes worn by aboriginal peoples. And sometimes, it would seem, by Lord Greystoke as well."

"So it would seem."

Looking down again, she said, "He was lying on the floor, exactly five feet, seven inches from his writing desk, and four feet, three inches from the balcony window."

"You measured the distance?"

Miss Fields looked up. "I always carry a measuring tape with me," she patted the handbag, "for occasions of just this sort."

"Yes. Pray, continue."

She looked down again at her notebook. "Also lying on the floor, five inches from Lord Greystoke's outstretched right hand, was a Colt .32 caliber semiautomatic pistol. A close examination of this weapon—"

"You didn't touch it?" said Marsh.

"Certainly not," said Miss Fields. "I got down on my hands and knees and I sniffed at the barrel." She looked at her notes. "A close examination of this weapon revealed that it had been fired recently. A close examination of Lord Greystoke's head revealed a hole in it, such as might have been made by the entrance of a .32 caliber slug. The hair around the hole was singed, suggesting that the muzzle of the weapon had been in proximity to the head when the gun was fired."

"Did you touch the body?"

"Briefly," she admitted. She smiled. "Well, yes, I know that I shouldn't have done so, of course, but I felt it necessary, you see, in order to determine the time of death. The body was cold, and rigor mortis had set in. I estimate that Lord Greystoke had died some six hours and thirty-five minutes before I found him. In other words, at one-thirty this morning."

"That is a very precise estimate."

Miss Fields' shoulders moved in a light, modest shrug. "I do have some small experience in these matters."

"And did that experience suggest to you that it might be advisable, at some point, to bring your discovery to the attention of the authorities?"

"It did indeed. It was quite clear to me that Lord Greystoke had been murdered, and that his murderer had attempted—rather clumsily, I might add—to make it appear that the man had committed suicide. I was about to seek out a telephone when that ridiculous Frenchman burst into the room and began to scream at me."

"Which ridiculous Frenchman?"

"That Pierre Reynard. One expects a certain amount of excitability in a Frenchman, of course, but Reynard was impossible. He stormed about the room, quite red in the face, waving his arms and screaming at the top of his lungs. And then, as though this weren't unpleasant enough, that American woman, Lulubelle Courage, the tennis player, *she* arrived and began to attack me as well."

"Attack you? Physically?"

"Verbally. To be honest, Inspector, I wish she *had* attempted a physical attack." Her eyes glinted as she smiled. "Over the years, you see, I have acquired a certain skill at jiu-jitsu."

"But why were Reynard and this Courage woman attacking you?"

"Simple jealousy, I imagine. They both fancy themselves sleuths—"

"Both of them?"

"Yes, it's absurd, of course. But there it is. And no doubt they were displeased that it was I who first stumbled upon the corpse."

"I see." Marsh glanced again at Sergeant Meadows, who shook his head in amazement. "Now, Miss Fields—"

Suddenly, the library door slammed open. In the doorway stood a small man wearing a beautifully cut three-piece black suit and, gleaming beneath the cuffs of his trousers, an immaculate pair of white spats. Tucked beneath his right arm was an ebony walking stick, and now, as he stalked forward, he swung it forward with a flourish and tapped it against the carpet. "Reynard," he announced, "will no longer be traduced by this ignoramus."

Inspector Marsh turned to Sergeant Meadows. "Sergeant, I thought that you had men watching the guests."

Standing, the sergeant set aside his notebook. "I'll handle it, sir."

The small man danced backward, toward the fireplace, swishing the walking stick through the air like a fencing foil, once, twice. "I must warn you, Monsieur. Reynard does not permit the touching of his person."

Meadows looked at Marsh, who waved him back. "You'd do well, Monsieur," said Marsh to the Frenchman, "to put down that device. Assaulting a police officer is a serious offence."

The Frenchman lowered the stick, rested its tip on the carpet, and rested his hand atop the handle. "And so is the assault upon my reputation by this *imbecile* of a woman. A face of red, she says. A waving of arms, she says. Lies, all of it. With the most icy of detachments, I calmly explained to her that her blundering about at the scene of the crime was entirely a *catastrophe*. I have, Monsieur, stumbled upon well over a thousand corpses, both here in England and on the Continent, and never have I ever seen such chaos. This numbskull had hopelessly compromised the evidence. Miles of measuring tape were draped across the body. Miles of twine, like the web of some deranged spider, connected the body to the writing table."

"You silly man," snapped Miss Fields. "You're only jealous because it was I who stumbled upon the corpse."

"Twine?" said Inspector Marsh.

"And how is it, you incompetent cow, that you *did* stumble upon the corpse before I? I had an appointment at eight-oh-five with Lord Greystoke, to discuss my book—but I was late." He tugged a gold pocket watch from his vest pocket and held it out to Marsh. "Observe, Monsieur. Someone has adjusted the hands backward by fifteen minutes, so as to prevent Reynard from meeting with Lord Greystoke at the appointed time."

Miss Fields sniffed. "You forgot to wind it, you idiot."

"Reynard *never* forgets to wind his watch. An accurate timepiece is essential to his success. No, you great nincompoop, it was you who—"

"*Enough!*" bellowed Marsh. Reynard blinked at him, apparently stunned. Marsh turned to Miss Fields. "What, pray, is this twine business?"

She waved a hand. "Nothing, Inspector, really. I was merely determining the angle at which the body must've fallen."

"And in the process," said Reynard, "she had stepped directly on the face of the corpse. The imprint of her walking shoe was clearly visible on Lord Greystoke's forehead. She had knocked over a bottle of wine, a Chateau Latour, spilling its contents across the desk, and also knocked over the wastebasket—"

"You pompous twit!" exclaimed Miss Fields. "I didn't knock over the wastebasket! The basket had been knocked over before I entered the room, as you would have known, you sniveling little dwarf, if it *had* been you who'd stumbled upon the corpse."

"*Dwarf?*" squealed Reynard. He raised his walking stick and advanced toward Miss Fields. Miss Fields tossed her handbag aside and leaped from the sofa to assume a jiujitsu fighting stance, her arms held before her in the air. Sergeant Meadows stood and moved to interpose himself between the two.

"She's right," said a voice from the doorway.

Heads swiveled.

At the door was an attractive young woman wearing a white silk blouse and a white silk skirt. Her hair was blond, cut very short, and in her right hand she held a tennis racquet. Lightly, she bounced the strings of the racquet against the palm of her left hand. She was chewing gum. "About the wastepaper basket," she said. Her accent was American. "It got knocked over before she went into the room."

"Who are you, madam," said Marsh, "and how do you know this?"

"Courage," said the woman. "Lulubelle Courage. And I know because I had myself stashed in the closet."

"Stashed. I see. May I ask why?"

"I had an appointment with Stokie at seven thirty. I—"

"By 'Stokie'," said Marsh, "you mean Lord Greystoke?"

"Right." She snapped her chewing gum. "He wanted to shoot the breeze with me, see, about a book I'm writing."

"Ah." Marsh nodded. "Miss Fields, are there, among the guests, any additional amateur sleuths?"

Miss Fields had returned to her seat on the sofa. Setting the handbag on her lap, she said. "Several, actually. There's Simon Lubner, the music critic. An absolute ninny, of course. And there's Father Greene. I shouldn't like to say anything unpleasant about a member of the priesthood, but—"

"There is also," said Reynard, "that great booby of an English lord, Wilbur Drimley. And his wife, the insufferable Edith."

"I see," said Marsh. "Sergeant, will you close the door, please, and lock it? Miss Courage, please sit there. Monsieur, please sit there. Now this is how we are going to proceed. I will ask Miss Courage some questions. She will answer them. No one will interrupt. Have I made myself clear?"

"But of course," said Reynard.

"Certainly," said Miss Fields.

"Sure," said Lulubelle Courage, and snapped her gum.

"Good," said Marsh. He glanced over to Sergeant Meadows, who had once again picked up his notebook. "Miss Courage, could you explain to me, please, what happened this morning?"

"Well, like I said," she said, tapping the tennis racquet against her knee, "Stokie wanted to see me at seven-thirty this morning. To gas with me about this book of mine. It's all about my adventures, right? Solving murder mysteries on the tennis circuit."

"And no doubt," said Marsh, "there are a great many of these."

"Hundreds. Believe me, it's a dog-eat-dog world, tennis. One time, I stumbled onto three corpses in the same day."

"Extraordinary."

"Yeah. But after a while it can really get on your nerves. That's why I've been thinking about getting into the writing game. Anyway, when I arrive at Stokie's room, no one answers the door. So before I go in, naturally, I check my watch. I always do that, just in case I stumble onto a corpse."

"*Your* watch, of course," said Reynard, with a significant glance at Miss Fields, "had not been sabotaged."

Marsh glared at him. Raising his eyebrows, Reynard held up his left hand and put the finger of his right to his pursed lips.

"And it's a good thing, too," said Miss Courage, "because I did. Stumble onto a corpse, I mean. Stokie's. He was dead meat, the poor thing, and I figure that somebody had aced him early this morning. Probably around two-thirty."

Miss Fields produced a contemptuous snort. Marsh glanced at her. Looking down, she adjusted the handbag on her lap.

"Whoever croaked him," said Miss Courage, "had tried to make it look like Stokie offed himself, but it was pretty obvious, from the way he was lying, and from where the gat was, that he'd been croaked, all right."

"The gat?"

"The roscoe," she said. "The heater."

"I believe," said Miss Fields, "that she means the pistol."

Marsh nodded. "At what point was it," he asked Miss Courage, "that you hid yourself in the closet?"

"At eight-oh-five. I checked my watch, so I know that's right. I heard someone at the door, and I figured it might be the shooter, coming back. They do that sometimes, you know—return to the scene of the crime. So I jumped into the closet, there in the entryway. And what happened, I guess, I knocked over the wastepaper basket. Anyway, so I'm inside there, right? I can see out, through these little slats in the door? And I see Miss Fields here come in. She spots the stiff—poor Stokie—lying on the carpet and right away she grabs that purse of hers and she starts hauling things out—a magnifying glass, some string—maybe a ton of string. I never saw so much string in my life. It looked like an explosion in a pasta factory. And she's got a tape measure that must be about four miles long."

Marsh said, "You remained in there the entire time that Miss Fields was . . . ah . . . conducting her investigation?"

"To tell the truth, I was laughing so hard I was pretty much paralyzed. You should have seen her. I mean, she was actually climbing on top of poor Stokie, so she could tie her string to the desk. A couple of times there, running back and forth, she tripped right over him. Finally, she plunks down in the chair and she grabs her purse again and pulls out a whole bunch of papers."

Marsh turned to Miss Fields.

"Tide tables," she said stiffly. "And railroad schedules." She gave Miss Courage a look that might shatter stone.

"But the sea is a good fifty miles away," said Marsh. "And there is no rail service within thirty."

"Better safe than sorry," said Miss Fields.

"Ah," said Marsh. To Miss Courage he said, "Please continue."

"So I'm in there, holding my sides and trying to keep quiet, right? Suddenly Frenchie here is in the room, screaming at Miss Fields."

"Untrue!" exclaimed Reynard. "With the most icy of detachments—"

"Yeah, well," said Miss Courage, "it sure sounded like screaming to me. And she starts screaming back, calling him a poncy frog pederast—"

"That's a lie!" said Miss Fields.

Miss Courage shrugged. "Maybe I had wax in my ears and didn't hear right. Anyway, while the two of them are going at it, I slip out of the closet and make like I'm just coming into the room."

"Mademoiselle Courage," said Reynard, smiling as he leaned slightly forward, "has neglected to explain precisely what she was doing in Lord Greystoke's room from seven-thirty, when she arrived, until eight-oh-five, when she was interrupted by the cow."

"Monsieur Reynard," said Marsh, "you are trying my patience."

"Forgive me," said Reynard. "In future I shall avoid any mention of cow."

Marsh scowled at him, and then looked at Miss Courage. "But what, in face, *were* you doing?"

"The same thing I always do when I stumble onto a corpse. I was snooping. I mean, it was pretty obvious who aced poor Stokie, and I wanted to find some proof."

"Obvious?" said Marsh.

"Sure. Look at the evidence. The gat, the bottle of wine, the singed hair around the bullet wound. That dumb curtain, or whatever, he had draped around his middle."

"A loincloth," said Miss Fields.

"Whatever," said Miss Courage.

"And whom," Marsh asked her, "do you suspect?"

Miss Courage shook her head. "Geeze, Inspector. I'm sorry, but it wouldn't be fair for me to say. I mean, you haven't even finished your investigation."

Pierre Reynaud chuckled. "I have no doubt, Mademoiselle Courage, that you have come to some conclusion as to the identity of the murderer. I have no doubt, also, that it is mistaken."

"Oh yeah?" said Miss Courage. "And you think you know who did it?"

"*Naturellement*."

"And would you care, Monsieur," said Marsh, "to share this knowledge with us?"

"Alas, I regret to say that I cannot. While Mademoiselle Courage is wildly inaccurate in most other respects, in this she speaks correctly. It would not, at this time, be appropriate for me to reveal the identity of the person responsible."

"What about you, Miss Fields?" asked Marsh. "Do you believe that you, too, know the identity of this person?"

"Of course," she said. "But, much as I dislike to do so, in this case I must agree with the Frenchman. And with *her*. It simply wouldn't be proper, just now, for me to reveal the killer's name."

"Is there, among amateur sleuths," Marsh asked her, genuinely curious, "some sort of code that forbids you to divulge the identity of a murderer?"

"It simply wouldn't be proper," she said.

At that moment, someone knocked on the library door.

Marsh said, "Get that, would you, Sergeant?" He looked at the others. "You do realize, I hope, that withholding information from the authorities could put all of you in a very bad light."

"Speaking for myself alone," said Reynard, "I withhold no information whatsoever. I withhold only my conclusions. And these are based upon evidence available to all. Although it is evidence, I admit, tarnished by the ineffable ineptitude of that . . . personage." He nodded toward Miss Fields.

Miss Fields said, "If you hadn't interrupted me—"

"Inspector?" Sergeant Meadows, at the door.

"Yes?"

"There's someone here to see you. It may be important."

Marsh cast a baleful glance at the three people assembled before him. "Please remain where you are."

He strode across the room to the door, where Sergeant Meadows gestured for him to step outside. In the hallway, Meadows pulled the door shut. "This," he said, "is Cleeves, the butler."

Cleeves was tall and imperious, the platonic ideal of a butler. "This just arrived, sir," he said. He held out an envelope. "It is for you, apparently."

Marsh took it. The heavy envelope was addressed as follows:

> To The Individual Investigating My Death
> Greystoke Manor
> Devon

Marsh said, "But surely there's no postal service on Sunday."

"No, sir," said Cleeves. "It must have been hand-delivered by someone. It has, as you see, no postmark. Simply that handwritten date in the corner. Yesterday's date."

"And the handwriting?"

"Is Lord Greystoke's, sir. Unmistakably. He taught himself to write, as you may know, while he was living with the great apes in Africa, and his handwriting displays several peculiarities of style which make it unique. You will notice, for example, those little smiling faces within the capital Ds. May I say something, sir?"

"Yes?"

"Well, sir, as it happens, I have a certain amount of experience with murder investigations. It has been my great honor to assist the local police with several of theirs. You have, perhaps, heard of The Middleton Muddle?"

Marsh sighed. "I'm afraid I haven't."

"Well, be that as it may, sir, I just wanted you to know that my talents, such as they are, will be at your disposal should you require them."

"Thank you, Cleeves. I shall bear that in mind."

"Will there be anything else, sir?"

"I think not. Thank you, Cleeves."

"Very good, sir."

Marsh watched the butler march away and then turned to Sergeant Meadows. "My mother wanted me to be a surgeon, you know."

"No, sir, I didn't."

Marsh nodded. He hefted the letter.

The sergeant said, "Looks like Greystoke already knew, yesterday, that someone was going to do him in."

"Umm," said Marsh, still staring at the letter.

"Who do you think they suspect?" Meadows asked him.

"God knows," said Marsh, looking up. "Perhaps none of them suspects the same individual. Perhaps they all suspect each other. An extraordinary lot, eh, Sergeant? Well. Let us see what his lordship has to say on the subject, shall we?"

Carefully he opened the envelope and removed from within it a packet of folded sheets of paper. He began to read. He frowned. He furrowed his brow. He continued to read. At last he looked up at Meadows. "You'd best call for reinforcements, Sergeant. I believe we're going to need them."

The Greystoke Letter, as it was called in the press, played an important part in the subsequent court trials. It is reproduced here in its entirety, minus its various addenda.

To Whom It May Concern:

You will forgive me, I hope, my little joke.

    The act of suicide is so inherently banal that, when its inevitability became clear to me, I decided that I should attempt to enliven, as it were, my own. It was partly for this reason that I invited to Greystoke the individuals whom by now you have met; and from whom, it pleases me to think, you must by now have derived a dollop or two of entertainment. It was for this reason, too, that I stood (will be standing) in the center of my room while I perform(ed) the act, and held (will be holding) the pistol in such a way that it fell (will be falling) somewhat ambiguously to the floor. Ever since I was a lad, swinging through the trees, I have admired the intricacies of the English language.

    But first things first. As a police officer, you will be understandably preoccupied by motive. Why suicide, you may well ask. To which I reply, why not?

    To anyone raised by the Great Apes, as I was, the contemporary European scene, political and social, can be perceived only as depressing. Where once I was surrounded by affection, sincerity, concern, and kindness, I am now surrounded by hatred, guile, envy, and a cruelty that is, to me, quite unfathomable. Reason enough, I should think.

    Additionally, however, over the years I have grown very, very tired. It is, perhaps, as simple as that.

    It was partly, as I said, to enliven my ending that I invited the guests I did. But there was another, more significant reason. Like all Great Apes, I carry within myself a powerful cultural taboo which effectively prohibits self-destruction. Among us, you see, like quite a lot of other "civilized" things, it just isn't done. I realized, therefore, very early on in my planning, that in order to proceed with the act I should be required to place myself in a situation, the unpleasantness of which was so intense that suicide became not merely an escape, but a celebration.

I could, of course, have invited to the manor a group of mere writers, chosen more or less at random. I did consider this. Speaking as a publisher, I can tell you that a weekend spent in a house filled with writers, and their whining, their petty grievances, and their childish envy (which invariably masquerades as something else, usually critical judgment), is enough to encourage the average person—indeed, the average saint—to leap merrily from the lip of a nearby cliff.

But it was, for me, simply not enough. I have been around them for far too long, unfortunately. I have grown immune.

And then, in a sudden blinding flash, it occurred to me: a weekend among amateur sleuths! I have met many members of this species. For some reason they all feel that their "adventures," whether penned by themselves or by some hired hack, are worthy of publication. I do not know whether you have had any previous personal experience with them, but I can assure you that they are, individually and as a group, wonderfully intolerable.

And so I invited the assemblage among whom you have, perforce, found yourself. I am pleased to report that they have worked, as we say, a charm. By Friday evening I had developed shortness of breath and a debilitating migraine headache. By this afternoon, following the tea, I had grown nearly incoherent with rage and loathing. The end will come as an enormous relief.

I have made arrangements to have this letter delivered to you tomorrow. If, for some reason, poor Cheetah is discovered in the act, please bear in mind that he has been, over the years, a good and loyal friend, and that he has virtually no knowledge of what the letter contains.

One thing more. The people gathered here are not (as I suspect you will be unsurprised to learn) quite so noble and so morally upright as invariably they like to present themselves. To this letter I have ap-

*pended proofs of this statement, proofs obtained by
several quite competent (and professional) enquiry
agents.*

*I've been dabbling, you see, in a bit of amateur
sleuthing myself. But I feel certain that, in the circumstances, the Gods will forgive me.*

*You will learn, for example, that the inestimable
Miss Fields has made, shall we say, quite a killing in
Lower Wopping real estate. That the remarkable
Monsieur Reynard is, curiously, without an alibi for
the evening during which his erstwhile companion,
Mr. Witherspoon, met his elaborate death. That the
splendid Lord Wilbur Drimley, and his equally splendid wife, Edith, have nourished the gardens at Drimley Hall with a form of fertilizer, the use of which is
considered, by most legal authorities, rather* de trop.

*You will learn, ultimately, that all of them, without
exception, have been guilty of precisely the crime in
which they all take such pride "investigating."
Guilty, in a word, of murder.*

*The facts are here. Everything is documented. I
wish you great fun.*

> *Ungowah,*
> *Lord Greystoke*

Carolyn Wheat pays homage to Christie's "ABC Murders" in this tale of alphabetical tourist murder. Wheat, author of the Edgar-nominated Dead Man's Thoughts, Where Nobody Dies, Fresh Kills, *and* Sworn to Defend *with attorney Cass Jameson, recently edited an anthology dedicated to Route 66, and won the Agatha and Anthony Awards for her chilling short story, "Accidents Will Happen," in* Malice Domestic 5.

Oh, To Be in England!

Carolyn Wheat

"Yes, it's my real name." I was getting an echo; I moved the mike an inch farther from my lipsticked mouth. I stood in the well of the tour bus, next to my driver, Clive, who sat on his inflatable donut and waited for me to finish my talk. "No, I never get tired of hearing the same old jokes told as if no one on the planet ever thought of them before."

I didn't say the last part, of course. I widened my toothpaste grin while the passengers made funnies and hummed tunes, lengthening the orientation portion of today's tour by the predictable five minutes. Every other guide on the Oh, To Be in England Motor Coach Tours made the welcoming speech in ten minutes flat; mine took fifteen on a good day. And since this morning's itinerary was The Beatles's London, it stood to reason we'd be in for a raft of puns and silly—

I like my name, really. I liked it before the Fab Four wrote that song and I still like it in spite of the jokes because it leads to nice big tips. Everyone on the coach simply must have a photo of themselves standing next to me, my name tag prominently displayed in the resulting snapshot. My breasts grace more photo albums in the States than—

But I digress.

Clive put the bus in gear and popped a cassette of *Revolver* into the tape player; we'd begin the tour by listening to the moptops and end it with *Abbey Road*. I'd have preferred to finish with the *White Album*, but the Charles Manson associations proved too much for the honchos at the head office.

Little did they know.

My thoughts, and Clive's, were far from Manson or the Maharishi or any other aspect of Beatlemania; we were planning, *sotto voce*, a new attraction to lay before the boss. An Agatha Christie tour, which would take in Brown's Hotel and Paddington Station and—

Well, there's where we were stumped. What else?

While Paul (or was that John?) emoted about how good Norwegian wood was, we made our way to St. John's Wood and I turned down the stereo, lifted the mike, and began my spiel about the history of Abbey Road Studios, which had not, I made dryly clear, been built expressly for the Fab Four. I was supposed to talk about the London Symphony Orchestra and mention that Glenn Miller had made his last recording there, but it was clear to me that this particular crowd cared only for the boys from Liverpool, so I trimmed a bit off the canned narrative.

There's not much to see except the outside of the lovely Georgian mansion where the EMI company maintains its recording studios, but it's a must-stop because they all need a photo of themselves striding across Abbey Road on the zebra crossing, four at a time. It's just a plain old crosswalk, truth be told, and everyone who was having a snap made would have to explain to their friends why this particular zebra crossing demanded a photograph, but the chance to line up and walk across the black and white stripes just like the Beatles on the album cover was irresistible.

Someone always took off their shoes.

You remember that whole crazy thing: *turn me on, dead man.* Paul is dead, decapitated in a freak accident, and the person pretending to be Paul is an eerie lookalike and one reason we know he's dead is that in some culture somewhere on the planet going shoeless is a symbol of death. And on the *Abbey Road* album where the Fab Four cross the street in single file, Paul is barefoot!

Case closed; the man's dead. Play your record backwards and mourn for the cute one.

So someone on the tour always gets this amazing inspiration—surely no one in the history of London sightseeing has ever had the same idea—and sheds footwear for his photo op.

It doesn't occur to them, and it never occurred to me either, that they were tempting fate.

What did surprise me was that Anne Ackerman, a fiftyish woman from Big Fork, Arkansas, shed her Birkenstocks for the occasion.

She didn't seem the type.

She was, as I'm sure they observed in Big Fork all the time, "a real hoot." She told amusing stories of her hometown in a loud, braying voice, laughing all the while at her own wit, and inviting everyone on the bus to share her pleasure over the doings of the quaint folks back home, many of whom had drained a drop too much mountain dew, and I'm not talking soda pop.

If you liked the late Minnie Pearl, you'd purely love Anne Ackerman. I had the feeling not many on the bus were huge fans of country-fried humor.

When Anne Ackerman failed to show the next morning for the Sherlock Holmes tour, I was annoyed but not worried.

I run a tight bus.

You're there on time or you're left on the sidewalk.

That's how it is under the rules laid down by the Oh, To Be in England Motor Coach Tour Company, Ltd., and that's how it has to be.

I can't deprive the other twenty-nine paying customers of a single golden moment on Sherlock Holmes and Dr. Watson's Baker Street because one tourist slept a bit late or grabbed an extra rasher of bacon at the full English breakfast.

But I waited ten minutes for Anne and I sent the hotel porter to knock her up. I heard plenty of complaints from the other passengers, who wanted me to get the show on the road, but the woman used a cane, for heaven's sake, and I just couldn't be so cold as to leave without at least trying to locate her. So I gave her a bit of leeway I wouldn't have allowed anyone else, in spite of Doug Didricksen's heckling.

The man actually held a stopwatch in his hand and called out the passing seconds in a raucous voice that reminded me of the famous ravens.

There's always one. One royal pain, one cross to bear— call it what you will, Doug was the one for this tour group. Loudly contemptuous of the Beatles in general and Ringo for some reason in particular, he'd peppered yesterday's trip with derisive remarks and off-key parodies of Beatles tunes. My offers to let him off at Harrod's for a bit of shopping or the National Gallery for a spot of art, or the Tower of London for a nice long visit—say, three months— met with no success. He was loudly and miserably bored and he had a fine old time telling the rest of the bus just how bored he was.

Now if somebody'd stripped off *his* shoes and left *his* body in the most famous zebra crossing in London, I'd have shed no tears.

But then his name didn't begin with *A*.

It was like that kids' game: My name is Anne Ackerman and I'm from Arkansas and I'm lying dead on Abbey Road.

The police caught up with us at the Sherlock Holmes Museum on Baker Street. I'd given my opening spiel before heading the bus down Oxford Street and was just about to buy the entry tickets when a female detective with short blond hair took me aside and told me about the shoeless corpse in the famous zebra crossing.

She showed me a Polaroid and I identified the body as Anne Ackerman.

Shaken, I picked up the mike and announced the news to the passengers, who had begun collecting their purses and tote bags in anticipation of shopping for Sherlockian souvenirs. When I finished my brief remarks, there was shocked silence at first, and then a chorus of questions I couldn't answer.

I handed the mike to the detective and stepped outside for a breath of brisk, damp, revivifying London air.

No one knew anything—that was the gist of a full hour's worth of Q and A conducted by the Inspector Tennison lookalike in the grey blazer. Anne roomed alone, having paid a stiff single supplement for the privilege, so no one knew her comings and goings. That she had left the hotel in the wee hours of the morning and made her way, for some insane reason, back to Abbey Road where she met her death at the hands of a hit and run driver seemed obvious, but no one on the bus could shed light on the motive for her crazy—

Except for one thing. One reason to go back, a reason only a tourist or a tour guide would understand.

I motioned the detective aside and asked a single question.

Her grey eyes widened and she called a uniformed bobby over. Taking his cell phone, she made a call, spoke quietly into the receiver, waited for an answer, and turned to me with a thin-lipped smile.

"Nice detective work, Ms. Lane," she said with an approving nod of her head. "It seems the crime scene team did find a camera halfway down the block, with the timer set on automatic."

"I thought that might be it," I murmured. "She realized the photo she had taken yesterday might not come out, and she went back to get a snap of herself in the zebra crossing." Taking her shoes off for maximum—

No, the word *impact* was too loaded. I'd seen what the

oncoming car had done, and there was nothing remotely amusing about it.

The tour was permitted to continue; I purchased group tickets for the Sherlock Holmes Museum and waited outside while they filed into the famous address, except of course that this building isn't 221B, because there *is* no 221B, a fact that never failed to be pointed out to me by someone who's convinced only he knows that particular fact. On this occasion, the enlightened one was Billy Brannigan, an Australian with a mahogany-tan face, a bent Aussie hat, and a chip on his shoulder the size of the Sydney Opera House.

Loudly proclaiming the superiority of all things Oz over any and all aspects of life in Britain, he'd spent yesterday telling Clive and me how the Beatles could never stack up to the Bee Gees. When he heard the two of us discussing Agatha Christie, he'd said she was but a dim candle compared to Dame Ngaio Marsh.

As for Sherlock Holmes, he was a pommy mountebank, easily out-detected by Inspector Napoleon Bonaparte.

One of the many little mysteries I have never managed to solve is why Australians call the Brits "pommies." I was about to ask Clive, but the forbidding look on his usually cheerful face warned me off. Instead, I reverted to the subject of Mrs. Christie while the tourists toured and shopped and took turns having photos made with the museum's official greeter, decked out in Inverness cape and deerstalker hat.

Predictably, Didricksen insisted on wearing the hat himself for his photo op.

Clive and I talked business. We needed more sites if we were going to convince the boss to add Christie to our regular schedule. I racked my brain, but came up empty.

"Wot about that Tommy and Tuppence, then?" Clive asked, pushing back his crushed cap and scratching his head. "I reckon they had adventures in London before they went into the spy game."

My knowledge of the collected works of Dame Agatha was a bit sketchy; I knew Miss Marple lived in the little village of St. Mary Mead, which wasn't a big help as far as London was concerned.

"How about the Inns of Court?" I countered. *"Witness for the Prosecution* and all that?"

"Ah, that's a good one, miss. We'll have to tell them who Charles Laughton was, mind. None of these young people remember the good old days and that's a fact."

Holmes himself or Hercule Poirot or the divine Miss M could have predicted what happened next. Either of them would have noticed at once that Billy Brannigan hailed from Brisbane. Elementary, my dear Penny.

Elementary in retrospect, anyway. Even when the police returned to our Baker Street parking spot and told us Billy Brannigan had been shoved under a train at the Baker Street Underground Station, where he'd gone to photograph the Sherlock Holmes tiles, the penny—pardon my unpardonable pun—failed to drop.

You try solving one murder and predicting the next when you've got twenty-nine hysterical tourists wailing and shouting and demanding and sulking all at the same time.

Stiff upper lips aren't part of American culture.

They whined. They demanded to be driven to Heathrow at once so they could go home to crime-free America; they yelled for their lawyers; they wanted to see the American Ambassador; they requested a free lunch to compensate them for the horror they'd almost witnessed. They—no, not they, that was Doug Didricksen all by himself—wanted to know if they'd miss any of the Chamber of Horrors at Madame Tussaud's.

By the time the police allowed the bus to leave, everyone was short-tempered. I made a cell phone call to the boss, who adamantly refused to refund anyone's money—they'd been to Baker Street as planned, hadn't they? We hadn't become a charitable institution, had we? Besides, there was still time to fit in Madame Tussaud's, provided we gave the tea at Mrs. Hudson's a miss, and that wouldn't be much of a loss, would it?

And it's your job to set'le all these lit'le fusses, now, innit, so wotcher boverin' me for?

Ah, the celebrated English politeness.

Even so, it didn't occur to me that tomorrow might be just as fraught. For one thing, we didn't have a theme for the next day's tour; it was just billed as London Shopping Spree and took in all the stores we could jam into six hours, from Harrod's to Laura Ashley, from Liberty's to Dickens and Jones, with a walk down Bond Street and a glimpse at the Burlington Arcade. They could pick up their macs at Aquascutum, their porcelain at Wedgewood, their scent at Penhaligon, and have a pub lunch at Shakespeare's Head.

I did have a little canned talk prepared about the Swinging Sixties, yet the minute the words left my lips, cold water trickled down my back as the implications hit home.

You guessed it: Carnaby Street. Parallel to Regent Street, right in the center of the most exclusive shopping area in London.

Well, I'm not stupid.

Of course I checked the passenger list for anyone with a *C* name, especially if they came from a *C* place.

Thank goodness Kate Crenshaw of Chattanooga spelled her name with a *K*.

How anyone could even pretend interest in Swinging London with two of their compatriots lying in the morgue was beyond me, but the Oh, To Be in England Motor Coach Tour Company, Ltd. wasn't paying me to conduct funerals, so I pattered on about Mary Quant and the mini-skirt and Op Art prints till my eyes bubbled, and still Ms. Crenshaw peppered me with questions.

When we reached the once-famous shopping mecca, her face fell.

"Is this all there is? I thought this was supposed to be a real high-class place," she said, tiny frown between her china-blue eyes.

"Everything changes," I said with a shrug. "We'll be moving on to Laura Ashley in just a few—"

"Laura Ashley! She is *so* over!" The blonde sniffed and said, "Why, every mall in America has a Laura Ashley. I didn't come all the way to little old England to buy things I could have bought back home. I want something everyone knows you can't get in America, something really English."

I was about to send her to the nearest Lush outlet, where

she could buy exploding bath balls, but she glimpsed an Op Art scarf in the window of an Oxfam shop and trotted off happily on her platform shoes.

It was true that there wasn't much left of the original Carnaby Street fashion center; a lot of stores with cheap merchandise displayed on wooden sidewalk tables lured my passengers into spending a few bob, and three of them bought those oversized street signs to take to the folks back home as evidence that they had visited the place.

I sometimes think that's what some people travel for: evidence. They don't seem to enjoy being there very much, and God knows they don't like the process of getting there, but once they are there (wherever *there* is), they are by God going to go home with something tangible for their efforts. A T-shirt, a mug, a mouse pad—and the latest must-have in souvenirs—anything that will convince apparently skeptical neighbors that one actually left home and hadn't spent the last two weeks in a closed-off bedroom watching television and pretending to be in England.

When the passengers drifted back to the bus, ostentatiously shaking the rain out of their umbrellas and looking at me with those unmistakably American we-didn't-spend-this-much-money-to-get-soaked-every-day glares, I ticked the names off one by one and sighed with relief as they all made it back until I had one unticked name left and realized it was Kate—no, as it turned out she was really Cate—Crenshaw.

Of Chattanooga.

Who had wanted to see Carnaby Street.

This time I didn't roll the bus out to the next stop on the tour; I grabbed the cell phone from Clive and dialed 999.

The body was still warm when they found her, in a little alleyway just off the famous street. She was between an Indian takeaway and a fish and chips place redolent of grease. She'd been strangled with the Op Art scarf she'd bought for two pounds sixty.

I made the identification. It could only be a preliminary ID, of course, since in truth I had no idea who these people really were. I only knew who they said they were, what name appeared on credit cards and passports. I only knew,

I told the Chief Superintendent, that the short-haired blonde with the oversized handbag and completely unsensible shoes, had called herself Kate/Cate Crenshaw and that the name on her luggage tags and passports confirmed that identity. For all I knew, she was really Dominique Dandridge or Sarah Jessica Parker or the Maharani of Ranjipur. For all I knew, she was smuggling drugs in the platforms of her impossible shoes or had The Plans sewn into the lining of the straw carryall or—

Yes, I was getting a bit hysterical. When the Chief Super, not unkindly, pointed this out, I didn't argue with her. I restated all I really knew: that the dead woman had presented herself to me as Catherine Crenshaw of Chattanooga. The Super thanked me and said she'd like to talk to all the passengers one by one.

While she bent to her task, I stood under an awning with Clive, morosely watching the rain drip from the striped canvas onto the sidewalk.

"Just like one of Mrs. Christie's books," he remarked, taking a last drag on his unfiltered cigarette. I couldn't help notice a touch of satisfaction in the way he smoked; the late Cate Crenshaw had dressed him down more than once for polluting her air.

Not, of course, that Clive smoked on the bus. But she complained that he smoked too near the bus, and that he reeked of smoke, both of which annoyed her to no end.

"Which one? I know I have to catch up on my reading if we're going to plan this itinerary, but I haven't had much—"

"*The ABC Murders*," he said, tossing his butt into the gutter where it fizzled and drowned. "You know, the one where everyone thinks the murders are done by a serial killer, but Poirot proves that the killer really had a motive for one of the murders and he just did the others to throw the police off the scent."

"I assume the ABC part means something?"

"You're too young to remember the ABC Railway Guides, but they were left at the scene of each murder." He warmed to his theme, his bright blue eyes alight. "And the victims were just like this lot, names beginning with A or B, and killed in places beginning with the same letter."

"So you're saying that one of these killings was done on purpose, and the others are just to throw the police off the track, make them think a tourist-killing madman is at work?"

"Could be," he said with a nod of his birdlike head. "Could definitely be. I think I ought to have a word with the Chief Super."

He had a word. She had a couple back, but I couldn't hear either side of the conversation.

I was too busy thinking about tomorrow.

After C came D. And even if Clive was right and the killer had a motive to kill only one of the passengers, he might still move on to D as a matter of versimilitude. Or perhaps the true object of his intention was Doug Didricksen and the other three deaths had been red herrings to mislead the police.

Either way, we'd have to be damned careful.

D is for—what? The next murder site, that was for certain, but where would the killer strike next? I puzzled over the question until the obvious struck me like a blow.

Only the most famous street in London, the one everyone in the whole world associates with the British government. The English equivalent of the White House—Number Ten Downing Street. And I was scheduled to lead the Whitehall tour tomorrow, complete with photo op as close as we could get to the PM's official residence, which wasn't actually Number Ten but Number Eleven, since Tony Blair changed houses with the Chancellor of the Exchequer.

Thinking of Downing Street, oddly enough, brought a measure of calm. The place had to be at least as well guarded as the Crown Jewels. And how hard could it be to convince Doug Didricksen that today would be a really good day to give the bus tour a miss?

Ha. Convince Doug Didricksen of anything? The tour leader wasn't born who could convince that man that his life was in danger. He had paid his money and he would take his chances, and I had no choice but to punch his ticket and escort him to his seat.

I did take precautions. I mentioned my suspicions to the

super and she assigned an undercover cop to keep an eye on Mr. D—who just happened to hail from Dover, Delaware.

The key to the whole thing was figuring out who had a motive to kill each of the dead tourists, and then finding out if anyone with a motive was actually here in London when the death happened.

Anne Ackerman had a sister back in Bug Tussle or whatever, Arkansas. No apparent connections in England. Brannigan had British relatives (the ones left behind when his ancestors had been transported?), and I could easily see where a week of his company might cause a lapse in hospitality ending in murder. As for Crenshaw, her ex-husband was supposed to be on holiday in Rome, but that meant he was close enough to fly to London and then back again, pretending he'd been there all the time.

Suggestive, as Sherlock Holmes would have said.

We passed the Admiralty, with its classic Adam design and ornamental sea horses; I pointed out the Banqueting House across the street and mentioned its Rubens ceiling. The Horse Guards stood just ahead, and directly beyond that, the tiny cul-de-sac that is Downing Street.

Two members of the Household Cavalry stood guard on horseback. I hoped none of my tourists would do what passengers from another bus were doing: trying to coax a smile out of the stone-faced men.

I pulled the mike a little closer and told the group that the Downing Street row houses had been designed by a Harvard graduate and that Benjamin Disraeli was the first Prime Minister to live there, his predecessors having used the buildings as office space.

I finished my remarks by announcing that this was a fifteen-minute photo stop only; we'd find bathrooms when we swung back toward Trafalgar Square for the National Portrait Gallery.

I stood with Clive while they trotted, two by two, much like the denizens of Noah's Ark, to the wrought-iron gate, where they dutifully peeked and snapped photos, then moved toward the horses to pose with the guards.

But peeking in through wrought-iron gates isn't good

enough for the Doug Didricksens of this world; they're going to by God get their money's worth regardless of the fact that the place they're visiting isn't a tourist model of reality, put there for the exclusive benefit of those with Kodaks. To them, the whole world is one big Disneyland, one giant stage set for them to pose against. Churches aren't for worship, ruins aren't for contemplation of the lost past, cities aren't for the people who live and work there. And Number Ten Downing Street isn't the seat of a real government, requiring major security; it's a sightseeing attraction and getting a picture taken right in front of the famous door with the famous number is worth breaking a law or two.

After all, it's not as if they were real American laws.

Well, that was my theory, anyway. The theory I expounded to the Chief Super when she came round after they found the body wedged in a little alleyway behind King Charles Street. He'd been coshed.

Didricksen's murder put paid to the ABC theory. A nice theory while it lasted, but the symbolism of the deaths was just too strong. Whoever killed Ackerman, Brannigan, Crenshaw, and Didricksen wasn't just using the trappings of tourism to enhance the notion of serial murders—he truly hated the tourists and what they represented. He hated the transformation of his country into a Disney attraction.

And since there was only one Englishman on the bus, and he'd been away "getting ciggies" when Didricksen was killed, I had no choice but to give Clive over to the authorities.

It took me a while to convince the Chief Super that I wasn't completely nuts. What with Dame Agatha and the ABC Murder theory and bodies without shoes, she was a tad confused at first. But finally I convinced her that the deaths were exactly what they seemed, no more and no less. Not a murder-in-a-haystack like the ABC Murders of Mrs. Christie's fertile imagination, but a deliberate, cold-blooded elimination of tourists who failed to treat their surroundings with respect.

Too bad; Clive was the best coach driver I'd ever worked

with, a Cockney to the bone and a man who loved his country.

And so, when I think back upon the most exciting period of my employment with the Oh, To Be In England Motor Coach Tour Company, Ltd., I recall the tourist deaths not as the ABC Murders but, more properly, I think, as The Patriotic Murders.

It seems a nice way to remember Clive.

Which I do every other Wednesday, the day I devote to the Agatha Christie Tour of London.

On this particular Wednesday, I lifted the mike to my lips, smiled broadly, and said, "Welcome to the Agatha Christie Tour. In addition to places made famous by the late Dame Agatha herself, we will also be visiting the sites of the so-called ABC Murders that happened right here in London a year ago this week."

A hand went up. I bowed to the inevitable and waited for the question.

"Yes, it's my real name."

World President of the International Association of Crime Writers, Susan Moody invokes Agatha Christie's alter ego Ariadne Oliver in this story featuring an enterprising crime writer and some very familiar Christie names. Moody began writing crime in 1984, with Penny Black, *the first of the seven Penny Wanawake crime novels. She also has written a number of acclaimed suspense novels, including the recent* Falling Angel. *She is the author of the Cassandra Swann series, featuring a weight-watching, bridge-playing amateur sleuth, and wrote* Misselthwaite, *a sequel to Frances Hodgson Burnett's children's classic,* The Secret Garden.

Oliphants Can Remember

Susan Moody

Mrs. Antigone Oliphants, the popular crime novelist, stared around the dining room with a considerable degree of satisfaction. So far, the Seaview had more than lived up to its reputation as one of the best small hotels on the South Coast. The food was excellent, the atmosphere peaceful, and her latest novel was proceeding smoothly toward its denouement. All she had to do now was gather her suspects together in the final chapter and let Nanook, her Eskimo detective, unravel the mysteries of the plot she had so painstakingly put together.

Over in the corner, behind a potted palm, she could see the most recent guest. He had arrived at the hotel that very morning and, as far as she could ascertain, had remained secluded in his room until the dinner gong had sounded. But even though he sat with his back to the rest of the diners, she had recognized him immediately. Clearly he wished to remain incognito. But how could Sir Launcelot Palango have hoped to avoid recognition? His star might be waning these days, and lately there had been hints that his financial affairs were in a parlous state, but the exotic actor-knight and theatrical impresario was still a public figure.

And judging by the conversation between the honeymooners at the table behind her, she was not the only one who had penetrated his anonymity.

"Of course it's him," Hattie King was saying in forthright tones. "I'd recognize him anywhere."

"I know, darling, but—"

"Especially," continued Hattie King darkly, "after what happened at Chichester."

"But he obviously doesn't want anyone to know he's here."

"You're being absolutely spineless," Hattie said.

"He may be a bit of a has-been—" Nicholas said.

"A bit of a bounder, you mean."

"But he's still got a lot of clout in the theatrical world."

"After what he's done to you, I'm surprised you don't go over and knock him down."

Antigone Oliphants listened enthralled to this dialogue, conducted in whispers which were nonetheless perfectly audible. How exactly had Sir Launcelot so enraged young Hattie? Or, for that matter, what had he done to the amiable Nicholas Bristow?

"And if you won't do it for your own sake, then you jolly well ought to do it for mine," Hattie added.

"If he was anyone else, darling, you know I wouldn't hesitate."

"But that's the whole point, darling. He's *not* someone else, he's Launcelot Palango, who tried to seduce your very own little wifie."

"*Dar*ling . . ."

"*Sweet*heart . . ."

At this point, as the whispers gave way to murmured endearments, the lady novelist turned her attention to another guest who sat near the window gazing mournfully out at the sea. She and Della Sweeting had traveled down together on the 4:50 from Paddington, but although they had shared the same first-class carriage, Mrs. Oliphants had been unable to break through Della Sweeting's air of sad reserve. She knew who she was, of course—the national press saw to that—but despite her best efforts, she had been unable to extract any information of a more personal nature. It was well-known that Della Sweeting had been a model for one of the great couture houses until she had fallen in love with a virtually unknown playwright and shortly thereafter, had dropped out of public life. Nothing more had been heard of her until her husband's death, hastened, according to the gutter-press, by the bankruptcy forced upon him by an unwise business venture. After a suitable period of mourning, Della Sweeting had become the third wife of Bernard Meredith, the property tycoon, and in this position, the brilliance of the soirées she held at their house in Grosvenor Square had made her the talk of London.

Wealth did not appear to have made her very happy, Mrs. Oliphants reflected: the beautiful mouth drooped and her green eyes were sad.

The hotel owner, dressed in her usual black silk, with a bunch of keys rattling at her waist, sailed into the room. Graciously she stopped at each occupied table to exchange a few words with her guests. Mrs. Quin was another person whose privacy Mrs. Oliphants had been unable to invade. Despite the fact that in the brochure, beneath the name of the hotel, appeared the sentence "*Sole Proprietors, Mr. & Mrs. R. J. Quin,*" Mr. Quin had so far not put in an appearance. Until yesterday, Mrs. Oliphants had been inclined to believe that "Mrs." was a courtesy title. But, idling purposefully in the hall, she had noticed that the door to Mrs.

Quin's private sitting room was ajar. Long nose twitching with curiosity, she had tiptoed closer and peeking in, seen a number of framed photographs set about the room, some showing a young girl in theatrical costume, others a balding man in a stiff collar. Was this the mysterious Mr. Quin?

"I do hope that dinner was to your liking," Mrs. Quin said now, stopping beside Mrs. Oliphants's table.

"Delicious, thank you." The novelist wished she could remember why the woman was in some way familiar.

"As usual, coffee will be served in the sun-lounge."

The novelist put a hand on Mrs. Quin's arm. "Tell me, is that really Sir Launcelot Palango over there?"

"Who?" Mrs. Quin seemed bewildered.

"Over there, by the palm. Sir Launcelot Palango," said Mrs. Oliphants. "The famous actor."

"I can't say I've heard of him." Mrs. Quin glanced over at the man. "He signed himself in the register as Mr. Roger Ackroyd. But we don't get much in the way of theatricals in these parts." She smiled benignly and moved away.

Antigone Oliphants rose. She would take two cups of coffee, and then return to her bedroom to revise the work she had done that day. She sighed. Nanook! What could have possessed her to create an Eskimo detective? If she had had the slightest notion that he would prove so popular with the public, she would never have dreamed him up. Never. He had been intended as a lighthearted frolic, a one-off, nothing more than that. She knew nothing—nor wished to—of Greenland or Iceland or wherever it was that Eskimos lived. Snow, ice, adorable fur hoods, and whale blubber: that had been almost the entire sum of her knowledge of the frozen wastes where Nanook supposedly operated. And then, to her horror, Pattinson & Knight, her publishers, had wanted more and more of him, until her detective now hung round her neck like an albatross. Or a polar bear.

As she proceeded to the sun-lounge, two of the other guests fell in on either side of her. Dr. Clitheroe and Inspector Williams. As they wished her good evening, Mrs. Oliphants graciously inclined her head. Although she had previously ascertained that the inspector was recently retired from Scotland Yard, he was still a well-set man. Po-

licemen never quite lost that air of authority and moral
rectitude which the uniform seemed to bestow. She had
been racking her brains since her arrival here in an attempt
to remember why his name was familiar to her, as, indeed,
was that of Clitheroe.

"Are you down here for long?" she enquired.

"We had planned on a week of golf," replied the Inspector. "But now . . ."

"Now?" Mrs. Oliphants's nose gave a preliminary wig-
gle.

"If we'd known that Sir La—Mr. Ackroyd would also
be here, we'd have gone elsewhere," said Dr. Clitheroe,
touching his pencil-line mustache. Life seemed to have
treated him badly and he gave the impression that he would
not be surprised if, in the future, it treated him even worse.
He moved away, shaking his head, followed by Inspector
Williams.

Dear me! thought Mrs. Oliphants. How intriguing! Her
nose quivered again as she subsided into one of the comfortable sofas and accepted a cup of coffee from the waiter.
As she raised it to her lips, the young woman who had
been at the next table came across and sat down beside her.

"How do you do?" she said brightly. "I'm Hattie King,
the actress—at least, I suppose I'm really Mrs. Nicholas
Bristow, but we decided that I would keep my professional
name. What do *you* do?"

"I am the crime novelist Antigone Oliphants."

Hattie looked blank. "Do you write under your own
name?"

The question all writers dread. Mrs. Oliphants tried not
to grind her teeth. "Yes."

"That's interesting." Hattie King's rather plain face was
transformed by her smile. "Nicholas, my husband—he's an
actor too—has written a really brilliant play. Maybe you'd
like to read it . . ."

Such impudence, thought Mrs. Oliphants. Why should
anyone suppose that I want to read their horrid little play?

". . . and if you liked it you might be able to advise us
where we could go to find someone willing to produce it."

I have ten perfectly good novels of my own, thought

Mrs. Oliphants, all of them crying out for stage adaptation, if only someone had the wit to recognize it. She did not allow these thoughts to become words. "I'd be delighted to read your husband's play," she said cordially. "But there are others here with much more influence than a mere crime novelist possesses." She leaned closer. "I couldn't help overhearing a little of your conversation at dinner. You agree with me, I think, that the gentleman who sat with his back to us is Sir Launcelot Palango. Perhaps you should give your husband's play to him."

Hattie's expression changed to a scowl. "I wouldn't give him the time of day, let alone Nick's play, the pompous bounder!"

"You don't seem very fond of him."

"I'm not."

"May one ask why?"

"He and I were at Chichester last year, playing in *She Stoops to Conquer*, and he kept trying to make love to me," Hattie said indignantly. "I *told* him I was engaged to be married but he didn't care. He does it all the time, especially with the younger, impressionable actresses. They're flattered by his attentions, you see. He even got one poor girl pregnant two or three years ago—Katie O'Reilly—and the poor thing . . ."

Memory stirred in Mrs. Oliphants's capacious bosom. "I think I read about it in the newspapers."

Hattie looked down at her hands. "When she told him about it, he wouldn't have anything more to do with her. Said it wasn't his child. In the end she . . . she *killed* herself."

"How did you manage to avoid his advances?"

"One evening he found me alone in my dressing room when everyone else had left. He started the usual thing, wouldn't take no for an answer, you know how it is. So I kicked him really hard in the . . ." She flushed. "If I hadn't, I think he would have . . . that the worst might have happened."

"He must have been annoyed."

"He was *furious*! And then poor Nicky found that whenever he auditioned for a part, as soon as he said who he was, they said they didn't want him."

"How strange."

"Not if you know that Sir Launcelot was deliberately sabotaging his chances by telling all sorts of lies. Said Nicky was difficult to work with, a hopeless actor, unreliable, and so on. Which is absolutely not *true*, he's a *brilliant* actor and not in the *least* difficult! And it's all because of me! So I thought that if I could get someone to put on his play, it might be a way for me to make up for completely *ruining* his life, the poor darling."

In a cloud of perfume, Della Sweeting appeared at the door of the lounge. For a moment, she hesitated, surveying the room, then moved towards Mrs. Oliphants and Hattie King. "Would you mind . . . might I join you?" she said hesitantly.

"Of course." Mrs. Oliphants turned to Hattie. "Perhaps Miss Sweeting might be interested in your play," she said.

"Play?" Della Sweeting's beautiful face changed. "You have a play?"

"It's my husband's," explained Hattie.

Della Sweeting looked over her shoulder toward the door through which they could all see the corpulent figure of Sir Launcelot making its way across the hall. Her fists clenched. "I would so much like to see it," she said, turning back to the young actress. "*So* much."

"I'll bring it to your room a little later," Hattie said, somewhat taken aback by the vehemence with which the former mannequin spoke.

"Death," Della Sweeting said, addressing Mrs. Oliphants. "As a crime writer, you deal in death, do you not?"

"Only in a fictional sense."

The other moved her well-coiffed head about. "I smell death in the air," she said somberly.

"I can't say that I do," said Hattie.

"Nor me." Mrs. Oliphants wondered if Della was slightly unhinged. After her first husband's death she had been left destitute. Perhaps the sudden change in her fortunes—after all, Bernard Meredith was *enormously* wealthy—had been too much for her.

"Nemesis," said Della vaguely. She seemed to have momentarily forgotten her two companions. "At last." And then, with a singularly sweet smile, she shook her head as though to clear it and began to talk animatedly about the round of golf she had played that afternoon on the local links.

After a while, Mrs. Oliphants got to her feet. Time to get back to Nanook and all that dratted snow! How many people knew that there were dozens of words for snow in the Eskimo language, undoubtedly because there was nothing else to talk about?

"Onwards, Antigone!" she exhorted herself as she opened her bedroom door. "Buckle down. Only one more chapter to go and then you may indulge yourself in some luxurious little treat."

She spent a pleasurable fifteen minutes contemplating what that treat might be: a silk scarf, a brooch she had recently glimpsed in a Bond Street jewelers, theater tickets? But thoughts of her fellow guests kept intruding. A strange group. Hattie and Nicholas, Inspector Williams, Dr. Clitheroe, Della Sweeting. And all of them appeared to have some grievance against Sir Launcelot Palango . . .

Briefly she considered talking to her publisher about a new series starring a flamboyant actor-manager of Italian descent as the detective. Then, sighing, she began to tap wearily at the keys of her typewriter. *"Frost sparkled on the sealskin lap-rug as Nanook's sledge pulled up outside Chingachook's igloo,"* she wrote. *"He spat out the piece of whale blubber he had been chewing and threw it away into the frozen darkness. Tonight, his investigations would finally bear fruit . . ."*

The following morning, the dining room was peaceful as Antigone Oliphants sipped a final cup of tea. Murmured conversations filled the toast-scented air. Suddenly, there was a terrified shriek from the upper regions of the hotel. And another. "Murder!" someone screamed. "Help!"

Mrs. Quin, who had just begun her usual stately procession among her guests, hurried out into the hall. Behind her, nose aquiver, came Antigone Oliphants, followed

closely by Hattie and her husband, Dr. Clitheroe, and Mr.
Williams. Della Sweeting brought up the rear.

They hastened up the front staircase to find Livvie, the
chambermaid, having hysterics on the landing. Behind her
was a half-open bedroom door. By craning her neck, Mrs.
Oliphants could see a rumpled pink eiderdown, a pair of
embroidered velvet slippers, and—she raised a hand to her
mouth—a pyjamaed arm dangling to the floor.

While Mrs. Quin tried to make some sense of the chambermaid's words, the detective novelist stepped swiftly forward and pushed the door a little wider. There, slumped
across the bed, half-off and half-on, lay Sir Launcelot Palango. His face was livid, his body contorted. Beside the
bed was a tray which held an empty glass and a bottle of
whiskey on a tray. He was clearly dead.

"The moving finger writes . . ." murmured Dr. Clitheroe,
bustling past her. He bent over the corpse. "There's nothing
I can do for the fellow, I'm afraid."

"Looks like poison," said Inspector Williams, who had
followed him into the room.

"I agree. The blue tinge to the lips, the contortion of the
body . . ."

Livvie screamed again. "First that murder at the vicarage
last year, now this!" she sobbed. "This place is accursed,
you mark my words!"

"Nonsense, Livvie," said Mrs. Quin. "Pull yourself together. The vicarage murder had nothing whatsoever to do
with this."

"Someone should ring for the police," said Mrs Oliphants.

"I agree." It was Inspector Williams.

Mrs. Quin raised her hands to her black-silk bosom.
"Think of the adverse publicity this will bring to my hotel."

"I'm sorry, Madam, but considerations of that sort cannot
be allowed to impede the progress of an investigation," said
the Inspector.

"Couldn't Doctor Clitheroe examine the body, and you,
Inspector, make a preliminary examination and tell the local
constabulary of your conclusion?"

"He was a public figure, Mrs. Quin," said the doctor

gently. "We cannot possibly keep this quiet."

The hotel proprietress looked stricken. "I've worked so hard to build up my business," she murmured. "Is he now going to destroy it, on top of everything else he has done?"

Hattie took the woman's hand. "You've heard about him too, have you?"

In the bedroom, the doctor lifted the corpse's eyelids, sniffed at the half-open mouth, felt the temperature of the body. "Sometime after ten and before midnight," he pronounced. "And I would stake my reputation on it being cyanide."

The inspector sniffed at the empty glass beside the bed. "I'm inclined to agree," he said. "Almost certainly ingested via the whisky." His sharp eyes glanced about the room, taking in the details. "Well, well," he murmured to the doctor, "Sir Laurence Palango poisoned. This'll certainly set the cat among the pigeons."

"Is it murder?" inquired the detective novelist. She wished she could remember where she had heard Dr. Clitheroe's name.

"Why would anyone want to murder him?" the Inspector asked.

"It cannot have been an accident, surely?"

"That remains to be seen." The inspector surveyed the group gathered outside the door. "If you would all be kind enough to descend to the sun-lounge," he said. "Perhaps I could adopt Mrs. Quin's suggestion by conducting a preliminary investigation while we wait for the police. Clearly there is no obligation upon any of you to answer my questions, but it could prove helpful in establishing where you all were when the murder of . . . of . . ."

"Roger Ackroyd," said Mrs. Quin. Her face was pale but composed as she surveyed the corpse of her erstwhile guest.

"*If* it's murder," said Mrs. Oliphants.

"He's not called Ackroyd," said Hattie. "He's Sir Launcelot Palango."

There was a kind of gasp from the crowd in the hall, which by now had been swollen by various members of the hotel staff. Even this far from London, reflected Mrs.

Oliphants, they kept abreast of the famous. She wondered how many of them knew Nanook's name. Let alone hers.

In the sun-lounge, Antigone Oliphants unobtrusively seated herself as close to Inspector Williams as she could, and pretended to be immersed in that morning's copy of *The Times*. After what she had learned about the dead man, she was not surprised to see that Livvie was the only person who seemed distressed by the news of his death.

"So, Doctor," she heard the inspector say, "justice at last seems to be done."

"I would have preferred it if he had been forced to face the music," Clitheroe replied.

"If you're right about the poison being in the whisky—"

"Or else in the glass from which it was drunk."

"—then the police have a problem on their hands. According to Mrs. Quin, the tray was taken up to his room about nine o'clock last evening, after which nobody appears to have seen him. The chambermaid has testified that the room was locked on the inside when she went in this morning to make the bed. Which would suggest that either glass or bottle was poisoned before it arrived in his room."

"Unless it was suicide."

"Agreed. Mrs. Quin has told us that she took a new bottle from her store cupboard and opened it herself, in the presence of the chambermaid. So when was the cyanide added either to bottle or glass? And by whom? Unless we are to suppose either she or Livvie is responsible?"

"The girl had the opportunity: did she have the motive?"

"I spoke to her. She told me she had once spent a year in London," the inspector said thoughtfully. "Had delusions of becoming an actress. Possibly she came across Sir Laurence during that time and somehow blames him for her failure to make it."

"What about the hotel keeper herself?"

"Again, opportunity but no motive. She didn't even know his real identity—she believed him to be a Mr. Ackroyd."

"Dash it all," said Clitheroe. "*I've* got more motive than either of those women."

"That point had not escaped me, Doctor."

"So, for that matter, do *you*."

Without moving her head, Mrs. Oliphants raised her eyes. The two men were staring at each other. And as she looked at them, she remembered why their names had been so familiar. A shiver ran down her back. Two years ago, little Gerald Clitheroe, only child of a widowed doctor who practiced in Camden Hill Square, had been run down and killed by a motor, driven by none other than Sir Launcelot Palango. At the subsequent trial, the actor had maintained that the child had darted out in front of his wheels in order to retrieve a ball and that he had been unable to stop in time. Witnesses had testified that Gerald often played in the gardens across from his father's surgery, though no one had ever seen him run into the road. The doctor, who had watched helpless from his window as the tragedy unfolded, maintained that the motor was being driven at a reckless speed and weaving from side to side, sometimes even mounting the pavement. He added that on running out into the square, he had smelled whiskey on the defendant's breath and had accused him of being drunk. Sir Launcelot had denied this, had brought character witnesses to state that he rarely drank, and then only a sip or two to steady his nerves immediately prior to a performance. Inspector Williams, the policeman assigned to the case, had not believed him, but despite this, the actor had been acquitted. The inspector himself had been removed from his position shortly afterward and had subsequently resigned from the force.

More than enough motive for murder, thought Mrs. Oliphants. But how had the cyanide got into the bottle or the glass?

Della Sweeting came into the room and joined the two men. "I want you to know," she said in a clear voice, "that I'm glad he's dead."

The inspector rustled the pages of his notebook and cleared his throat. "Why is that?"

"He killed my first husband," said Della.

"Your husband was murdered?"

"More or less. Poor Harry was an innocent; he knew

nothing about business. That . . . *monster* persuaded him to invest all our savings in backing some dreadful play. He swore that with his name up in lights, the public would pour in and all our fortunes would be made. My husband believed everything he said. And then, for no reason at all, Sir Launcelot found something better to do and pulled out. We lost everything. Everything. It killed my poor Harry. The shame of being made bankrupt—Harry never got over it."

"I'm sorry, Miss Sweeting."

"If I'd known he was going to be here, I'd happily have procured some poison and killed him myself!"

"Between the time of Sir Launcelot leaving the dining room and the whisky being carried up to his room, where were you, Miss Sweeting?"

"In here," said Della. She looked vaguely round the room. "With some of the other guests—they'll tell you."

"And after that?"

"I went up to my room, had a bath, and went to bed. Hattie King had given me a copy of a play that her husband has written and I read that. It's good. It's really good. I want to persuade my husband to back it—I was going to get Sir Launcelot in on it and then, at the last moment, I would have kicked him out. I would have . . ."

"The maid, Livvie, has informed us that she left the tray with the glass and whisky on a table on the landing while she went for some fresh towels which Sir Launcelot had requested. When she returned, she says she saw you just going to your room. Are you sure you didn't—"

"If I had, I'd tell you," said Della. "I'd be proud of it. Since Harry died, I haven't known a s-single h-happy moment." She raised a lace-edged handkerchief to her eyes.

With another discreet glance from behind her paper, Mrs. Oliphants saw that the beautiful woman's hands were clutching convulsively. Didn't being a top model require a certain ability to act? The haughty stare, the loping sway along the catwalk—were they not as much a performance as any actor's?

When she had left, Dr. Clitheroe said, "If the glass or

bottle was left untended, Miss Sweeting is not the only one who could have added the cyanide."

"But so far she's the only one with both motive and opportunity."

"Would she be so open about her hatred for the victim if she'd done it?"

"Could be a double bluff."

Nicholas Bristow and Hattie King were next to be questioned. Both said that they were not sorry to learn of the demise of the actor-knight and cited as the reason the information that Hattie had given Mrs. Oliphants the previous evening. "But we didn't kill him," Hattie said vehemently. "And we were together all evening, either down here or in our room." She threw a tender glance at her husband, who began to blush.

"He doesn't seem to have been a very popular person," observed the inspector when they had gone.

"I can see why," said the doctor.

To Mrs. Oliphants's eyes, he seemed nervous. A pulse twitched in his cheek. It occurred to her that a doctor might well have access to cyanide or one of its derivatives. As might a policeman. And both men had motives. Did they have the opportunity, though?

"What about you, Mrs. Oliphants?" The inspector interrupted her thoughts. So he had noticed her, after all! "What did you do last night?"

"Much the same as everyone else," she said. "Had coffee here in the lounge—in the presence of witnesses—and then went up to my room to complete some work."

"Alone?"

"Naturally," bridled Mrs. Oliphants.

"By work, you mean your next crime novel?"

"You know my name?"

"Featuring Nanook, I do hope," interrupted the doctor. His eyes were warm. "I'm a tremendous fan, Mrs. Oliphants."

A groan escaped her lips. "But why? He's so maddening. I'm sure that if I ever met him in real life, I'd murder him myself."

"It's your sense of place," said the Doctor. "I can practically smell the snow, shiver in the cold, smell the whale oil. I always feel myself transported to another world when I start the latest Antigone Oliphants."

"So do I. And it's a world I do not wish to inhabit. Don't you think Nanook is boring? And insufferably smug?"

"Not at all. Where *do* you get your ideas from?"

Mrs. Oliphants raised her eyes to heaven. "Have you come to any conclusions with regard to this much more dramatic happening right here on our own doorstep?"

"I'm afraid not."

"It seems that those with the motive did not have the opportunity, and vice versa."

"Indeed it does. We shall have to wait for the local police to arrive."

The police, in the form of a local inspector and his sergeant, conducted their inquiry along the same lines as Inspector Williams had done. By late afternoon, they had interviewed everyone, including Sir Launcelot's man of affairs and his theatrical agent, both of whom had been contacted by telephone and had come hurrying down from London.

The accountant informed them gravely that owing to some ill-advised investments, the actor's debts had become unmanageable, and that he was currently being dunned by any number of creditors. His agent added that despite his fame, no parts had recently been offered and it appeared that the actor's career was in severe decline.

"I'm afraid he is a man who has had his day," sighed the agent, his mouth pursed. "Unfortunately, Sir Launcelot refused to believe it and, despite his precarious financial situation, insisted on living in the grand style to which he had become accustomed."

"I told him that he must cut down on his expenses immediately," chimed in the accountant.

"Do you think," asked the local inspector, "that this might have caused him to contemplate suicide?"

The agent and the accountant gazed at each other doubtfully. "It's possible, I suppose," said the agent.

"But I wouldn't have thought him the suicidal sort," added the accountant.

"We found a letter in his room, which must have come from your office. The hotel owner has confirmed that it arrived yesterday afternoon." The inspector studied the piece of paper in his hand. "You wrote that the situation had become critical, that his creditors were acting together and unless he paid off some of his debts he could very well find himself in prison."

"This is true. You don't think that could have pushed him over the edge, do you?" asked the accountant, looking disturbed.

"I'll put my cards on the table, and admit that this is the conclusion to which our investigations are leading us."

"Suicide, eh? Poor old Launcelot. Nobody likes to accept that they're past it." The agent looked downcast. "What a pity he never made any motion pictures. Given the manner of his death, we could have made a fortune by reissuing them."

A couple of days later, Antigone Oliphants stood with Mrs. Quin at the edge of the hotel's cliff-top gardens, waiting for the cab which was to take her to the station. Below them, the sea sparkled in the sunshine. "Your gardens are so beautiful. You must work hard to keep them so free of weeds."

"We use a strong weed-killer at about this time of year. It keeps them down."

"Suicide," said Antigone Oliphants thoughtfully. "It can't do your hotel any harm."

Mrs. Quin nodded soberly. "Quite the opposite. I've already taken a record number of bookings since Sir Launcelot's death. People seemed oddly intrigued that such a famous man should have traveled to my hotel in order to put an end to his life."

"But that's not why you did it, is it?"

"Did what?"

"Why you put poison in his glass."

"I'm sorry, I don't understand."

"The police reached their conclusion based on the fact

that his career was in decline and that his debts had grown beyond his capacity to repay them. But why would someone as flamboyant and self-regarding as Sir Launcelot wish to do away with himself? And if he did, why come to this seaside resort to do it? And having come, why not jump off the cliffs, rather than die a painful death by poison?"

"What do you mean?"

"Last night, I suddenly remembered why your face was so familiar," said Mrs. Oliphants. "I'm a great theater goer, and I well recall the lovely young actress called Peggy O'Reilly, who took London by storm for a few seasons and then married and retired."

Mrs. Quin gazed at her steadily.

"No doubt your daughter Katie inherited your acting ability, as well as borrowing your stage name," continued the crime novelist. "And then, at the very start of her career, before she could begin to fulfill her promise, she was seduced and betrayed by a famous actor. And killed herself."

"You're making a great many assumptions, Mrs. Oliphants."

"You had the opportunity. You knew who he was, even though you pretended you didn't. You know as well as I do that a man like that would never willingly deprive the world of his presence."

Mrs. Quin sighed. "Katie was the world to us," she said softly. "The light of our eyes." She gazed out at the sea moving gently below them. "When we heard the news of her . . . death, and why it had happened, my husband collapsed. He died in my arms. I buried them together, him and his darling Katie."

"None of this was premeditated?"

"Of course not. Sir Launcelot gave a false name when he arrived here, but I knew him at once. Though he did not remember me, he played Hamlet to my Ophelia, years ago. It seemed as though Fate had brought him here. I felt that I'd been given an opportunity to even up the score."

As the cab pulled up in front of the door, Mrs. Oliphants looked into the face of the other woman and then turned away. There are so many steps to death. It was not up to her to pass judgement on any living creature. If the police probed more deeply into Mrs. Quin's past, they might make the connection between her and the dead actor.

And if they did not, then at least justice of a kind had been done.